Viking One

A New Homefront Novel

By Steven C. Bird

Viking One

A New Homefront Novel

Published by Steven C. Bird at Homefront Books

Illustrated by Hristo Kovatliev

Edited by Sabrina Jean at Fastrack Editing

Print Edition 2.14.17

www.homefrontbooks.com

www.stevencbird.com

facebook.com/homefrontbooks

facebook.com/stvbird

twitter.com/stevencbird

scbird@homefrontbooks.com

Table of Contents

Disclaimer

The characters and events in this book are fictitious. Any similarities to real events or persons, past or present, living or dead, is purely coincidental and are not intended by the author. Although this book is based on real places and some real events, it is a work of fiction for entertainment purposes only. None of the activities in this book are intended to replace legal activities and your own good judgment.

Some items in this book have been changed from their actual likenesses to avoid any accidental sharing of Sensitive Security Information (SSI). The replacement values serve the same narrative purpose without exposing any potential SSI.

Dedication

To my loving wife and children

Monica, Seth, Olivia, and Sophia

As we continue to walk through the doors that God leads us to, I can't help but think about how blessed we are as a family. Since embarking on a career in writing, our family has seen many incredible changes, and I hope the path he has laid out for us continues to carry us where he ultimately wants us to be in this world. Thank you each and everyone for the love and support you have shown me during this transformation of myself both personally and professionally. I wouldn't be who I am today without both God and you.

Introduction

The winds of change had been sweeping through America for some time now. Certain political factions controlling the mainstream media had been working toward their goal of redefining the nation into their own image of government-centered collectivism. Through the media, public schools, and a near fascist use of political correctness, they had been changing the opinions of the uninformed and blissfully distracted public and the way they see traditional American values.

A constant assault on the nation's traditional religious faiths, as well as chipping away at America's pride in its history, work ethic, and rugged individualism, had left the country divided. To those who paid attention, this division seemed hopeless to repair. Add to that, out-of-control government spending and political leaders who seemed intent on collapsing America's economy with burdensome social programs and business-killing regulation, and it's understandable why so many constitutional and libertarian-minded Americans were uneasy about the future.

Survivalists and doomsday preppers, once on the fringe, were joined by a low-key wave of mainstream conservative and constitutional libertarian Americans. Cable TV programs, as well as a myriad of websites and both fiction and non-fiction books, proliferated, depicting prepping and survivalist skills and their anticipated importance in coming days, feeding this hunger for answers in an insecure world.

Americans from all walks of life were preparing for the uncertainty ahead. One of the more widespread fears was the almost certain coming collapse of the house of cards on which the nation's economic security was based. Whether this fragile situation was brought on intentionally to enable those pulling the strings from the behind the scenes to rebuild America into a new form after the collapse, or unintentionally by inept politicians who sold their oath of office to any special interest group that would bankroll their careers, one thing was sure; it just could not go on like this forever.

Jim and Damon Rutherford, two brothers who lived in Delaware City, Delaware, were two such people. Jim, a self-employed electrical contractor, and Damon, an electrical engineer, were preparing themselves and their loved ones for what seemed to be the inevitable event that would push the nation over the edge. From where or just what that event would remain a mystery, but they both felt deep down inside that the country could not continue down its current path for long.

Chapter One: Send Off

Reaching into his bag and removing his compact Smith & Wesson Model 60 five-shot revolver chambered in .357 Magnum, Damon placed it off to the side, thinking to himself, *No, if I get caught in New York with that, they'll put me under the jail.*

Begrudgingly placing it on his nightstand, he noticed his cell phone light up and begin to play AC/DC's *Thunderstruck.* Picking up his phone and answering with a swipe, Damon said, "Hello there, brother."

"If you don't hurry, we're gonna get stuck in traffic!" Jim blasted through the phone. "Philly is a nightmare these days. With our luck, we'll get caught up in a highway shutdown protest or something like that."

"Yeah, yeah. I know. I'll be right over," Damon muttered. Hanging up his phone with a swipe, he placed it in his shirt pocket and picked up his bag.

Pausing before walking out of the house, Damon looked around once more to make sure he had turned everything off and that everything would be secure while he was away at his week-long conference in New York.

Climbing into his Chevrolet Silverado pickup truck, he started the engine and began scanning through his FM radio pre-select channels while waiting for it to warm up. "Ah, screw it!" he said aloud, shutting off the radio, discouraged by all of the negativity on his favorite talk radio channels.

~~~~

Arriving at his brother's home a few minutes later, Damon was greeted in the driveway by Jim and his wife, Lori. Giving
~~~~

Damon a big hug around the neck as he stepped out of the truck, Lori said, “You be careful up there. I hate the thought of you traveling for work with all that is going on in the world.”

“I’ll be okay,” he said, giving a reassuring smile.

Throwing Damon’s bag in the seat of his Ford F-250, Jim said, “Come on, man. We’re gonna get caught in traffic for sure.”

Looking at Jim with a perturbed look, Lori said, “You’d better get going before Mr. Cranky Pants over there gets any more irritated. It’ll be a long drive for you if he gets himself any more worked up.”

Answering with a smile, Damon said, “Oh, he’s all talk. He’s been a grouch ever since we were kids. I can handle him.”

Climbing into the passenger seat of Jim’s truck, Damon waved goodbye to Lori as they pulled out of the driveway and began their forty-five-minute drive to the Philadelphia International Airport, just north of Delaware City.

Before Damon could say a word, Jim pounced. “I still can’t believe you’re flying to New York. It’s only a three-hour drive. I’d feel much better if you had a vehicle up there with all that’s going on.”

Dismissively, Damon replied, “Hell, it’s three hours on a good day, not to mention all of the toll roads and bridges along the way. No, I’d rather not give them a penny more of my money than I have to. Besides, my company is paying for the flight, so I’m out nothing. And if something did happen while I was there, do you honestly think I could get from Long Island to Manhattan Island, then across to New Jersey to drive back down here? That place is a nightmare to drive through on a good day. That, and I don’t want my truck up there having people bang into the bumpers every time they try to squeeze into a parking spot on the street next to me that is two sizes too small for their compact car. Work is paying for the flight, so that is that.”

"I still think you should come to work for me. You'd never have to travel again."

"Jim, you're too cheap to pay me what I'm worth," Damon said with a crooked smile.

Grinning, Jim said, "Hell, I've got five bucks. That ought to do it."

"Dream on," Damon said with a chuckle while turning to look out the window.

Taking a more serious tone, Jim said, "Did you hear about the shooting last night?"

"What shooting?"

"Four more sheriff's deputies were killed—execution style."

"Ah, damn," Damon said while shaking his head. "No, I didn't hear about that. It's gotten to the point that I can't stand to turn on the news anymore. Even if I did believe you could trust the news, which I don't, there's always a protest, a riot, or stuff like that going on. All while our government sits back and does nothing and seems to support the wrong side."

"Seems?" Jim queried sarcastically. "They're damn near promoting all of the hate and violence openly. It's a case of divide and conquer right out in the open. Hell, people wouldn't hate each other so damn much if the powers-that-be weren't always giving us reasons to. Just when things start to settle down, they come up with a new reason for us to all hate each other."

"That's just it, Jim. It's futile. Watching the news just pisses me off these days, and it's gotten to the point that I know I can't do anything about it anyway, so why bother? That, and it's making me grouchy all the time, like you!"

"As Jefferson said, 'If a nation expects to be ignorant and free in a state of civilization, it expects what never was and never will be. If we are to guard against ignorance and remain free, it is the responsibility of every American to be informed.' You see, brother, you can't just sit back and ignore it all and then complain when it all falls apart."

"Brakes!" shouted Damon, pointing at the road ahead.

Violently bringing the big F-250 to a stop just before rear-ending a small hybrid car, Jim shouted, "Damn it! What the hell is going on up there?"

Hearing police sirens and seeing flashing lights in their mirrors, Jim and Damon watched as several police cruisers raced by on the shoulder of the road.

"I wonder where they're headed in such a hurry?" Damon said, thinking aloud.

"Somewhere I don't want to be," replied Jim. "I just can't imagine how those guys do it anymore."

"Do what?"

"How they go to work every day, knowing full well it could be their last. I know that's always been a risk of their jobs, but these days, they go to work with targets on their backs. Their hands are tied by the same ruling class that blames everything on them while fanning the flames of hatred against them. And of course, all of this while expecting them to still do their jobs. It's insanity."

"Well, I guess they're just hoping this social nightmare will all blow over after the election. Maybe they hope it's all being fed by election year tactics, and if they can hold on a little longer, it'll pass. Especially if the people stand up on election day and toss those tyrants out."

"Election day? I'll be surprised if there is another election day," Jim said, replying in a sarcastic tone. "No. My guess is something will go down before then to bring this pesky democracy thing to a screeching halt. That ole' constitution thing is just in their way. They need something big to happen to give them a way around it."

With a crooked smile, Damon asked, "How do you sleep at night with all of those conspiracy theories swirling around in your head? I mean, doesn't the tin-foil hat get in the way of your pillow? Besides, we're a republic, not a democracy."

Huffing and puffing, Jim defiantly said, "Make fun of me now, but when it all starts to hit the fan, you won't be laughing."

With a look of understanding, Damon said, "No, in reality, I agree with you. I just don't want to admit it to myself. Maybe it's the ignorance is bliss thing."

"Ignorance is slavery, brother," Jim said sharply.

~~~~

After working their way through traffic on I-95 North to Philadelphia, Jim and Damon approached the departing passenger drop-off area for the F terminal where Damon's commuter flight was scheduled to depart.

Stepping out of the truck with his bag in hand, Damon turned to Jim and said, "Take care. I'll see you in a week."

"You too. Stay safe up there and don't get out and about much!" replied Jim. Leaning across the cab of the truck to shout to Damon over the noise of the traffic echoing off the concrete above, he added, "Oh, and check on my boat while you're there. It should be nearly finished. It's at the Rockaway Point Yacht Club."

"Will do, brother. Take care!" Damon said, waving and rushing into the terminal, nearly late for his flight.
~~~~

Chapter Two: Standstill

Driving south toward Delaware City, Jim pressed the wiper/wash switch to clean the dust from his windshield as the sun was now low on the western horizon, seeming to illuminate every dust particle, obscuring his view. Pressing the switch several times in an act of futility, he shouted, "Damn it!" as he realized his washer fluid reservoir was empty, smearing the dust and dirt across his windshield in streaks, making his visibility even worse.

Seeing the glow of red taillights a few feet in front of his truck, Jim slammed on the brakes, screeching to a stop. His heart raced as he heard his wallet and phone slide off the seat and thump onto the floor. Regaining his composure, Jim could now see that he was mere inches from the Hyundai Sonata in front of him. "What the heck?" he shouted, wondering why traffic on I-95 South was at a standstill.

After a few moments of impatiently rapping his fists on the steering wheel as if he was the drummer of a rage-filled rock band, Jim opened his door, exiting the truck to join several other motorists who were now standing outside. He joined the crowd of people, who in an act of futility, seemed to be trying to determine what was going on further south, turning the entire Interstate into a parking lot.

A man in his mid-thirties spoke to Jim. "The northbound lane is empty. What's going on?"

"You've got me," Jim replied as he reached into his truck to turn his radio to the local news/talk station.

> *"The standoff between police and protestors has created a gridlock on both the north and southbound lanes of I-95. Authorities are recommending that motorists use*

alternate routes or to remain in place until movement is restored.

The Governor's office will release a statement shortly. Sources close to the Governor state that his position supporting the protestors has not changed. He stands with them, yet asks for peace and calm."

Turning his attention back to his fellow motorists, Jim asked, "What protest? What are they talking about?"

A middle-aged man in a light blue Chaps polo-style shirt and light tan pants spoke up, and said, "It's about the proposed cuts to EBT benefits to avoid insolvency. In addition to protesting the cuts, they're demanding that more options be made available to those on benefits who have certain religious food requirements."

"What the heck?" Jim exclaimed, feeling himself begin to lose his temper. "This country is on the verge, no, not on the verge, it *is* on its way to bankruptcy, and people want to demand more free stuff? No matter how hard I work, I can barely keep my business'es doors open, yet my taxes, fees, and expenses to comply with the ever-increasing layers of regulation continue to rise. Maybe we should be the ones blocking the freeway?"

"Yeah, right," the man said, placing his hands on his hips and looking at Jim with a raised eyebrow. "They'd send SWAT teams or drones in to deal with us if we did the same thing. Besides, these people know the administration has their backs. The president does everything but openly tell them to riot. The message is loud and clear. It's never his fault things are getting worse and worse. It's always the other side of the aisle."

"It's both damn sides if you ask me," Jim said in disgust.

Interrupted by the sounds of gunshots in the distance, they stood silent, quickly turning their attention to the sounds of a police helicopter flying overhead toward the scene of the protest, further south on I-95.

Watching as several of the motorists hurried back to the perceived safety of their cars, one of the men said, “That glass and sheet metal ain’t gonna stop bullets. If someone starts shootin’ at me, I’m shootin’ back. I’m not hiding in my damn car.”

Adjusting his hat with a smile, Jim replied, “Amen to that. There’s no need to go out in the fetal position when you can go out swinging.”

Standing on the bumper of his truck, a man in a red ball cap and a white t-shirt cupped his hands around the bill of his hat in an attempt to shield his eyes from the sun as he looked south toward the situation ahead.

“What do you see?” asked one of the others.

“Nothing you can’t see from there,” he replied, stepping back down to the road. “All I know is I’m glad I’m not in the front row of this mess. The way things have been going with the other protests around the country, I’d imagine the first few rows of cars aren’t having a good day.”

“Well, guys, I’ve got to call my wife. Maybe she can tell us what’s going on. It’s probably on TV, and I’m sure she’s worried.” Sliding into the seat of his truck, Jim reached to the floor and retrieved his cell phone. Dialing his wife, he heard the message:

All circuits are busy; please try again later.

“Figures,” he said, tossing his phone onto the seat next to him. Noticing that his phone’s battery indicator was blinking red, Jim rolled his eyes, and said, “Just great. That’s just great.”

Seven hours later...

Pulling into his driveway with his headlights illuminating his home in the darkness of the night, Jim saw his wife Lori step outside with a perturbed look on her face. "Where have you been? I've been worried sick. There has been all sorts of chaos out there today. Why didn't you call? Why didn't—"

"Shhh, calm down, calm down," he said while reaching out to her.

"Don't you shush me, mister!"

"I'm sorry. Some protest had the freeway shut down, and my phone died," he sheepishly explained.

"I've been telling you to get another car charger forever!"

"Let's go in the house and stop putting on a show for the neighborhood to watch," he said, as he hugged her close and began leading her inside.

Closing the door behind them, Jim said, "This is exactly why I didn't want Damon leaving town right now. Things seem to be getting worse by the day."

"I've been worried sick," Lori said, wiping a tear from her eye. "I was watching the news reports about the protest on I-95. They said one of the motorists tried to push through the protesters with his car. The protesters dragged him out of his car and began beating him. The reporters said the man pulled a gun and shot one of the protesters. The others took it away from him and continued beating and stabbing him right there in front of everyone," she said as she began to sob.

Holding Lori close, Jim asked, "Why didn't anyone stop them?"

Regaining her composure, she said, "One of the reporters said she heard that the police were under strict orders not to intervene. They just stood there while the man was beaten to death right in front of everyone. Children were watching, for God's sake! Finally, several of the officers refused to stand by and watch any longer and broke up the protest using some sort of tear gas and tasers."

"My God, what has this country become?" Jim said, sitting down on the couch in disbelief. "They were told not to intervene?"

"Yes, and to make it worse, the only people arrested were the officers who acted in defense of the man who was being beaten. They are being held pending a full investigation by the DOJ."

"Arrested? For what?" he asked. "And why is the DOJ involved? This is a local matter."

"I don't know. Probably for violating the civil rights of the protestors or something," she said with a defeated tone. "Who knows? Nothing makes sense anymore."

Pausing for a long moment, Jim looked Lori in the eye. "We've got to have a long talk with Damon when he gets back. I think it's time to pack up and move."

"Move?" she interrupted. "What are you talking about, move? Our friends, our family, everything is here."

"We live too close to the city, and things keep getting worse and worse. I love it here. I love the people. I love our neighbors. But I just can't sit back and watch while things crumble apart around us. If I had been sitting in the front row of traffic today, that would have likely been me you saw being beaten. Only I would hope they wouldn't have gotten my gun until it was empty and smoking with all of my empty magazines laying on the ground around me in a pile of warm brass."

"Tough talk won't keep you alive, Jim. You can play things out in your head the way you want to see it, but that doesn't mean that's how it will happen. I would hope you would keep your wits about you better than that."

After a moment of awkward silence, seeing that Jim was biting his tongue, holding something back, she continued,

"What about the business? It's all we have. It's what we've always worked for."

"I've been meaning to talk to you about that. Our revenues continue to decline, while our costs and expenses continue to rise. We're having a hard time keeping our heads above water, and we can't afford to hire more accounting and compliance folks to help us deal with the layer after layer of regulations they keep piling on top of us. They're making it impossible for the little guy to make it. Large corporations have the legal and accounting staffs to deal with it all, so they're not in the same boat as us little guys. Not to mention the fact that they get special carve-outs due to their most generous campaign and foundation contributions. The little guy is simply getting crushed under the weight of it all. It's nothing but cronyism anymore. It's pay to play, and the payers aren't the best players, so it's all going in the tank."

Pausing to gather his thoughts, Jim took Lori's hand. "To make a long, rant-filled story short, our business won't be around much longer the way things are going. I think we need to cash in our remaining chips and walk away while we still have the shirts on our backs."

Turning to look out the window, Lori sighed. "Let's talk about it more when Damon gets back."

Chapter Three: Confusion

Two days later...

Pouring himself a steaming hot cup of coffee, Jim stirred in his favorite mixture of heavy whipping cream and honey. He took a sip, enjoying the aroma of the obnoxiously strong brew. Settling in his recliner, Jim picked up the remote control and turned on the TV as he propped his feet up in front of him. Flipping through the channels, he paused on Channel 6 Action News, catching what appeared to be the middle of a special report.

"...series of explosions, as well as reports of gunfire in New York City, Philadelphia, Washington D. C., and yet to be verified reports of similar occurrences in cities all across the nation. The president has declared a state of emergency, and the Department of Homeland Security urges everyone to shelter in place and follow further instructions as they become available. All major airports have been closed, and the National Airspace System has been severely restricted to government and expressly authorized civilian aircraft."

"Lori!" Jim said, shouting toward the bedroom. "Get in here!"

"What?" she replied as she hurried into the living room. "What in the world are you yelling about?"

"Shhhh," he said as he gestured with his index finger across his lips. "Watch. Just watch."

"We now turn to our KBC News affiliate in Washington D. C." Pausing and waiting for their affiliate station to take the

handoff, the local anchor repeated, *"Andrea, are you there? Well, folks, we seem to be having some technical difficulties. We'll check in with—"*

Jim watched with anticipation as the television went black. Quickly looking around, he noticed that the familiar hum of the home's heating and refrigeration systems were silent as well.

"Damn it!" he exclaimed, standing to flip the light switch on the wall on and off in an act of futility.

"What?" Lori asked. "What's going on? What were they saying?"

"Something about explosions and gunfire in New York, Philly, and D. C., as well as some others. They didn't go through the entire list. They said the DHS told everyone to shelter in place and that the National Airspace System is basically closed. It sounds like something big, but I only caught the tail end of it."

Pacing around, as if trying to develop a plan, Jim said, "I've got to run over and grab Carl. I'm sure he's thinking what I'm thinking. We'll head over to Bruce Thomas's house to see what the airwaves have to say about all this. Get your shotgun and stay put. I'll be back soon."

"Wait...what? Stay put?" With her hands on her hips, she scrunched her forehead and nose, giving Jim a look he had seen many times over the years.

"I'm sorry. I mean, please stay here until I get back," he sheepishly replied, correcting himself.

"Why are you going to Bruce's place?" she asked.

"He's got the CAP and HAM radios. We need to find out what's going on. This is something big. I can feel it," he said as he pulled up his blue jeans and slid his Kimber TLE 1911 pistol into his inside-the-waistband holster.

Turning back to Lori as he ran toward the door, Jim said, "Lock the door behind me. And remember, keep the shotgun with you. Oh, and I love you, babe."

"I will. I love you, too," she said as Jim disappeared out the door, slamming it shut behind him.

Quickly running to the door, Lori secured the deadbolt. Pulling the curtains back slightly, she looked out the window, seeing several of their neighbors starting to congregate outside. With a stress-filled sigh, she said to herself, "I hope he's just getting himself all worked up for nothing, again."

~~~~

Hearing someone knock at the door several times, Carl peeked out the curtain adjacent to the door. Recognizing Jim, he quickly opened the door, ushering him inside.

"Jim, so glad to see you. What the hell is going on? Did you see the news?"

"Part of it," Jim said as he hurried inside. Looking over to the dining room table, Jim saw Carl's woodland camo painted Arsenal SLR-104, a semi-automatic, civilian legal version of a Bulgarian-made AK-74. The rifle, with its paracord-wrapped, tubular-style side-folding stock was propped up against a kitchen chair, along with several loaded magazines laying on top of the table. He also noticed that Carl was already wearing his Glock 35, also painted woodland camo, in a drop leg holster atop his tiger-striped camo BDU pants. Taking note of Carl's tall, formidable frame, and his equipment of choice, Jim said jokingly, "I'm sure glad you're on my side. You look like you mean business."

"Hey, man, we've always talked about what we were gonna do if it all hit the fan, and well, I think it did last night. It's time to put your game face on."
~~~~

Nodding that he understood, Jim replied, “Personally, I hope we’re just jumping to conclusions, but you’re right. We might as well get our heads wrapped around the possibilities.”

“So, what’s the plan?” asked Carl.

“I was thinking we should head over to Bruce’s place and see what he’s heard over the radio. Between the CAP frequencies and HAM, he should at least have a basic clue what’s going on.”

“That sounds like a good idea,” Carl said sharply.

Reaching to grab his rifle, Jim looked at Carl and asked, “Don’t you think the Glock will be good enough? We’re just heading down the street.”

“Trouble doesn’t always send you an invitation,” Carl replied as he picked up his rifle and threw it over his shoulder, hanging it from its sling in front of him. “Besides, I’m sure the sheriff will understand, all things considered.”

~~~~

Reaching Bruce’s house, Jim and Carl saw Bruce and several other men on the front porch having a heated discussion. As they approached, they heard Bruce saying, “Look, I don’t know what to tell you. All I know is that the powers-that-be told us to stay off the CAP frequencies for now. As far as HAM goes, a lot of the guys who usually yap a lot have gone quiet. The few that remain simply wished each other luck as if they all know something big is going down. One of the few guys I got to talk told me that based on what he had heard, there was a series of coordinated attacks all across the country. He said they hit just about every component of our basic infrastructure. Transportation, distribution, power generation, medical, financial, government, you name it. Nothing went completely untouched.”
~~~~

"Who's they?" Jim asked as he and Carl walked up the steps and onto the front porch.

"We don't know. At least not yet," Bruce answered. "Some people theorize it was terrorists, but to me, it seems too big for it to be just that."

"I don't know about that," Jim said in a sarcastic tone.

"Don't know about what?" one of the men asked.

Looking the man in the eye, Jim said, "I don't know about it being too big for that. Too big for terrorists, that is."

"I agree," Carl said, interrupting before anyone else could chime in. "This country has had its collective head up its own ass for so long, worried about one fabricated social issue after another, that we've all but stopped paying attention to the world around us. Sleeper cells could have been setting up shop here for years just waiting for the right opportunity to set it all into motion. I mean, think about it. The Middle East is on fire. The rise of groups like ISIS has gone unchecked while we sit around worrying about who is going to be forced to bake a cake for who or who can take a dump in what restroom. The fact that we haven't been hit big before now is what's hard to believe for me."

Jim smiled, noting the silence from the other men. "So, where's the police? I expected to see a presence by now."

Lance Miller, a member of the local city council, said, "Considering that there are only five of them, including the chief, they are spread a little thin. The chief is with the mayor and her staff at the town hall. The other four are taking shifts guarding the refinery. We've received unsubstantiated reports that some refineries may have been hit. With that in mind, the mayor and the chief thought it best to augment the security staff there."

"What about the sheriff?" Carl asked.

"As you can imagine, Wilmington is their primary concern at the moment. Chief Winsted relayed to us that Sheriff Nariño sent a group of deputies to aid with the reported chaos in the Philadelphia area. That was, of course, at the request of the Philadelphia County Sheriff when reports of the attacks first started coming in. At that point, they thought it might have been isolated to Philly. Otherwise, they would have kept their resources here in Delaware. The last word I got was that the sheriff had yet to receive any updates from them, but I'd imagine they're still in the middle of all that mess and it'll be a while."

"If that's right, and knowing how thinly spread the state boys are and will be for the foreseeable future, we need to keep an eye on things around here ourselves," Jim said, looking around at the group.

"What do you have in mind?" Lance asked.

"Let's meet up this evening and discuss it when more people can be present," Jim replied. "Each of you spread the word to your neighbors and anyone you can think of that may be willing to get involved. I'm not talking about some vigilante-style group. I'm talking about a legitimate citizen's militia, recognized by the city. I'm sure Lance here can help with that. Right, Lance?" Jim said, looking to Lance for an answer.

"You've got my support," Lance replied, "but there are others that won't be as easy to sway. The fact that you two are already carrying guns around will put them on edge. Instead of setting up a meeting on your own, why don't you attend the city council's emergency town hall meeting tonight? They called for a special meeting to address everyone's concerns. That's actually why I was here. I can tell you now that having an armed militia patrolling the streets will be a tough sell, though, regardless of the logic in your argument."

"So, even though we've had reports of widespread terror attacks..."

"No one officially knows what it is," interrupted one of the men.

Correcting himself while giving the man a perturbed look, Jim continued, "So, even though it's '*possible*' that we've been hit by a series of widespread terror attacks, the city council might have a problem with the townspeople defending themselves? That's insane."

Looking at Jim and Carl, Lance shrugged. "That's the world we live in today, guys. There are those among us who believe only the government should have guns."

With anger building inside, Carl quipped, "Yeah, and those are the same assholes that call cops—who carry guns on behalf of the government—racist murderers when such remarks can gain them political capital. Screw those people! They can deal with us now as fellow citizens who just happen to believe in and cherish our right to bear arms in defense of ourselves and others, or they can deal with us after the fact in a court of law and public opinion. Either way, we're not just gonna lie down and be rolled over by whoever decides to do our loved ones harm. When the sheriff gets back, he can call the shots, but for now, we need to call them for ourselves. If the city council wants to vote on some stupid sign ordinance or the like, let them argue about that, but when it comes to the defense of ourselves and others, well, they can—"

"Okay guys, we get it," Jim said, trying to diffuse the rage that he could clearly see building inside Carl. "We're all a little stressed at the moment. Let's just go back to our homes and families and work on our individual emergency plans, then meet back up at Town Hall tonight for the meeting. If it ends up being a waste of our time, we'll meet privately with anyone who chooses to after the meeting adjourns. Does that sound good to everyone?"

With a few mumbles and replies in the affirmative, the men disbursed and went their separate ways.

After a moment of awkward silence, Jim looked at Bruce and asked, "So, based on what you heard before you were cut off, do you think it's all as big a deal as we seem to think?"

Looking Jim directly in the eye, Bruce replied, "Remember how I always said I wanted a hunting cabin way off in the woods?"

"Yeah," Jim replied with a nod.

"Well, if I had such a cabin, I'd be on my way there right now."

Chapter Four: Debate

Walking up Clinton Street toward Delaware City Town Hall, Jim, Lori, and Carl watched the sun drift below the western horizon. Breaking the silence, Jim said, “They didn’t come on.”

“What didn’t come on?” Lori asked.

“The street lights. I was wondering if the power was going to come back on anytime soon. I guess I was subconsciously hoping the lights would come on, and we’d realize things weren’t as bad as we thought, that we were all getting worked up because of our lack of twenty-four-seven news and internet that we’re so conditioned to have at our fingertips.”

“We’ll find out soon enough,” Carl added. “Hopefully something useful will come out of the meeting tonight.”

“I have a feeling that’s not going to be the case,” Jim said dismissively.

“Well, if not, we’ll still deal with things as we see fit, but first, we can at least try to talk some sense into people.”

Trying to bring a positive note to the conversation, Lori said, “Maybe the sheriff’s deputies made it back. If so, I’m sure they’ll be able to help the local police, and we won’t have to worry about it.”

“I appreciate your optimism, Lori,” Jim said, flashing her a smile, “but I wouldn’t count on it. If things are as wide-spread as they seem, the sheriff and what few deputies he has will be spread thin over the entire county. With Wilmington being their primary concern, a little town like Delaware City will barely be on their radar, well, except for the refinery. That may make us at least somewhat of a priority.”

Nearing Town Hall, they saw Bruce standing out front with Rick Parsons, C.J. Smith, Martin Partagás, Ken Reed, Paul and Marcie Funk, and Rob and Barbara Whitmore.

Smiling and glad to see them, Bruce said, “Oh, hello there. I knew you folks wouldn’t miss the festivities tonight.” Turning to Carl, Bruce said, “I see you left your rifle at home this time.”

Replying with a crooked smile, Carl said, “This will probably be the last time you see me without it for a while. I’m trying to be cordial tonight, but if things get worse, I won’t be worried about offending people’s delicate sensibilities.”

Looking back to the Town Hall building, Bruce said, “Well, we’d better get inside. We’re still early, but tonight’s gonna be a packed house, and I imagine the questions are already starting to flow.”

Entering the main assembly room, the group worked their way through the crowd that had already grown to standing room only. The chatter throughout the room was overwhelming, as a very anxious public argued amongst themselves and shouted questions at the podium. Standing behind the podium was Mayor Christine Hammond’s assistant, Marceline Rosenberg. Attempting to quiet the noisy crowd to no avail, Marceline looked to the side of the stage to ask for help, as Carl shouted in a loud and authoritative voice, “Everyone shut up!”

Silence fell across the room with all eyes now squarely on Carl. He pointed to the podium as Marceline looked at him with a smile, saying, “Thanks.”

Clearing her throat, she continued, “Anyway, thank you all for coming on such short notice. I know many of you may have only heard about the meeting within the last hour as our cell phones and land lines remain down. Our apologies, but word of mouth is all we have at the moment. Let me start by saying we’re glad to see you all here.”

Before she could continue, a man on the other side of the room shouted, “Where’s the mayor?”

Responding to his rudeness and impatience, others around him quickly silenced him.

Answering the room, Marceline said, “Mayor Hammond and Chief Winsted will be at the podium momentarily. What I can tell you, is that they have both had extensive briefings with the governor and other mayors around the state of Delaware, and they...oh, here they are now,” she said as she saw Mayor Hammond and Chief Winsted enter the room from her left.

Taking the podium, Mayor Hammond said, “Thank you all for coming. As you have probably seen and heard, our nation is facing many challenges at this very moment.” Pausing while several people in the audience impatiently shouted questions, she then continued. “If you let Chief Winsted and I speak, we will tell you everything we know. But please, hold your questions until the end. At which time, we will answer any questions you may still have, and we will stay here all night sorting this out with you if need be.”

Faking a cough, she looked around the room in an attempt to read the crowd. As the rumble of conversations quieted, she continued, “Like I was saying, our nation is currently facing many challenges at this very moment. As many of you have no doubt already seen and heard, at least before the power went down and we lost our cell phone and landline services, there has been a series of attacks all across the country. I’m not going to go into an all-encompassing list of each attack, but I will highlight several key things that are affecting us here in Delaware City.

“Before I begin, let me say that I also know that many of you are concerned about friends and loved ones in other areas of the country. I share those concerns. I really do. But for now, with the limited time and resources we have, I will focus on what’s affecting us here in Delaware City.

“First off, several major population centers were hit with devastating attacks. Most importantly to us and our concerns here in Delaware City, due to our proximity to them, are the attacks in New York, Philadelphia, and our nation's capitol. We aren't sure of the origin of the attacks, nor do we know the extent of the damage or the nature of the attacks. All we can say is that the situation is nothing like we've seen in our lifetimes."

Feeling stress and apprehension sweep through the room with every word that escaped her lips, Mayor Hammond paused, giving what she had already said time to sink in before continuing.

Adjusting her eyeglasses, she looked down at her notes and continued, "Transportation, power generation, communication, and nearly every other vital aspect of our country's infrastructure, including our oil refineries and natural gas assets, have been affected by the attacks.

"As of now, the national airspace system is closed to civilian air traffic unless specifically authorized by the Department of Homeland Security. Additionally, both cellular and land-based forms of telecommunication will be down for some period of time. The utilities concerned hope to restore service over time, but as of now, that is all we know. We have received reports of the intentional contamination of municipal water supplies in some cities, so we recommend filtering or boiling your water before you drink it. This is merely a precaution, however, as we have no reason to believe that the integrity of our own water supply has been compromised."

As the room erupted with questions and concerns, Mayor Hammond banged the podium gavel loudly, attempting to restore order. "Ladies and gentlemen, please. I know this is more than any of us ever thought we could be facing, but I'm telling you everything that I know so that you can make informed decisions in regards to the safety of yourselves and your families. As I stated before, Chief Winsted and I are going to stay as long as it takes to answer your questions and to listen to your concerns, but you have to let me speak."

Pausing momentarily, she continued, “Thank you. We also recommend that you consume the foods you currently have in your homes based on the remaining shelf-life. Rotate refrigerated and frozen foods, as well as breads, fruits, and vegetables to the front of your meal planning, while foods more suitable for long-term storage should be kept in reserve as the availability of resupply for our local stores remains uncertain.

“We are in the process of working with local law enforcement, first responders, and emergency management personnel to set up a series of daily briefings right here in Town Hall to keep everyone up to date. In addition, we will use those daily briefings to educate the citizens of Delaware City on how to deal with the hardships created by this situation.

“Since security will undoubtedly be on the forefront everyone’s minds, I yield the floor to the head of our police department, Chief Samuel Winsted.”

As several people started shouting questions to Chief Winsted, he held his hands up. “Please, like the mayor said, let’s hold all questions until the end of the briefing.”

Once the crowd silenced, he continued. “As the mayor said, we are facing a disaster unlike any seen in our lifetimes, except of course, for many of our veterans in the crowd here tonight. Some of you saw similar chaos in the performance of your duties overseas. I ask that everyone remain calm and that we stick together as a community to see us through this situation and the tough times that undoubtedly lie ahead.

“Needless to say, Delaware City, like most other small towns, has limited resources. The New Castle County Sheriff’s Department sent a support team to the city of Philadelphia when the reports first started rolling in. In hindsight, I’m sure Sheriff Nariño would have kept those deputies right here in New Castle County had he known the extent of the attacks. For now, we have to play the hand we’ve been dealt. That being said, the remaining Sheriff's Department assets will be focusing on the vital resources throughout all of New Castle County and will not be able to provide much in terms of a response to individual crimes or events.

"The same can be said of us here in Delaware City. I will remain with the mayor and the city's leadership, so I can stay up to speed with the ever-changing information as we receive it. The other four police officers will take rotating shifts at the refinery to supplement the civilian security staff already in place there. When not on duty, our officers have friends and families to attend to just as the rest of you do, so please, let's all grant them the courtesy of our understanding when they are in their own homes."

Shouting from near the back of the room, a man said, "So, your officers are going to guard the refinery and leave the rest of us to fend for ourselves? That's bullshit! We pay your salaries with our taxes. You owe us, not the oil companies!"

"Calm down and listen," Chief Winsted shouted in response to the man. Pausing for a moment to ensure he had the room's full attention, he retorted, "I asked you all to hold your questions until the end. We will never get through everything we need to cover tonight if you keep interrupting with such outbursts. Though I shouldn't, I will take a moment to address that comment." Looking squarely at the man, he said, "What do we have here in Delaware City that may be of interest to an organized group of individuals out to create mayhem and destruction? It sure as hell isn't the local diners or stores. It's not even our marina. It's the refinery. What do you think would happen if all the oil and refined products at the refinery were to be ignited somehow? How close are you and your loved ones? Where would the ensuing fires spread? Which direction would the thick, harmful billows of black smoke drift? The most important thing we can do to ensure we are not a target is to keep the refinery secure."

Regaining his composure, Chief Winsted looked around the room at the mostly thankful crowd, and said, "I know this is a lot to take in all at once, but we need each and every one of you to pitch in and keep your eyes and ears open to keep us all safe. Keep an eye on your neighbors. Take care of the sick and the elderly. Let's all pull together to make sure none of our less fortunate are forgotten during these trying times.

"With the exception of travel that is absolutely necessary to check on and care for others, we recommend and ask that you avoid any unnecessary travel and remain in your homes.

"I know we haven't answered all of your questions. I know we've been speaking in generalities instead of specifics. We have been receiving a lot of information from various sources, and as we sift through it all and can paint a more clear and accurate picture of the crisis we face, we will do our very best to keep you updated.

"Like Mayor Hammond said, we will hold daily briefings here at Town Hall. We ask, however, that each household sends a representative, rather than everyone attending. This will reduce the crowd and any unnecessary travel through town, conserving our valuable resources.

"Now, if anyone has any questions regarding the information that we've shared, please raise your hand. I'll ask you in advance to keep your questions brief and simple."

As conversations throughout the room began to grow, Chief Winsted called on a woman in her mid-forties accompanied by her two children, and said, "People! Please, let's try and keep the volume down so that this young lady can speak."

"Thank you, Chief. My name is Anita Parker. My husband is a member of the Delaware National Guard. He is currently on his two-week annual training orders, and we haven't heard from him since the phones went dead. Do you have any contacts for information regarding Guard personnel?"

"Thank you for your husband's service, ma'am. That's a good question. Unfortunately, I don't have an answer for you at the moment. I do, however, recommend that if anyone else in the audience is or has family members who are Delaware National Guard or Air National Guard personnel, that you or they attempt to make contact with your units as soon as possible. In addition to the declaration on the national level, Governor Markley has declared a state of emergency for Delaware. With that, of course, comes the need for our men and women in uniform to pitch in and lend a hand while the nation struggles both during the crisis and in the subsequent recovery. I ask that you attempt to contact or join up with your respective units as soon as you get your own families squared away to see where you're needed most."

Raising his hand, Jim waited patiently for his turn while Chief Winsted worked the room, doing his best to answer a majority of the questions as vaguely as possible.

Looking to Jim, Chief Winsted asked, "Mr. Rutherford, what's your question?"

"Thank you, Chief, and thank you for being here tonight. We all really appreciate it. My question goes along with your statements about how thinly spread our local, county, and state law enforcement agencies are at the moment, and for that matter, in the foreseeable future. With that in mind, I would like to ask that you and Mayor Hammond formally recognize a citizen organized patrol of the city. You've got your hands full. We know that, and we appreciate your efforts. But with the situation as it is, and without the benefit of cell phones or even landlines, if someone runs into trouble, they may have a hard time getting help. If we have a patrol of able-bodied men and women out walking the streets, we could alleviate that problem."

Interrupting Chief Winsted before he could answer, Mayor Hammond addressed Jim. "Thank you for your question. However, what we don't want to do is jump right into having untrained and armed militias running around our streets. For now, just remain in your homes, and we will ensure the appropriate authorities do everything they can to keep you all safe."

As Mayor Hammond once again yielded the floor to Chief Winsted, and he attempted to call on another person who had their hand raised, Jim said in a loud voice for all to hear, "Thank you, Mayor Hammond, for so clearly letting us know your personal position on the subject. And Chief, I understand you are an appointee of the Mayor, so I won't ask that you give us your own opinion as I understand your situation. However, can you tell me if it is currently illegal for groups of individuals to peaceably assemble and walk the streets of Delaware City?"

"No...it is not illegal...at this time," Chief Winsted answered.

"Can you also tell me if the open carry of a firearm in Delaware City is currently prohibited by law?"

Pausing for a moment, looking at the mayor, and then clearing his throat, Chief Winsted answered. "The State of Delaware regulates the issuance of concealed carry permits, but it does not have laws governing the open carry of firearms, and neither does Delaware City at this time. So, to answer your question, that by de facto, makes such carry lawful. However, New Castle County does have laws in place restricting firearms in publicly owned facilities such as parks and government buildings like Town Hall. That being said, I strongly advise against openly carrying firearms in town. With the situation as it is, we do not want our citizens becoming alarmed when they see someone they may not immediately recognize carrying a deadly weapon."

With a smile, Jim replied, "Thank you, Chief. And your opinion, as well as Mayor Hammond's, is duly noted."

As Jim's comments began causing an uproar of discussion throughout the room, Jim shouted above the noise, "Folks, some of us are going to peaceably assemble outside if you want to join us!" Turning to leave the building, Bruce, Carl, Lori, and Jim worked their way through the crowd.

Looking back before exiting the assembly room, Jim could see that Mayor Hammond was visibly furious and was shouting at Chief Winsted while pointing in their direction.

Sorry about that, Chief.

Chapter Five: Meeting of the Minds

As a group of residents of Delaware City joined Jim, Carl, and Lori outside Town Hall, Jim shouted, "Let's all go around to the side of the building. There's no use being right in front when the mayor and her entourage leave. I've ruffled enough of her feathers for tonight."

Behind the old, red brick Town Hall building, Jim gathered everyone around the Delaware City Police Department's patrol boat, parked on a trailer just behind the facility. He began counting heads and taking note of who he saw. "One, two, three...looks like an even dozen," he said.

In attendance, in addition to Jim, Lori, and Carl, was, of course, Bruce Thomas, Lance Miller, Paul and Marcie Funk, Rick Parsons, C.J. Smith, Thane Rogers, Martin Partagás, Brett and Elizabeth Marsh, and Dr. Dinesh Patel.

"Okay, first—before I waste my time arguing with people who are just here to shout me down—if you have something negative to say, get it out there."

Pausing for a moment as everyone looked around, Brett spoke up after being nudged by his wife, Elizabeth, as if she was prompting him to speak. "Let's just get something clear," he said. "Are you proposing that we have people carrying deadly weapons on our streets around our children?"

Taking over for her husband, Elizabeth interrupted before he could continue. "Don't you know the statistics of gun deaths? If what you're proposing is what we think it is, we simply won't stand for it."

"Okay, then," Jim said with a smile. "You two have a nice day. You did your part to save the world. Now run along."

"Who the hell do you think you are?" shouted Brett while pointing his finger at Jim.

Jim's smile transformed into a cold, hard stare. Squaring off in front of Brett, he replied in a serious tone, "I'm someone who understands that the United States of America is facing a tremendous threat, the full extent of which isn't clear to us at this time. I'm someone who understands that, exactly like Chief Winsted said, our law enforcement assets are spread thin on a good day. Now, with all that is going on around us, they simply won't have time to ride in and save the day like the cavalry in an old west movie. We have major cities that have been hit all across the country, and it's still uncertain how many have been killed or injured. Our supply chain has likely faced a severe disruption, and even some of our water supplies have been hit."

Growing more agitated, Elizabeth shouted, "But we've got to remain civil about this!"

With a perturbed look on his face, Jim replied, "Just what exactly is uncivil about our own citizens, the people you know and trust, taking measures to protect their neighbors? If a police officer walks down the street with a gun, you think nothing of it. Why? Does that uniform somehow transform the gun into an instrument of peace, while in my hands it's a tool for evil? Your line of thinking is flawed, ma'am."

"Who put you in charge?" asked Brett. "We've had elections to put people like Governor Markley and Mayor Hammond in place to deal with situations like this as they come up. They will handle it. Vigilantes like you need to stay out of it."

"Give it about a week and everyone around you will be running out of food. In the major cities nearby, where they have seen first-hand the devastation of the attacks, there are probably people already being forced to flee their homes with little more than they can carry. Motorists are already in gridlocks. The disruption in fuel supplies will strand people alongside every major roadway, including I-95, which isn't that far from here. We will no doubt be hearing from those people soon. Whoever it is that's doing this has hit many of our major refineries for heaven's sake. This isn't something that's just going to blow over like a bad storm. What do you think those people stranded out there without fuel will do? Do you think they'll just sit in their cars and wait for help that already has its hands full with more pressing issues? Hell no they won't! They'll be looking for food and shelter anywhere they can find it, and as each day goes by without help arriving, they'll get more and more desperate."

"That's ridiculous!" Elizabeth shouted as she turned to talk to the people around her. "The government isn't just going to let people sit in their cars on the side of the road and starve."

"What the hell do you think the government is gonna do about it?" Jim retorted, his face turning red. "Did you not hear what the rest of us heard in there and on the news, while we still had news? There have been major attacks in some of our most populated cities. What don't you understand? The last thing the government will have time to worry about will be people stranded in cars. Hell, even if they did somehow manage to send a fleet of Uber drivers to pick them all up and take them home, what would they use for fuel? And what about everyone else? When people begin to really feel the hunger, they'll get desperate. And when they get desperate, you'll wish you had a fellow citizen like one of us standing in front of your home with a gun to protect you."

Pulling Elizabeth by the arm, Brett said, "Come on. Don't waste your breath on them."

"Waste your breath?" Jim said as he lost his patience with Brett and Elizabeth. "According to the U.S. Government, CO2 is a harmful pollutant that's destroying the world, which, based on your opinions on guns, is probably a view of yours as well. When you breathe, you exhale CO2. Why don't you do us all a favor and stop breathing for a while and do your part to save the planet."

"Jim!" Lori said sharply, tugging at his arm.

"Yeah, buddy," Carl said in a calm voice. "If you say things like that, the next thing you know, those two idiots will be reporting you for death threats or something."

"As if the police would even care right now," Jim replied sarcastically.

"Oh, they'd care," Carl said with a crooked smile. "I'm pretty sure I saw Mayor Hammond put you on her list back there. You're flagged now, brother."

"Hell, Carl, you know damn well you and I are both already on every watch list out there," Jim said as his voice began returning to his normal, laid back state. "If nothing else, the UPS and FedEx guys had us put on the list simply because they were sick of carrying all those orders of bulk ammo."

Speaking up for the first time, Lance Miller said, "Hey, folks, thanks for the entertaining show, but I've got to be getting back inside. Things are gonna be crazy around here for the foreseeable future. I personally can't patrol the streets with you, which I assume is what you plan to do, but I'll do my best to keep you in the know."

"Thanks, Lance," Jim said, shaking his hand.

Turning to leave, Lance added, "Oh, yeah. Carl isn't that far off. I'd say Mayor Hammond has you flagged for sure. Whether that amounts to anything, in the long run, remains to be seen, but if anyone complains about you and your group, she'll make sure to address it. That I can guarantee."

Replying with a smile, Jim said, "If my gut feelings are correct, she'll have bigger problems on her hands than a non-compliant citizen like me before long. We'll all have a lot more to worry about." Turning to the rest of the group, he said, "Okay, does anyone else want to throw stones at me before we begin?"

Looking around, Jim saw that everyone was doing their best to keep a straight face after what had happened. "Good. Anyway,

I, for one, don't feel right just hiding inside my home while we wait for the world to burn down around us. What say you?" he said to the group, looking around amongst them.

Bruce spoke first. "I want to be part of whatever you've got going on here, but I have severe degenerative disk disease in my back. I can' t stay on my feet for extended periods of time, or I begin to get pain in my left hip and left leg. My crooked spine interferes with some of my nerves. However, I will do my best to contribute in any way I can. Jim and Carl here are already aware that I'm sort of a radio geek. I'm the comms guy for our local Civil Air Patrol squadron at the Newcastle County Airport. The CAP uses private DoD frequencies, but from way up in the chain of command, we received word that we're prohibited from transmitting at this time. I do have a HAM setup and can still hear some chatter about what's going on out there. Unfortunately, many of the regulars have gone silent. Anyway, to keep a long story short, I will do my best to contribute any intel about what's going on around us. Maybe that will help us to better prepare for whatever may come."

"Great, Bruce," Jim said with a smile. "You'll be a tremendous asset to the entire town, and not just us. I'm sure of that. We're glad to have you on board."

"I've got something to say," said Dr. Patel, a medical doctor of Indian descent.

"Sure thing, Dr. Patel. Go right ahead," Jim said with enthusiasm.

"I came to this country because I know all too well the ugliness that the instability of a society can bring. I grew up penniless in India, near the border of Pakistan in the city of Ludhiana. Ludhiana is near Kashmir, which if any of you know history beyond your own borders, has been the scene of disputes between India and Pakistan, and now China, for quite some time. I was just a child during the Indo-Pakistani War of 1965."

Pausing as anguish passed over his face, he collected himself and continued. “I’m sorry. As I was saying, I was a child then, but I saw things no child should see. Most people around the world believe the United Nations intervention ended the conflict. Well, it may have ended it officially and on your television screen, but our lives were a living hell for quite some time.”

Standing up straight, Dr. Patel said, “I came to this country seeking a better life. I came to this country to pursue the opportunities that many people around the world dream of. You see, to those of us who have lived through the horrors that are all too common in the rest of the world, we don’t take this country for granted. I know what it is to do without things that most modern people consider fundamental human rights. Where I come from, if you are poor, you are skinny and starving. If you eat meat once a month, it’s a luxury. A flushing toilet and running water are merely a fantasy. I’ve done well for myself here, using the opportunities this great nation gave me. But none of that matters if I lose my freedom and security. Air conditioning, Wi-Fi, and the other comforts people have come to expect are nothing without freedom. I cry inside sometimes when I see the youth of America be so willing to squander away their freedoms to the political elite in exchange for entitlements. I love this country. I am now proud to be a citizen of the United States of America. I feel it deep inside every time I utter the word, citizen.”

Now beaming with pride, he concluded. “I may not be proficient in the use of arms or such things that may be necessary in the realm of physical security and defending our neighbors, but I can offer you the services of first aid and medical treatment. If you are in need, I will come running to your side to render whatever aid I can. And if necessary, I will take up arms alongside you to defend our fellow citizens. Count me in on whatever you plan to do in any capacity that I may help."

Reaching out to shake Dr. Patel's hand, Jim said, "It's an honor to have you as a friend and neighbor. We need more people like you these days, and we will gladly take you up on your offer. We will work out the details later, perhaps a portable radio version of 9-1-1 where we can reach you if we are in need. We'll think of something, and we're sure glad to have you aboard, especially considering the strain on our medical resources that is likely coming."

After listening to everyone's input and concerns, Jim pulled a small notepad and pen out of the cargo pocket of his dark green, Dickies work pants. Passing it around the group, he said, "I know where most of you live, I think, but if you could, please jot down your physical address. We'll then copy this and hand it out to everyone else when we meet again. We need to have each other's backs. When it comes to the point of doing physical patrols, it will be important that we check in on one another."

After everyone had signed it, Jim flipped open the flap of his shirt pocket, placing the notepad inside. "Okay, we'll get together again real soon, but for now, head on back to your homes and take a good look around. Consider what you need to address regarding physical security. Carl and I would be glad to come by to offer our advice if you feel you need it. Take an inventory of what food, water, first aid, and weapons, or other items you have like flashlights and headlamps. I also recommend putting together a bug-out-bag with any critical items you may need if you have to leave your home in a hurry.

"I know to some of you, it may seem as if I am being overly dramatic, but all of these items may save your life and the lives of your family at some point. I also recommend that you have a several day supply of food and water, as well as any medication you may need. You should also include a blanket or sleeping bag, any specialty light-weight camping gear you may have, a change of clothes, and spare glasses or contacts, if you wear them, in the bag at all times. Try not to over pack, though. Keep in mind you may have to carry that bag, preferably a backpack, while walking long distances if the chaos of the Philadelphia area spills over to us. This isn't an all-encompassing list of what you need, but it is a beginning. Think about your own situation and what you would need to feed yourself, defend yourself, and stay alive while on the move. Keep it simple, but keep it smart."

Remembering an item of importance, Jim awkwardly added, "Oh, and ladies, well, you know. You've got additional supplies to consider. You may not need such things this week, but what if you're on foot for three or four weeks?"

With a nervous look on her face, Marcie Funk spoke up, and asked, "Do you think it's going to come to that? I mean, we don't even know what's really going on yet."

In a reassuring voice, Jim said, "Marcie, you're right. We don't know for sure what will happen in the near future, but I've seen nothing like this in my lifetime. I want to be ready for whatever may come. I want you to all be ready. When I think back to Hurricane Katrina and more recently, Hurricane Sandy, I reflect on how quickly people came together to help each other, like we're doing here, but also about how quickly people turned on each other.

"The hell those people suffered through in New Orleans was magnified by those who preyed on them in their vulnerable state. Hell, the Super Dome, a place that was supposed to be a place of refuge, ended up being the scene of rapes and sexual assaults so numerous the authorities couldn't deal with it all. And that's where the help was supposed to be. After Hurricane Sandy, a much smaller disaster and much closer to us, people pulled weapons on each other in mile-long lines for fuel the very next day. And that's with help guaranteed to be on the way.

"In this case," Jim said reluctantly, "I don't have a good feeling that anyone will be coming to the rescue anytime soon. From what Mayor Hammond and Chief Winsted both said, as well as what we've all gathered from the television and internet before the signals went down, the shit has quite literally hit the fan, and it's a big fan. Any problems we may face here in Delaware City will be nothing compared to what the state and federal authorities will be most worried about. Just be ready to both stay in your home and defend it or to leave it if necessary."

Chapter Six: Teamwork

Early the next morning while sipping a hot cup of coffee, Jim pushed back the curtain while sitting on the loveseat in his and Lori's home. Seeing Chief Winsted pulling up to their driveway, he took another sip of coffee before placing it on the end table next to him, and thought, *I wonder what Mayor Hammond has him up to?*

Opening the door before Chief Winsted had a chance to knock, Jim found him standing there with his hand awkwardly in midair and his knuckles formed into a fist.

Chief Winsted said, "Holy crap, Jim. You scared the daylights out of me."

"Sorry about that, Chief," Jim replied with a chuckle. "Come on in."

As Jim stepped out of the way and opened the door for Chief Winsted to enter, Jim's Kimber 1911-style .45 ACP pistol was prominently displayed on his strong-side as he closed the door behind him.

Noticing the weapon, as well as the AR-15 leaning against the sofa, Chief Winsted asked, "Is that thing loaded?" as he pointed toward the rifle.

"That's a silly question," Jim replied.

"What's silly about it?" asked Chief Winsted.

Walking over to the curtains, drawing them back to allow more light in the room, Jim said, "What good is an unloaded weapon while the world crumbles apart around us? Besides, that thirty-round magazine should have answered your question. I don't know many people who would insert an empty mag on purpose during a national crisis. She ain't there for a photo op."

Answering with merely a look of understanding, Chief Winsted added, "Jim, I know what the mayor said last night, but I just want you to know that I disagree with her completely."

Pouring his guest a cup of coffee, Jim asked, "Do you like it black, or with cream and sugar?"

"Cream, please," Chief Winsted responded. "Anyway, I know she went on like she meant business, but I think her mind was changed pretty quickly last night after she spoke with the governor."

"She spoke with him after the town hall meeting?" Jim queried, handing Chief Winsted the coffee.

Reaching out to take the warm mug, Chief Winsted replied, "Yeah, by phone."

"Phone?" Jim said in a curious tone. "I thought the phone lines were all down. Neither of our cell phones or our landline is working."

"Satellite phone," Chief Winsted replied.

"Well, at least my tax money is paying for something tangible," Jim replied, taking a seat on the loveseat. Pointing at the sofa, Jim said, "Please, sit."

Balancing his cup of coffee, Chief Winsted sat down, clearly appreciating the break after his long, grueling night. "Last night at about one in the morning, Mayor Hammond received a call from the governor's office in Dover. The staffer who called asked her to remain on the line and that the governor would be with her shortly. After sitting impatiently on hold for about a half an hour, she was finally transferred to Governor Markley. He appeared to be giving her an updated intelligence briefing on the current situation."

"What did he say?" Jim asked, interrupting.

"I only got bits and pieces. The only thing I know for sure is whatever it was that he told the mayor made her pretty upset. She immediately started packing her things and shouting orders to me and the rest of her staff. I had to pull an officer out of bed to join me in escorting Mayor Hammond to Dover, where she said she will be meeting with Governor Markley in the morning...well, this morning."

Yawning, Chief Winsted put his hand over his mouth, and said, "Sorry. Needless to say, I've been up all night. On the drive back, while Officer Hinton slept, I began to realize that I think Mayor Hammond isn't coming back anytime soon. She's 'in the club' with the governor. She's an up-and-coming star in the party. I believe Governor Markley gave her an opportunity to get somewhere safe as if he knows the full extent of what's going on out there."

Placing his now empty cup on the end table, Jim asked, "What makes you think that? And why are you sharing this with me? I'm not necessarily the most popular guy around town in the eyes of the city government. I've always been a thorn in their side."

"Jim," Chief Winsted said, looking him directly in the eye. "I seriously don't think she's coming back. At least not until everything shakes out. Her opinion of you means about as much to me as—" Interrupted by another yawn, Chief Winsted said, "Damn it. I'm too sleepy to even finish a sentence. Anyway, she doesn't mean shit to me right now. And if she wants to fire me, if and when she gets back, then so be it. My number one concern is for the safety and security of our town and the people in it. I don't give a damn what some political hack with high hopes of a prestigious political career thinks. Frankly, I don't give a damn if she comes back, either."

Jim couldn't help but chuckle at Chief Winsted's attempt at a tirade while struggling to keep his eyes open. "When's the last time you've slept, Chief?"

"I can't even remember. Probably before it all started, except for a quick nap or two. Anyway, the reason I'm here is that I wanted you to know I'm all in on your offer to patrol the town; however, I've got a favor to ask."

With peaking interest, Jim asked, "What might that be?"

"Instead of patrolling the streets, I want to ask you to secure the marina."

"The marina?"

"Yeah. You're a boater. You know the marina as good as anyone. You know the ins and outs of who comes and goes. You also know that the refinery is just up river and around the bend. Some of the reports and recommended courses of action that I've managed to receive from my liaisons with the state have revolved around high-risk targets such as power plants and oil refineries. The refineries in the Philadelphia area have already been hit."

"So, that's the black smoke on the horizon to the northeast?" Jim asked.

"More than likely," Chief Winsted replied. "Hell, that could be the entire city burning by now. Our small-town department is spread thin. Instead of posting my officers as sentries at the marina and the refinery, leaving the townspeople vulnerable to inland threats, I'd like to utilize them as first responders, while you and your folks keep an eye on the marina and the refinery. Just think of yourselves as Delaware City's very own citizen's coast guard."

"We'd be more than glad to help, Chief."

"I'd also like to make sure my officers are in place to guard what's left of the city's food inventory as well as the other essentials. With it being doubtful that any supplies will be coming in anytime soon, it won't take but one more nudge for our own folks to be ready to begin to ignore that whole 'follow the rules' thing. I imagine the average pantry around here will start to run dry in a few days. We've got to be ready to respond when people get desperate. Also if, and that's a big if, the state or federal governments get involved, we need to be available to help distribute any emergency supplies they may bring, as well as ensure they have Delaware City's citizens' interest in mind with whatever it is they do." Pulling his glasses down on his nose, Chief Winsted looked Jim directly in the eye, and said, "I bet you don't have an average pantry. Do you?"

Feeling a bit uncomfortable with the question, Jim answered, "Oh, we're no different than everyone else. I'm just a gun nut. Not a doomsday prepper or the like."

Changing the subject, noting Jim's awkward response, Chief Winsted asked, "You've got a good-sized boat, don't you?"

"I've got a forty-three-foot Viking double cabin. Well, forty-three feet of load bearing water line, but when you count the swim platform and the bow above water out to the pulpit, it's a tad over forty-seven feet. But, as luck would have it, it's up on Long Island in New York having the canvas redone around the flybridge. Or was, anyway. Who the hell knows what's happened to it in all of this mess?"

"Well, if any of the others have a boat, or if we simply need to commandeer one, I'd like to add that to the tools you have available to you to cruise up and down our side of the river from the city waterfront to the refinery."

"I'm sure we can get that worked out," Jim replied confidently.

Yawning once again, Chief Winsted said, "Hell, I've got to get some sleep, or I'll be no good to anyone. You've got my full support, Jim. Get your people together as you see fit and get a rotating watch going. I'll check in on you from time to time, but for the most part, you run your own show down there. I'm sure I'll have my hands full, and I have confidence that you can handle it on your own."

Standing to escort Chief Winsted to the door, Jim gave him a firm handshake, and said, "I'll get to work setting everything up right away. I appreciate your faith, Chief. But to be honest, regardless of what Mayor Hammond said, we'd be protecting our own here."

"Yeah, I know," Chief Winsted said. "That's why I'm glad she left," he said with a tired smile, fighting off another yawn. "Her only concern is the political ladder she sees in front of her, and all of her decisions revolve around that. I'd rather have you on my side than have her riding my ass to deal with what she calls you crazy, right-wing militia types," he said with a grin.

Sharing a laugh, the two men waved goodbye as Chief Winsted began walking toward his patrol car. Closing the door behind him, Jim heard Lori ask, "What was that all about?"

Walking over to her, Jim put his arms around her squeezing her tight. He looked down at her, smiling softly as he gently brushed her hair out of her eyes, and said, "It looks like things are about to get busy around here."

Chapter Seven: Standing Guard

Taking the last bite of his cheeseburger grilled over his backyard charcoal grill, Carl savored the juicy goodness. Looking into the trash can where he had tossed the packaging, he sighed, and thought to himself, *Damn, I'm gonna miss fresh meat.* Having used the last of his fresh meat from his now thawing freezer, Carl thought about his unrealized plan of buying a solar-powered chest freezer from Chuck Weatherman, a man he had met down in Florida during a survival training course the previous year.

"Coulda, shoulda, woulda," he said, regretting his lack of follow through. "I bet those things are worth their weight in gold today if Florida is facing the same crap we are. Chuck's got to be the barter king right now."

Tossing his paper plate in the trash, he said, "Oh well, that won't be the last of my regrets. That, I'm sure of."

Hearing a knock on the door, Carl picked up his AK-74 and slipped through the house to the front door. Pushing the curtain out of the way with the barrel of his rifle, he saw Jim, anxiously knocking again.

Opening the door, Carl said, "Let me guess—more bad news?"

"No, well, I guess partly," Jim stammered.

"Come on in," Carl said, stepping out of the way as he scanned the neighborhood before closing the door behind Jim.

"What's the deal?

Smelling the aroma in the air, Jim's face lit up and asked, "Burgers?"

"Sorry, that was the last of it," Carl replied. "So, other than the smell of my grill, what brings you by on this fine day?"

With a chuckle at Carl's 'fine day' comment, Jim said, "Chief Winsted came by this morning. He said the mayor seems to have bugged out on us. He doesn't expect her back."

"So, it's good news," Carl said with a chuckle.

Grinning in reply, Jim said, "Yeah, there's a silver lining in every cloud, I guess. But seriously, he believes the Governor offered her safe haven to ride out the storm."

"Being in a club has its benefits," Carl replied.

"Yep. It sure does. Especially ours," Jim said with a crooked smile. "Speaking of which, have you seen Carmen? I've not seen her since all this started."

"No, I haven't," Carl said in a concerned voice, "but she's always headed up to Philly or New York on the weekends, so who knows?"

"Hmmm, I guess I was doing a lot of that at her age, too," replied Jim. "Well, she's tough. I've got faith in her. Anyway, from what the chief has gathered, both from the mayor and his contacts with the state, things are getting uglier out there by the day. With no resupply on its way, Chief Winsted expects the townspeople to start getting desperate soon. He wants to utilize his department to mitigate that desperation if things continue to go south. With that in mind, he asked that we keep watch over the marina and the refinery."

Scratching his chin as if consumed by deep thought, Carl said, "Well, that makes sense. I'd rather not have to scuffle with my neighbors if I can avoid it. Besides, he's right about the marina. It's basically right in town and leaves us pretty vulnerable, especially considering where the refinery is located."

"Exactly," Jim said. "Anyway, if you have a few spare minutes, I could use a hand knocking on doors. I'd like to announce a meeting at the marina at four this afternoon for anyone interested in joining our group."

"Sure thing, Jim," Carl said as he began to gather his things.

"Great. Your place is near the midpoint of town. I'll work my way southeast while you work your way northwest. That's a lot of doors to knock on, so try to recruit others to spread the word as you go."

"Roger that," Carl said sharply.

~~~~

For the next few hours, Jim and Carl worked their way through town notifying the residents of Delaware City of their plans and intentions, as well as asking for their assistance. Being a small town with a population of only seventeen hundred people, spreading the word the old-fashioned way would not be too burdensome once others got involved.

While most of the residents were warm and receptive to their plans, some had very little good to say about what they perceived to be a militia takeover of their town. Regardless of the explanations and assurances that the group would be working hand in hand with Chief Winsted and the Delaware City Police Department, many simply could not be swayed.

Undeterred, Jim and Carl, along with several other townspeople who volunteered to spread the word, walked the streets tirelessly in an attempt to get the word out to as many people as possible. They wanted their fellow residents to know what the city was doing to prepare itself to handle the current situation, as well as what they may all be facing in the very near future. They did their best to explain the importance of preparing for the uncertainties that may come.

As four o'clock approached, Jim and Carl met back at the Delaware City Marina where people had begun to gather.

Walking up to Carl, Jim said, "This looks like it's gonna work out nicely."
~~~~

"I've counted twenty-seven so far, but I think a few others may have slipped in since then," Carl said while looking into the crowd.

Nodding with a pleased look on his face, Jim said, "I imagine once we get things up and running, and everyone is able to see that this isn't some radical knee-jerk reaction, more will be willing to join. People have had it engrained in them for too long that only the government should be armed and capable of protecting its citizens. They forget that our government is supposed to be made up of citizens on behalf of the citizens, rather than some entity that sees itself as being over the citizens. These days, the word militia or anything that resembles one has a negative connotation to it, despite the fact that this country was literally founded by militias."

Putting his hands on his hips, Carl said, "They'll come around in a few days when they realize the government is busy protecting its own assets and could care less about theirs."

Nodding in agreement, Jim said, "Well, let's get this party started." Stepping up on the fender of an empty boat trailer, Jim cleared his throat, and in a loud voice began addressing the crowd. "I'd like to thank you all for coming. I'm sure if you're here, you're the kind of person who's been paying attention, so there's no reason for me to rehash the information you've likely already received from Chief Winsted's briefings at Town Hall. We all know it's ugly out there. We all know that people across the country have been hit from different angles, and they're suffering."

Interrupting Jim's address, one of the attendees shouted, "Is it true that no more gas is coming? And what about the electricity? When will it be back on?"

As mumbling grew throughout the crowd, Jim tried to regain control of the situation by shouting, "Okay, okay. I know we've all got a lot of questions and are desperately seeking answers, but I'll have to defer those to Chief Winsted. In my own opinion, though, I believe that since Delaware is an energy importer, the restoration of our electrical power is probably low on the priority list. And if the terrorists, or whoever the hell is behind all this, has gone as far as taking out the actual power stations themselves, well, we're screwed. We'd all better get used to doing things the old-fashioned way for a while. As far as fuel goes, refineries all over the country, even as close to us as Philadelphia, have reportedly been destroyed. With that in mind, we're all going to have to find and use alternate forms of transportation because this is gonna take a long time to all shake out."

Pausing to look at the crowd, attempting to gauge their mood, he continued. "Like I said, any other such questions I'll defer to Chief Winsted. He's got connections with the state, and as far as I know, he's the only person around here that can give you more than just hearsay and conjecture. I'll be glad to relay your questions to him. Now, back to the point of our gathering here today. I spoke with Chief Winsted this morning, and he has decided that now that Mayor Hammond has left—"

"What do you mean Mayor Hammond left?" another man shouted.

Feeling regret that he had mentioned it, Jim explained, "Mayor Hammond left to meet up with Governor Markley at an undisclosed location. There is no ETA for her return."

Looking to the crowd, as another man began to speak, Jim interrupted with a firm voice. "Look, folks. Those types of questions are best left to the good folks at Town Hall. I'm one of you. I'm just trying to help out where I can. Now, back to my point, Chief Winsted needs his officers in town to respond to whatever may come, be it threats from the outside or from within. As people begin to run out of food and essential supplies, he fears crime will skyrocket. Also, he would like to be in place at Town Hall in the event state or federal agencies send assets to Delaware City. He needs to be in place to deal with such things in the absence of Mayor Hammond."

Seeing that he now had the crowd's attention, Jim got back on track. "With that in mind, he asked us, the citizens of Delaware City, to form a militia-type group to secure the marina and keep an eye on the refinery. With our food and fuel supplies already low, we can't be having boats from the north attempting to pull in here in search of such things. We need to maintain what we have for ourselves. Also, if we are monitoring the length of the canal out to the river, we can keep an eye on suspicious activity that may be headed to the refinery."

Just then, James Horton spoke up. "I can help with that! I've got a Savage 110BA Stealth chambered in .338 Lapua Magnum that'll poke holes in a boat's hull from as far away as we'll need on the river."

With a chuckle, Jim replied, "James, we'd be glad to have you. I knew you'd be itchin' to put some of those toys of yours to use."

Getting a scowl from a woman in the crowd, Jim asked, "Is there something I can address for you, ma'am?"

Looking around before she answered, she put her hands on her hips and took a deep breath. The dark-haired woman in her mid-forties replied, "Are you bunch of idiots going to send away people in need and resort to violence so fast? This is insanity! We can't close our town to those in need. Mayor Hammond wouldn't stand for this."

"You're exactly right, ma'am," Jim said in a patronizing manner. "Mayor Hammond wouldn't stand for it. She would allow our city to be overrun with refugees at the expense of our fellow citizens, and she'd do it just to score political points."

"Refugees?" she interrupted. "Those people you are talking about are our fellow Americans!"

"I'm sure many of them are," he replied. "But who the hell knows who else will be among them? Just think about all the horrible things that have happened over the past few days throughout the country. A uniform-wearing army didn't just come marching across our border. Those who did this were among us. They may have even been standing in line behind you at the grocery store. They lived right alongside us, watching and waiting for the day when they could fulfill their obligation to whoever the hell it is they give allegiance to. Chief Winsted said his sources have confirmed that the refinery in Philly was hit by boat. If our refinery is taken out, it would be capable of burning our entire city to the ground. We can't have that. We can't let a boat pull up pier side only to have it explode while we're asking them how we can help. And even if they aren't here to do us harm, they'll be wanting resources. Resources that are already scarce. If we give away what little food, medicine, and fuel we have in this town, we'll end up being the refugees."

Seeing that the woman was obviously taken back by his bold statements, he attempted to convince her to see reason. "When you're on an airplane, the flight attendants always brief you to put your own mask on first before helping others. There's a reason for that. If you're dead, how will you help others? If you are starving, how will you help others get back on their feet once the dust settles? Trust me, I understand what you're saying, but I'll be damned if I stand by and let anything happen to this town or anyone in it if I can help it. We've got to secure ourselves first before we do anything to help others. This is a very small town, and if word gets out that it's a safe-haven, we'll be overrun in no time."

With a huff and puff, the woman shouted, "I'm gonna talk to Chief Winsted and demand he get in touch with Mayor Hammond to put a stop to this lunacy!"

"Good luck with that, ma'am," Jim said as he turned his attention back to the rest of the crowd, watching the woman stomp away in his peripheral vision. "Now, back to what I was saying, Chief Winsted wants us to keep an eye on the marina, to include all of Canal Street, as well as the inlet to the refinery. It looks like we've got around thirty people here, give or take. I've seen a few others arrive after we last counted."

Pointing to Carl, Jim said, "Carl here has the beginnings of a watch roster. We should be able to run three shifts of five-man watches—" Seeing the reactions of several women in the group, he corrected himself, saying, "Uh...I mean, three shifts of five-person watches, making it an every-other-day watch rotation. We know everyone will have a lot to do around their own homes with all that's going on, so we want to build the schedule accordingly."

Stepping up to the crowd with his notepad in hand, Carl said, "Okay folks, I've scribbled out a rough draft of a watch schedule. There are three shifts for both today and tomorrow. If you could each sign up for a shift one of the days, we'll start the every-other-day rotation accordingly."

Passing the notepad to the group, Carl and Jim watched as each of the townspeople in attendance eagerly selected a watch shift, and then passed the notepad to the person beside them. Once the roster was mostly full, Carl retrieved the notepad, gave it a quick look, and nodded in the affirmative to Jim.

Stepping back onto the fender of the empty boat trailer, Jim said, "Thank you all very much for coming and for graciously volunteering to help your community. Everyone meet here at the marina no later than fifteen minutes before the commencement of your shift in order to relieve your fellow watch standers on time as well as to receive a proper passdown. We'll pass off the duty of senior watch stander to someone on each shift to settle any disputes or to make any necessary decisions that may arise. Again, thank you all for coming, and God bless."

As the crowd dispersed, leaving only the first group of watch standers, Jim handed the notepad to one of the men he recognized to be Matthew Heinz and said, "Congratulations, senior watch stander of the shift. If you could just spread everyone out evenly along the sidewalk spanning the length of Canal Street all the way out to Battery Park, that should work just fine. Adjust as necessary as the shift goes on."

Taking the notepad with a nod in the affirmative, Matt took charge of the group and began posting his watchstanders accordingly, as Jim and Carl began to walk back into town.

Looking at Carl, Jim asked, "What did you sign up for?"

"The late shift, 0100 to 0900," Carl replied.

"Good. I'll see you in the morning. I took 0900 to 1700."

With a chuckle, Carl said, "Banker's hours?"

"Heck, that's the rough shift. You don't have to wear sunglasses in the middle of the night. I've got to deal with squinting in the sun all day."

"Whatever you gotta say to make yourself feel better, man," Carl said as he and Jim went their separate ways, each of the men heading home to begin to prepare for whatever may come.

Chapter Eight: A Turn for the Worst

Just as Jim was rounding the corner toward his home, he heard what sounded like several gunshots coming from a few streets over. Pulling his Kimber TLE pistol from his inside-the-waistband holster, Jim ran toward the direction of the shots. As he neared, he heard a woman screaming. Looking toward the sound of the cry, he saw her standing on Dr. Patel's front porch, pointing frantically toward a man who was running away from the scene.

"He killed him!" she shouted. "He killed Dr. Patel!"

Running after the man, Jim shouted, "Stop! Stop, or I'll shoot!" Having only what the woman said to go on, Jim didn't feel he was justified in shooting the man in the back as he ran away. *What if she was mistaken?* he thought as countless scenarios bounced around in his mind.

Jumping over a fence and into the backyard of a house on Adams Street, the man tripped and fell into a kid's sandbox full of toy trucks, allowing Jim to gain ground on him. As Jim began to jump the fence, he noticed the man pointing a nickel-plated revolver at him, seemingly preparing to fire.

Flicking the safety off with his thumb, always carrying his Kimber 'cocked and locked' with a round in the chamber, Jim extended his right arm and point fired the gun at the man without taking the time to acquire his sights. As the .45ACP+P cartridge fired and ejected the spent casing from his pistol, Jim saw a flash of light from the man's revolver. Jim's world fell silent for a moment, hearing only his own breathing and heartbeat as if his world had come to a stop around him. Firing a second shot, Jim watched as the man jerked violently as his body absorbed the two-hundred-and-thirty-grain hollow-point projectile, it smashing into his torso, sending him onto the ground behind him like a rag doll, bouncing as he struck a metal toy truck beneath him.

Running over to the man with his sights now trained on him, Jim kicked the revolver to the side and watched as the man struggled to breathe, his lungs filling quickly with blood and his life slipping from him. As the man's struggles ceased, Jim could hear only the sound of air escaping the massive chest wound as he came to terms with the fact that he had just taken this man's life.

Picking the man's revolver up from the ground and placing it in his waistband, Jim turned to see several other townspeople coming over the fence behind him. "I had to," Jim said. "I had to. He was about to shoot."

Recognizing the man and the woman who had joined him in the yard as Tim and Felicia Johnson, Jim turned to see that the homeowner was standing at the back door of the house, hurrying his children back inside. Turning back to the couple, Jim asked, "What happened? What happened back at Dr. Patel's home?"

"Dr. Patel is dead," the man said. "His wife is very shaken up and in tears, but she managed to tell us this man busted into their home with his gun drawn demanding pain killers. Dr. Patel insisted that he didn't keep anything at his home, that he only wrote prescriptions, but the man wouldn't believe him. Mrs. Patel said the doctor went for a gun hidden in his desk drawer and he and the man exchanged fire. That's all she could tell us for now. She's extremely distraught."

Removing the magazine from his Kimber and replacing it with a fresh magazine from his back pocket, topped off with eight more rounds of Remington Golden Saber jacketed hollow-points, Jim slid his pistol back into his holster. Placing the partially spent magazine in his back pocket, Jim looked around as if to gather his thoughts and to process what had just happened. Looking back to the others, he said, “With no pharmacy in town, and the nearest one being at the grocery store in Bear, people around here with substance abuse problems, prescription or not, are gonna get desperate fast.”

Looking Jim in the eye, Tim said, “With the DART buses no longer running, I’d say that desperation is upon us already. Not being able to get to their suppliers, whether that’s a legitimate pharmacy or a ‘street pharmacy’, I’d say we’re gonna see more of this.”

Looking back at the dead man, Jim expressed his disappointment. “Being in a small town, one hopes to be shielded from this sort of thing. I guess we are, to a point. But, we can’t kid ourselves. We’ve got to be on the ball. We’ve got to be prepared for not only what we fear may come from the cities to the north, but from within our own community as well. The ugly side of humanity may be more evident in the larger cities, but it’s everywhere. That fact can no longer be ignored.”

Chapter Nine: The Encounter

Lying in bed, staring at the ceiling after a nearly sleepless night, Jim felt Lori cuddle up next to him. In her calm and loving voice, she asked, "It's Damon, isn't it?"

"What?" he asked, caught off guard in his sleep-deprived state.

Putting her arm around him, she said, "The reason you can't sleep. It's Damon, isn't it? You've barely said a word about him being up there in New York this whole time. I could tell it was eating at you inside. I just didn't want to mention it. I know how you deal with things."

Kissing her on the forehead, he said softly, "Yeah. That's a big chunk of it."

"Damon's just like you," she said reassuringly. "He can handle himself. You know that."

"Yeah. I do know that, but things like that don't always matter. Being a resourceful person doesn't save you when you're standing next to a bomb when it goes off, or when some scumbag gets a shot off at you before you're able to react. Real life isn't Hollywood. Good people will get hurt and killed. That's just how it is."

"I know, but—" she said, trying to interject.

"Just like today," he continued. "when that junkie killed Dr. Patel. Dr. Patel was a great man. He had his head on straight. He was armed, but, he was still murdered. That same pill head pointed his gun at me. My life was saved by a mere fraction of a second or a fraction of an inch. I'm not sure which one. Today could have had an entirely different outcome."

With a sigh, Lori said, "I know, but it didn't. We need to keep our thoughts as positive as we can."

"I'm not being negative. At least, not intentionally. I'm just being realistic. We can't kid ourselves about what's going on out there. This is big. It's huge. I just don't want to be operating with a false sense of reality. That's all."

Feeling Lori squeeze him tightly as she kissed him on the cheek, Jim tilted his head toward her and smiled. He watched as she closed her eyes. Not knowing what the future would bring, Jim pushed his negative thoughts aside and enjoyed the moment, watching the love of his life falling asleep beside him.

~~~~

Early the next morning, after eating breakfast with Lori, Jim approached the marina with his AR-15 slung around his neck and under his shoulder from a single-point sling, and his Kimber .45 in a strong-side, Kydex positive retention holster.

Seeing Carl as he approached, Jim heard Carl shout, "I see you're not hiding that thing anymore," gesturing toward his sidearm. "And the AR, that's a step in the right direction."

"We moved past that stage quicker than I expected," Jim replied. "I'm not taking any more chances. Yesterday shook me out of my false hopes that everything would shake itself out anytime soon."

"You knew better than that, anyway, Jim," Carl said as he walked up and patted Jim on the shoulder. "That's why you're a hoarder and have a stockpile that could feed and arm a small army in your basement."

Looking around to ensure that no one heard Carl's statement, Jim said in a quiet but serious tone, "Don't make me have to consider you a threat to my OPSEC." Pausing briefly, he smiled and said, "I'd hate to have to 'lose' you as an asset."

Nodding and smiling in return, Carl laughed and changed the subject. "We had a few boats attempt to port last night."
~~~~

Raising an eyebrow, Jim asked, “What did you do?”

“We looked them over closely. If it wasn’t a boat homeported here, we waved them off. A few were persistent, yelling profanities at us. We used ‘ballistic persuasion’ to get them to go elsewhere. We made it clear we were serious.”

“No one threatened to use force themselves?” Jim asked.

“One boat full of loud-mouth jerks acted as if they were gonna give us a little pushback, but then the rest of our guys appeared from the darkness. If the numbers didn’t scare them away, the aiming lasers from a few of the guns dancing all over their boat did.” Pausing briefly, Carl added, “Oh, and what appeared to be a group of low-flying helicopters flew by to the east of here.”

“Which direction were they heading?” Jim asked.

“They appeared to be following the coast on a northerly heading.”

“What type were they?”

“We couldn’t tell. They were off in the distance. They were turbine powered, though, and they had some weight and size to them. They weren’t little piston-powered Robinsons, that’s for sure.”

“Hmmm,” Jim wondered aloud. “They could have been National Guard, I guess.” Looking at his watch, he said, “It’s past your bedtime. You’d better get some sleep while you can, Carl. You know you can’t count on an uninterrupted day.”

With a yawn, Carl nodded, patted Jim on the shoulder, and said, “Take care, man. Send for me if you need me.”

“I will,” Jim said as he surveyed the marina.

Assembling his watch standers, Jim turned to Paul Funk, one of his friends and volunteers, and asked, “Who all do we have for this shift? I guess I should know that already.”

Handing Jim the notebook they had been using to keep track of the watch, Paul placed his pump-action, Mossberg 590 shotgun over his shoulder, and said, "It looks like it's me, you, Rick, and Phil Gooch. Phil missed our meeting, but met up with some of the other guys to put his name on the list."

"What's Marcie up to today?" Jim asked.

"She's keeping an eye on our house as well as beginning to get things together in the event we have to get out of here. We're getting pretty nervous about how things are going out there. Did you hear the thud last night?"

"Thud?" Jim asked.

"Yeah, it was a big, deep thud. Marcie was up doing a little collapse-of-society induced Bible study when she heard it. I didn't hear it myself. I was asleep. But she's practically got bionic hearing anyway."

"I guess I've had too many gunshots and too much loud machinery in my past to hear it," Jim replied.

"Anyway," Paul continued, "It sounded like it came from the northeast, from the direction of New York or Philly. If it were Philly, though, it would have probably been louder."

Feeling his heart skip a beat when he realized the direction from which Marcie believed the sound came, thoughts of Jim's brother Damon raced through Jim's mind as he snapped back into reality, asking Paul, "Have you heard any more credible news from outside of Delaware City?"

"No. Marcie and I have been holed up getting our house locked down and a few easy to carry bags packed."

"Bug out bags?" Jim asked.

Paul nodded. "Yeah, if you want to call them that. We've not been prepping for the end of the world or anything, but we've been paying attention. Our government, our society, our financial system, the threats from around the world that our elected officials seem to favor over us, I mean, hell, if you add it all up, how could you not have expected things to fall apart at some point?"

"So, you're saying you've been prepping for the end of the world," Jim said, tilting his head down while looking at Paul through the top of his sunglasses.

With a chuckle, Paul said, "Yeah, I guess. We've just been quiet about it because of the stigma such a thing carries in this part of the country."

"The last thing any of us should care about in this jacked up world is what people think. But, I know what you mean," Jim replied as he looked out toward the Delaware River. "By the way, make sure you keep that to yourself. And be careful who you choose to partner up with. If word gets out that you've got things stashed away, which I'm assuming you do, once people get hungry, they'll want it."

"Yeah, I wouldn't have said that to just anyone just now," Paul said, giving Jim a nod of mutual understanding.

Pausing for a moment to think carefully about his next statement, Jim said, "Carl, myself, and several others around town have been watching the world around us over the last year or two and kind of formed a group for just such an occasion. If it gets to that point, I think you and Marcie would fit right in."

Watching Paul's reaction, he then added, "Our original plan was to head out to sea, away from the masses. With my boat being away for canvas work, well, let's just say that's really bad timing. If and when, the time comes, head for the marina. That's our rally-point, regardless of which plan of action we take. We keep things very low key. No one would ever recognize us as a group. That's the way we want it. I'll make sure we get you acquainted with the others between now and then, if you're game?"

"Yeah. That would be great," Paul replied.

Hearing a shout from behind him, Jim turned to see Ken Reed walking toward him. "Jim," Ken said, "Chief Winsted wants to see you."

"What's going on?" Jim asked. "I just relieved someone for watch, so I'm sort of obligated at the moment."

"I'll stand in for you while you're gone," Ken said.

"Thanks, man," Jim replied. "I'll try not to be long."

~~~~

Reaching Town Hall, Jim jogged up the steps and inside where he found Chief Winsted swarmed by residents of Delaware City.

"The store shelves are empty! How are we going to feed our children?" a woman shouted.

"When are the gas stations going to open again?" asked an agitated man.

Attempting to extract himself from the crowd, Chief Winsted held his hands up with his palms toward the angry mob, insisting, "Folks, folks. I'm sorry, but I don't have all the answers you want. We are receiving little to no communications from the state, and nothing from the federal government. I know what you know."

Seeing Jim approach, he then said, "I'll be right back. I've got to confer with the river watch."

Ushering Jim into the mayor's office and closing the door behind them, Chief Winsted said, "Did Ken send you?"

"Yeah, he's down there right now filling in for me," Jim replied.

"Good," Chief Winsted said as he took a seat, removing his hat and rubbing his face with his hands.

"You look like hell," Jim said, reading the lines on Chief Winsted's face.

"I sure feel like hell," he replied. "Sorry for having you walk all the way here. I was just afraid the mob of angry people
~~~~

demanding that I provide them with services that I just can't provide would follow me."

"It's no problem. I understand," Jim said, taking a seat across from him.

"Something went down last night," Chief Winsted said, getting right to the point.

"What do you mean?"

"There was a major explosion last night."

"Paul mentioned that. He said Marcie heard it during the night."

"I received word from my contacts with the state that New York was hit hard last night."

"The city?" Jim clarified.

"Yeah. Manhattan, they believe," Chief Winsted said. "They weren't exactly sure of the source, but it was hit hard. It was big. They also told me that they, my contacts, were going to run silent and dark for a while. Most people on the front lines believe the attacks have been coming from jihadists; although, the federal government has been putting out conflicting reports, blaming right-wing militia groups. There have also been accusations that insiders were involved, allowing these attacks to be carried out unimpeded.

"And that's not all. More and more reports are coming in about attacks on our infrastructure from coast to coast. It seems as if nothing has been left untouched. Several of my sources have indicated that the president, using the state of emergency as justification, has basically declared martial law. Not officially, mind you, but the executive actions he's taken are flying in the face of our constitution. Never let a crisis go to waste, right?"

"Aren't accusations of an inside job a 9-11 conspiracy kind of thing?" Jim asked skeptically.

"Normally, I would brush such things off as lunacy, but for some reason, I have a feeling in my gut that there may be something to it. Something just isn't right about the whole thing. I can't go into everything I've been briefed on, but trust me when I say you should use a skeptic's eye on anything you see or hear from here on out. Question everything."

Looking down at the floor with thoughts of his brother's likely fate swirling in his mind, Jim asked, "Is that why you called me here?"

Pulling out a map of the Eastern Seaboard, Chief Winsted tapped his finger on the New York City area, saying, "New York and the surrounding areas are filled with marinas and boats that could be looking for a place to go. I have a feeling the marina is going to be a hot spot for people trying to port and fuel up before heading further down the coast. My guess is that by now, a lot of boats would have gotten underway unprepared, and they'll need to acquire food and fuel to get wherever it is that they need to go—food and fuel that we just can't spare."

"So, you're saying it's gonna get busy around here really soon."

"Basically," Chief Winsted replied. "All we can be sure of at this point is that change is coming." Changing the subject, Chief Winsted asked, "Does your family have plans?"

"Plans for what?" Jim asked.

"Plans for whatever may come?"

Leaning forward, Jim placed his elbows on his knees while looking at the floor. "We've always had a plan, but that plan isn't available at the moment, so we'll have to improvise. But yes, we don't have illusions that this will all blow over leaving Delaware City untouched. Those illusions were shattered at the crack of the first gunshots. They were shattered when I—"

Jim's thoughts were interrupted as memories of the man he shot came rushing into his mind. Jim could see him there, lying in a pool of his own blood, the children on the back porch being rushed inside by their father. Snapping back to the present moment, Jim said, "We know eventually we may have to leave. Don't get me wrong. I was born and raised here. I love this town. But, with Philly and New York being so close to us, well, you've done the math."

~~~~

Back at the marina, Ken and Paul watched as a large cruiser entered the channel leading into town with a sailboat in tow. "What the heck?" Paul said as he raised his binoculars, scanning the boat for threats.

"There are two men on the flybridge," he said. "What the heck is up with the sailboat, though?" he said as he studied the situation.

Walking toward the approaching vessels with his shotgun slung over his shoulder, clearly visible, Paul waved his arms, shouting, "No services! Go away!"

Watching as one of the men on the flybridge of the cruiser stood, Paul raised his shotgun, pointing it squarely at the man, and repeated his warning, "I said no services! Go away!"

"Do you know Jim Rutherford?" the man shouted back to Paul, undaunted by his warnings. "We have his brother and a very sick man who needs help."

Looking at each other in a moment of confusion, Ken asked, "Doesn't Jim own a boat like that?"

"Yeah, a Viking," Paul replied.

Shouting back to the man, Paul asked, "Who is his brother?"

"Damon Rutherford," the man on the boat said without hesitation.

"Go get Jim," Paul said. Walking along the pier to get a view of the boat's name art, seeing the words *Mother Washington* boldly displayed on the vessel's stern, Paul murmured to himself, "Well, I'll be damned," as he watched the boat begin to
~~~~

dock broadside along a long section of the unoccupied pier with the sailboat still in tow.

Looking to Phil and Rick, Paul shouted, “Hey, you two, give me a hand.”

As the *Mother Washington* closed to within a few feet of the pier, the man at the helm shut the engines off as the boat glided silently up against the parking bumpers spaced evenly along the pier. As Phil and Rick tied off mooring lines to the cleats on the *Mother Washington,* Paul ran to the sailboat, which bore the name *Little Angel,* and tied it off as well.

Holding the shotgun at the ready, Paul asked, “Who are you and why are you on Jim’s boat?”

The man at the helm replied, “I’m Evan Baird, and this is Jason Jones,” he said as he motioned to the other man occupying the bridge. “Down below is Peggy Marshall. The couple who own the sailboat is Bill and Judith Hoskins. They’re onboard as well. Bill is in terrible shape and needs to see a doctor ASAP. He may be having a heart attack. We met them a few miles out to sea in distress and pulled them here for help. We were on our way to bring Damon to Jim as well as return Jim’s boat.”

Confused, Paul shouted, “What the hell do you mean *bring Damon to Jim*? Where is Damon?”

“He was shot while sitting on the bridge. A boat attempted to hijack us out at sea,” Evan said as he pointed to the bullet holes on the flybridge. “He didn’t make it, and we wanted to get him back to his family where he belongs.”

Lowering the shotgun, Paul said a silent prayer, cleared his throat and wiped a tear from his eye. In a somber voice, he asked, “Where is he?”

“He’s in the stateroom,” the man said. “But let’s get Bill taken care of first.”

"Right, of course," Paul said as he turned to Phil, shouting, "Get the cart and get it now!"

A few minutes later, Phil returned driving a propane-powered, golf cart style, utility vehicle with a small dump bed on the back that they had been using to support their watch operations. The men hurried onto the boat and down into the salon, where they picked up the man named Bill and rushed him onto the pier, and into the utility bed of the cart.

Looking at Judith, the man's wife, Paul said, "Ma'am, they're going to take your husband to my sister's house just up the street. We recently lost our doctor, but she's an ER nurse, and she will do everything she can to help. You can ride with them," he said, motioning toward the cart.

As the cart sped away, Paul turned his attention to Evan, Jason, and Peggy. "You three come with me. Jim is just a few blocks up the street. He's gonna want to hear everything you can tell him."

Getting Rick's attention, Paul said, "See if you can intercept Ken and Jim. Have them meet us at Jim's place. Jim is going to need to sit down for this."

With a nod, Rick ran off in the direction of Town Hall.

~~~~

Arriving at Jim's home, they exchanged pleasantries and introductions as Evan and Jason sat down with him in the living room, breaking the news to him about his brother. Jim sat silently, his face rigid and cold, his skin pale and flush.

"Peggy, Jason and I, as well as a coworker that went missing after the attacks began, were staying at the same hotel as your brother," Evan said. "We were an overnighting airline crew. We were supposed to be on our way the very next day. Anyway, once it all started falling apart, I bumped into him downstairs in the
~~~~

breakfast area of the hotel. We both watched as the other guests began to mob the hotel staff, taking every bit of food that they could. We recognized that we each shared the same level of disgust for the scene as it was playing out, and began to chat."

Jason then added, "As things began to unravel, we joined up with Damon after he offered us a way off of Long Island. That way off, of course, being your boat. After having a violent run-in with some people who were going room to room throughout the hotel in search of food, we left in the middle of the night. Damon had a route all planned out for us, and it worked like a charm. We only had to make minor deviations along the way."

Looking around the room, Evan paused before looked Jim in the eye, and said, "Things went to hell quickly after that. We had several encounters that required that we take less than desirable actions to ensure our own safety. One of which was with DHS officers."

"What happened?" Paul asked.

Evan seemed as if he was searching for the right way to explain the situation before he spoke. "Let's just say if you've ever wondered about the intentions of our own government, your paranoia would have immediately been justified. They were confiscating food to redistribute as the government saw fit. At one point, two of the goose-stepping bastards were seen using deadly force to secure the food they were confiscating from a local corner store. We couldn't just sit there and watch it happen."

Seeing Evan pause, thinking back to that day, Jason continued. "Once we got to the boat, Damon got us out of there just as something big went down in Manhattan."

Looking to Paul, Jim asked, "The thud?"

"If you heard a big thud, there's a good chance that was it," Jason replied. "We're not sure what it was, but it was devastating, and Manhattan will never be the same again. That, I can promise you."

Resuming their explanation, Evan said, "Once we got underway and got some distance from the hell we had left behind, we noticed a vessel approaching rapidly from the rear. After making several evasive turns to verify that they were indeed intercepting us, they made repeated demands in several languages over a loud speaker. They were attempting to force us to stop and be boarded. Damon, of course, wasn't having that.

"Once they were convinced we weren't going to comply, they opened fire on us. Jason and I used the M1's Damon found in the forward V-berth to hold them off while Damon pushed the *Mother Washington* as hard as she would go, turning wildly to avoid the barrage of lead they were sending our way."

"Unfortunately, Damon was struck during the hail of gunfire. There was nothing we could do," Evan said as he lowered his head and wiped away a tear.

"Early this morning, once we had Damon's body taken care of as best we could, we were hailed over the radio by Judith from the *Little Angel*. We could hear the desperation in her voice. Knowing it may have been a trap, we used caution, but there was a sincerity in her voice that told us we could not simply motor away without investigating first."

"Getting within sight of them, we saw Judith, frantically waving her hands in the air. The tears and pain on her face was clearly no ruse. Once we boarded them, we tied their boat off securely and found Bill down in the cabin, barely clinging to life. That's when we fired back up and headed for Delaware City, hoping to find Damon's family and to seek help for Bill."

"How is Bill?" Peggy asked, speaking up for the first time.

"We're not sure yet," Paul replied. "He's in good hands, though."

“I need to see Damon,” Jim said, clearly distraught. “We need to get him off that boat.”

“Of course,” Evan said, standing to lead the way.

~~~~

Accompanying Jim to the *Mother Washington*, Paul, Ken, Evan, and Jason waited on the pier as Jim boarded the boat. They wanted to give him the privacy they knew he would need to come to terms with his new reality. After a few minutes, Jim stepped out of the salon, with tears in his eyes, climbing the steps to the rear deck. Closing his eyes for a brief moment, Jim allowed the breeze to dry his tears. Taking a deep breath, he opened his eyes and waved the group aboard.

~~~~

After respectfully removing Damon’s remains, Jim looked at Evan and Jason, and said, “We will have a proper ceremony and have him buried within a day or two. I would like to ask that your group stay for the service.”

“Of course, we wouldn’t dream of missing our chance to pay our respects to our friend and hero,” Evan said with trembling in his voice, overwhelmed by the emotions of the moment. “We wouldn’t have made it out of New York without him. That’s no exaggeration. Meeting Damon in the hotel lobby changed the outcome of our situation. We will never forget him.”

Gathering their things from the *Mother Washington*, the group stepped down onto the pier as Jim said, “Normally, I wouldn’t do this, but I’d like you all to stay with Lori and me tonight. A meal and a warm bed are the least I can do. In my heart, I’m forever in your debt. The power has been out all week, so all of the fresh food is gone,” Jim said humbly. “Luckily, we’ve kept our home, as well as the boat, fairly well stocked for emergencies. There is plenty of freeze-dried and long-term storage food to eat so you won't go hungry, but please forgive us for the lack of a decent meal tonight."

"Oh, don't worry about feeding us," Jason said. "We'll manage. We've got some tuna and stuff we can eat; we don't want to take your food."

"Nonsense!" Jim replied, dismissing their concerns. "You risked your necks to bring my brother and my boat back. You didn't have to do that, so you are welcome to dinner. I insist!"

Chapter Ten: The Ugly Truth

After a simple but filling meal of rice that was boiled in a pot on a propane-powered grill, in addition to some canned ham, Jim led Evan and Jason to the garage while Peggy helped Lori clean up after dinner.

Closing the door behind him, Jim asked, “So, what do you know about what happened? What did you see up there?”

Looking him in the eye, Evan responded, “All we know is that there seemed to be a coordinated series of terror attacks scattered throughout the city that virtually destroyed the city’s infrastructure. Manhattan Island appeared to have been nearly burned to the ground from what we saw on our way out. A massive explosion rocked the city. I can’t imagine there’s much left.”

Clearing his throat after a brief pause, the three men standing there in silence, Evan continued, “Judith and Bill relayed the same sort of scenario from the Norfolk area, which is what forced them out to sea. Atlantic City, and pretty much everything else we could see from several miles out, seemed to have been experiencing the same sort of turmoil.”

“Well, guys,” Jim said, “It’s actually a lot worse than what you saw. It’s much more widespread than that. I’m with the Civil Air Patrol, and while not a source of intel on its own, we do have an extensive radio network.”

“Ham?” Jason interrupted.

“No, not HAM,” Jim replied. “HAM is governed by the FCC, but Civil Air Patrol radios are regulated by the National Telecommunications and Information Agency (NTIA). CAP uses private DOD frequencies, which can only be used by CAP members. Our radios have a range of one hundred and fifty, to two hundred and fifty miles, and that is multiplied by an extensive network of repeaters. We are basically capable of relaying messages coast to coast.

"Anyway, in addition to what I've heard from our local Chief of Police, our guys with the CAP were reporting what they saw all across the country. Several major metropolitan areas, such as L.A., Dallas, Detroit, and Boston, as well as some smaller areas in the Midwest, have had their water supplies poisoned. There have been thousands of people killed and sickened from drinking tap water."

Raising an eyebrow, Jim continued, "Of course, that now means that bottled water and water purification supplies are life and death issues and are being fought over. Bottled or purified water is the new money in a lot of the country, with people being afraid to drink tap water.

"Also, nearly every major city has had numerous transportation system bombings, like the subways in NYC and the trains in Chicago. There have even been Greyhound buses explode, or be shot up while carrying passengers. There have been mass shootings, by what has been described as jihadist type individuals, in schools, shopping malls, and other crowded public places. Police departments, fire departments, and hospitals have been bombed or burned.

"You said you're airline crew, right?" Jim asked.

"Yes, sir," replied Evan.

"This will be near and dear to your heart, then," Jim continued. "Several large airplanes were stolen and used as flying bombs. A Boeing 737 was intentionally crashed into the terminal at the JFK airport, shutting it down."

"Damn," Evan replied, shaking his head. "I hope it wasn't full of passengers."

"I never heard if it was or wasn't," Jim said. "As if all of that isn't bad enough, power plants have been attacked, and at a minimum, taken offline. Several major power plants were completely destroyed. Some coal-fired plants had their coal stores ignited, creating enormous fires that took the plants down for the long haul.

"In addition, including just north of us in Philadelphia, oil refineries have been hit as well, ranging from harassing attacks to keep employees away to all-out assaults. Some received only small-scale damage, but others were completely destroyed. That's not good considering the last oil refinery built in the U. S. was completed in 1977!"

"Damn," Jason said in dismay as he shook his head.

"Yeah. They've basically hit every facet of our infrastructure and every safety net that we had in place. The transportation, energy, fuel, food distribution, financial system—everything. Everything has been hit. Gas stations that still have gas don't have electricity to pump it, and the ones that have generators are already out from all of the well-justified panic buying. On top of that, we all know resupply won't be coming anytime soon, and from what we have heard from both sources, the majority of the remaining food and fuel stores have been seized by the federal government to distribute and or stockpile as it sees fit. Which, of course, will probably be reserved for its own use and for its supporters.

"Think about how bad Katrina was, yet people in nearby cities and states were able to come and help. In this situation, whoever is behind this, has made sure that virtually every populated area in the nation has been hit in one way or another, which means that wherever you are, no one is coming to help because they are dealing with their own problems.

"By the second day, the president basically suspended the Constitution and declared martial law. Not officially, but he might as well have with some of the moves he's made. Some of that sounds like what you witnessed in New York.

"Even our CAP radio network was ordered off the air in the name of national security. Our fleet is also grounded, as the entire national airspace system has been considered a no-fly zone, except of course for government authorized traffic.

"This is bad, guys—really bad. Our financial system, which was already teetering on the edge of collapse, is simply no more. It's not that the stock market has collapsed. Based on what you're saying you saw in New York, the stock market was literally destroyed.

"As widespread as this is, I just don't see how we can bounce back." Slumping as if he was carrying the weight of the world on his back, Jim continued. "Some of the final chatter on the CAP radios, before we were shut down, was that the government was rounding up opposition groups and labeling them domestic terrorist groups. They were ignoring the fact that most of the reports from eye witnesses stated the attacks were jihadist or military in nature."

Shaking his head, Evan huffed and said, "It's not like facts have meant much over the past few years anyway."

Just then, Peggy burst into the garage with tears in her eyes, reflecting the light of the candle she held to light her way in the dark house. "Bill didn't make it," she said. "He died in the nurse's home. Judith is a mess. She's having a nervous breakdown. I'm going to stay with her tonight at the nurse's house because she refuses to leave Bill's side. I will meet you guys back down here in the morning."

With a sigh of disappointment, Evan said, "Okay, Peggy. Thank you so much for helping her."

After both he and Jason gave her a hug, he then said, "Be careful tonight. We will see you two in the morning."

As Peggy left the garage, escorted out of the home and to Judith's side by Lori, Jim looked to Evan and Jason, and asked,

"So, where will Judith go now? And what about you guys? What's your plan?"

"Well, our plan is to head west to Ohio to collect Jason's family and bug out vehicle. We will then head south to my family's property in Tennessee to weather out the storm," Evan explained.

"Bug out vehicle?" Jim queried in a curious tone. "Were you guys into that doomsday show or something?"

"No. No, we were a little more subdued than that," Evan said. "In hindsight, though, I'm glad we became 'crazy preppers.' We've planned for things and stockpiled tools and supplies accordingly. We developed a 'get home' plan, or rather, a strategy, since we both traveled for a living with the airline. All of that is now coming into play. Anyway, as far as Judith is concerned, both of her children are thousands of miles away in California and Texas. Bill was all she had in regards to family on the East Coast. That sailboat was basically their retirement plan. Without him, she really has nothing to fall back on that I know of."

"Well, guys," Jim said with a grave expression on his face. "We don't have enough food for ourselves here as it is. I mean, I've also prepared for what may come, as you have, but it was with Lori and myself in mind. We would love to take her in, but trust me, the situation is going to become dire around here soon. We're too close to the masses to our northeast. No amount of preparation can truly prepare for the hordes that will come flowing out of the major population areas now that the food supply has been cut off. I suggest you take her with you."

"Absolutely!" Jason replied. "She's part of the group now if she wants to be, as far as we are concerned. Whether or not she follows us all the way to Tennessee is up to her, but she has a place to go if she wants it."

"So, you guys are pilots?" Jim asked with a raised eyebrow.

"Yes, sir, why? responded Evan.

"I may have a proposition for you. Are you familiar with a Maule?"

With peaked interest, Evan replied, "The four-seat rag and tube taildraggers? Those things are cool. They make great four-seat bush planes. They're quick to get off the ground, too, aren't they?"

"Yes, they are," Jim replied. "I have a 1980 Maule M-5. It's out of annual, and technically, the engine is a tad over its recommended time before overhaul, but now that the world has fallen apart around us, that doesn't seem to be much of an issue. The engine still runs strong and has an automotive gasoline supplemental type certification. Being able to run pump gas will help a lot with the scarcity of avgas. I also had oil samples taken on a regular basis, right up to the point where the annual expired, and I stopped flying it. There were no metal deposits or anything indicating an imminent failure. It's got a simple panel, but it all works."

Getting back to the point, Jim said, "Anyway, if Judith has no need for that boat without Bill, and if she wants to go with you, I'll trade her the boat for the plane. You guys can fit all four of you and your bags inside and low-level yourselves all the way to Ohio."

Raising an eyebrow, Jason said, "But didn't you say the entire airspace system is a no-fly zone now?"

"Well, yes, technically. But, if you fly at the tree tops, stay low over the cornfields, and follow the terrain along the way, you should have a fairly radar-free route from here to there. Besides, I've heard of other guys going up in rural areas to survey their surroundings, and they haven't had a problem. The feds don't have the time or manpower to chase every little gnat in the sky at the moment. And to be honest, I just don' t believe you'll do very well traveling by land the way things are."

Looking to Jason, Evan said, “Well, that actually might not be a bad way to go. We have to give Judith a chance to get over this big change in her life, though, before we offer to trade her out of her retirement dream.”

“What are you going to do with her boat if she says yes?” Jason asked.

“We’ll load it up with friends and supplies and together, the *Mother Washington* and *Little Angel* will be our bug out armada. We are getting the hell out of here and heading for the islands down south. We are way too close to Philadelphia. If we stick around much longer, the people there will be spreading out in desperation, and we’ll be right in their path. This little town will be overrun by next week at the latest.”

“Hmm, this might just be a win-win,” Evan replied. “Oh, and one more thing; we desperately need to get to a HAM radio. Jason and I both have HAM setups at home, and our wives have always known that if something were to happen while we were away, the plan is for them to listen every morning at nine o’clock and every night at nine o’clock until we make contact.”

“So, that’s why Jason asked if our radios were HAMs,” Jim replied. “Like I said, our official CAP communications aren’t, but we have a HAM guy in town. He lives just two streets over. I’ll take you there in the morning. There is no power on his street, but he can fire up his generator for a few minutes. We will try and have you set up before 9 am.”

~~~~

After leaving Evan and Jason to themselves, Jim greeted Lori at the front door as she returned from escorting Peggy to stay by Judith’s side for the night. Glad to see that Lori was wearing her Smith & Wesson revolver on her hip, Jim gave her hug and a kiss. “I’m so glad you’re home.”
~~~~

"Me too," she replied, holding Jim tightly. "That poor woman is torn to pieces. I can't imagine what she's going through. I can't imagine the hell she's suffering, combined with the uncertainty of her future without him."

"I'm sure her new-found group will take good care of her," Jim said as he went on to explain the offer he had made to Evan and Jason.

"Are you sure heading out in the boat is the right thing for us to do?" she asked. "I mean, I know we always planned for the *Mother Washington* to be our getaway if things came to that, but based on what they said, based on how Damon was killed, can we be sure it is the right choice?"

"I'm not sure there is a solid right choice at the moment," Jim replied. "But, at least with the second boat, and maybe a third or fourth if we can convince others in town with boats to join us, maybe we'll have a fighting chance. More eyes, more capacity for food, more guns."

With reluctance in her voice, Lori added, "Or a bigger target."

"Possibly," Jim replied. "But it also may be seen as a more formidable target—not an easy kill. Like I said, there may not be a right choice that's evident at the moment, but it's what we've planned for. There just aren't many choices presenting themselves to us right now."

"It's getting late," she said, changing the subject. "We can talk about this more after you talk to Judith. Right now, it's still all up in the air."

With that, Jim and Lori retired to their room for the evening—anxious about what the following day might bring.

Chapter Eleven: Making Contact

Early the next morning, Jim and Lori prepared breakfast on an old Coleman camp stove. As Lori stirred the cream of wheat, the aroma of fresh coffee filled the home as the old, tin campfire style percolator bubbled and puffed.

Wrapping a potholder around the hot metal handle of the percolator, Jim poured both he and Lori a cup of coffee, saying with a chuckle, “I can’t believe such an old relic can still cook such a good breakfast.”

Giving Jim ‘the eye’ while placing her hands on her hips, Lori said, “What did you say?”

Not understanding why she was upset at first, his mind processing the situation slowly as he savored his first sip of hot coffee, Jim finally came to the realization of how she had heard what he’d said. Quickly putting his free hand up simulating a defensive block maneuver, Jim said with excitement in his voice, “No! No! Not you! The camp stove. I was talking about the camp stove. I’ve had that thing since I was a kid.”

Turning her attention back to the bubbling pot of cream of wheat, she resumed stirring it, and said, “Nice save.”

“No. Seriously,” he said, laughing so hard he nearly spilled his coffee. “I was just sitting here thinking about how old that stove and percolator are. I mean, that’s back when Coleman wasn’t just a logo slapped on cheap Chinese camping gear. That’s back when stuff was made to last a lifetime. I’m just glad we’ve got the good stuff, not the newer crap you buy at the big box stores that falls apart after the first season—if it even lasts that long.”

Looking up to see Evan and Jason enter the room, with a warm smile, Jim said, “Good morning, gentlemen. The coffee is ready and the food is simple, but it’s hot.”

"Sorry, guys," Lori said. "It's just cream of wheat, no toast or anything; all of the fresh stuff is already gone."

"Oh, don't worry, ma'am. These days, any morning you wake up alive to eat breakfast at all makes it a good breakfast," Jason said with a smile.

Nodding in agreement, Evan said, "Yes, and we are very thankful for anything at all."

Filling each of them a bowl of the creamy concoction, Lori handed it to them, and said, "Be careful. It's still hot."

"The cream of wheat is instant, and the butter is too, but it sure tastes good to me," Jim added.

"Instant butter?" Evan asked.

"Yeah, it's dehydrated. We have some friends that run a store in Waynesville, North Carolina called Carolina Readiness Supply. They've got everything you can imagine to ride out the end of the world. We get large cans of dehydrated staples from them on a regular basis. Or, we did. The butter is powdered. You can reconstitute it, or you can just sprinkle it directly on your food as it cooks. It tastes like regular butter in a dish like this. And when you're in a world of hurt, as we are, any little luxury—like the mere taste of butter—goes a long way toward keeping your morale up."

~~~~

After everyone had eaten, Jim helped Lori put everything away, and said, "Well, gentlemen, I'm sure you want to get a move on so that we can be at Bruce's place before nine. Lori will be here while we're gone, just in case Peggy and Judith come by." Looking at his watch, he suggested, "We'd better get a move on. The morning is burning."

Setting out on foot, Jim, Evan, and Jason walked several blocks to Bruce Thomas's place to see about using his HAM
~~~~

radio. “We pretty much walk everywhere now,” Jim said. “Gas is too hard to come by to burn going somewhere you can get for free. Most people around here only have what’s in their tanks, and when it’s gone, who the hell knows when there will be a chance to get more, with the attacks on the refineries and all. I imagine that’s gonna be a long, long time.”

“I guess America is about to lose a lot of weight,” chuckled Jason.

“And a significant portion of the population,” replied Jim in a somber manner. “There are way too many folks out there who could barely keep it together during a three-day power outage. Imagine when the permanence of all this settles in. There will be absolute chaos.”

“It didn’t even take that long for New York City to turn to chaos,” Evan replied.

“Yeah, well, in places like that, where the population density is so great that without constant resupply the shelves go empty immediately, there’s just no avoiding it. Add to that, the fact that many of those tiny New York City apartments have less of a kitchen than a decent motorhome, and people just don’t have a way to store much more than a few days worth of food. Hence going out to dinner being a recreational activity for most people living in a major city like that. It’s bad enough being here in Delaware City. We might feel like we live in a small town, but our proximity to Philly, New York, and Washington D.C. means the sand in our hourglass is about to run out. Those people are probably already migrating out of the cities, and many are likely heading our way. Even if they only mean to pass through, we just don’t have the resources to deal with it all.”

“Based on what we’ve seen already,” Jason added, “you won’t want to be around when that happens. Desperate people will do anything for food and water. Unless you’ve got enough to share, they’ll take it, or at least try.”

Nodding in agreement, Jim pointed up ahead and said, "That's Bruce's place, there."

As they approached the front door, it opened from within, with Bruce standing there with a smile on his face. "Come on in, gentlemen. Please, make yourselves at home," Bruce said as he ushered them in, closing the door behind them.

Once inside the home, Jim introduced everyone, and they all quickly got down to business. Having heard of their plight, Bruce was eager to help.

Leading them down the hall, Bruce said, "We don't usually have the lights on these days, but I fired the generator up to get the radio all warmed up for you. It's this way, just down this hall."

As they entered the room, following closely behind Bruce, they were impressed by his radio equipment, as well as the military memorabilia that he had displayed all over the room. "Now, who are we calling first?" asked Bruce.

Pulling a small notebook from his pocket, Jason flipped through the pages to find the frequency he needed in order to contact his wife in Zanesville, Ohio. "Do you mind if I go first?" Jason asked, looking at Evan.

"No, man, of course not. Go for it," Evan replied.

Sitting down at the radio, Jason watched the clock tick by. It felt to him as if time was moving in slow motion. It was currently 8:55 a.m., and it seemed as if the next five minutes would take an eternity. At exactly 9:00 o'clock, just as he was about to key up the microphone, he heard, "JJ220... are you there?"

Jason's heart nearly skipped a beat as he realized that the soft, female voice on the other end of the radio was his wife, Sarah.

Standing up from his seat in excitement, Jason grabbed the microphone as he broke down in tears. "Yes, baby, yes, I'm here. Oh, thank God you're there! How are you? How are the kids?"

The next thing he heard over the radio was "Daddy! Daddy! Daddy!"

Bruce, Jim, and Evan stepped out of the room for a moment to give him some time to talk to his family in private. It had been a stressful time for everyone since the attacks had begun, and they knew Jason needed a few precious moments alone with his family.

When they came back in, Jason was all smiles. He asked Sarah, "Have you heard from Molly?"

"Yes," Sarah said. "We talk every day on here. She contacted me shortly after it all started and we have been keeping each other up-to-date ever since. She said that Griff and his family have joined up with them on the Homefront and that with the extra security they are providing, everything is going well."

Evan wiped a tear of joy from his eyes as he heard the good news. "I owe you the beer now, Griff," he said aloud with no one but him getting the inside joke.

"How are things throughout Ohio?" Jason asked.

"Not so good," Sarah replied. "There is no electricity, and it's starting to get uncomfortably cold at night. Crime and looting have been getting worse and worse as each day goes by, too. From what I hear, the masses are starting to leave Columbus in search of food and water. They are hitting and looting the outlying towns and neighborhoods pretty hard. I've been afraid to drink the tap water after all that has happened, so the boys and I have been filtering the rain barrel water and using it instead. We are doing fine, but we really need you to get here soon, before the city rats, as Evan so eloquently puts it, make it as far as Zanesville."

"We're working on that, baby. We might be there sooner than you think. I can't give details now, but just so you know, we are on our way. I'm not sure when the next time we can get to a radio will be. Keep checking in just in case, but cut your frequency down to just the morning call," Jason said as he wiped another tear from his eye. "I love you, Sarah! I love you, boys! Take care of Mommy. Daddy will be home soon." With that, he signed off.

As Jason and Evan exchanged seats, Evan made his call, and right on schedule, Molly was right there waiting. They also shared a special, emotional moment. She let him talk to their kids, and then she caught him up on the situation in Tennessee. She explained what had happened prior to the Vandergriff's arriving, and how the extra security had really helped take the burden off of her. Evan then updated her on the fact that they were, indeed, going to retrieve Jason's family from Ohio, and would be heading south very soon.

After a very emotional few minutes to say goodbye, he signed off as well, regaining his composure. "Oh, thank the Lord they are all okay," he said with elation in his voice.

Chapter Twelve: Pressing On

Upon returning to the Rutherford home, the men found Peggy, Judith, and Lori sitting at the kitchen table having a cup of tea. The mood was somber due to Judith's loss, so Evan and Jason kept their happiness gained from their contact with their loved ones subdued. She looked as if she had been crying all night. Her eyes were swollen and red, but the expression on her face showed that she was trying to be strong and keep herself going.

Before anyone could say a word, Peggy stood, and said, "Judith is coming with us. I told her she can stay with Zack and me at my parents' home in Cincinnati," she said, referring to her young son who awaited her return back home.

With a smile, Evan replied, "Well, that makes it easy then. We were just about to try and convince her to come along."

Judith smiled for the first time since they had met her. "I prayed for angels, and oh how the Lord sent me my angels," she said, holding Peggy tightly.

~~~~

After lunch, Evan and Jason caught Peggy and Judith up on their contact with home, and they solidified their plan to head initially to Zanesville, and then on to Cincinnati before heading south to Tennessee. Jim took advantage of this moment and made his offer to Judith to trade the airplane for her boat, and she graciously accepted.

"Please, use the boat," she said. "Please let it take another family to safety like it delivered me to my angels. I have no doubt that Bill and I would have both died in Norfolk if we didn't have our *Little Angel* to whisk us away. And my poor Bill
~~~~

died because of his efforts to get me to safety. Just take good care of her and don't change her name."

"Yes, ma'am," Jim replied with a smile. "I will take great care of her, and since she will be taking care of us as well, she will be our *Little Angel,* too," he said as he gave her a warm hug.

~~~~

The next morning, several dozen people from town gathered for a memorial ceremony for both Damon and Bill. The pastor of the church that the Rutherford family regularly attended presided over the simple, yet beautiful ceremony. Jim and Judith both said their final goodbyes and Evan and Jason both thanked the Rutherford family publicly for having been led out of New York by Damon. To them, he truly was their hero.

The next day, Evan, Jason, Peggy, and Judith gathered their things and began to prepare for the next leg of their journey. Lori gave them each two packets of instant oatmeal and a packet of instant cream of wheat, and said, "I'm sorry it's not much to help get you on your way, but it's all we can spare. Everything else is going on the boats with us, and since we've got several people going with us, we will need our remaining provisions for them."

"Oh, nonsense," Peggy replied. "We are thankful to receive anything at all. Besides, you and your husband have been too kind to us already, and we will be forever in your debt. We appreciate everything you have done more than you will ever know."

Changing the subject, Jim looked at Evan and Jason, and said, "The plane is out at a little make-shift grass strip at a friend's farm. It's only about a thousand feet long, but the Maule is good for that."

"Are there any trees or obstacles at the end?" Evan asked.
~~~~

“No, just a fence. There are some trees along the side, but nothing to interfere with your departure,” Jim replied. “We will need to drive out to the farm. It’s about twenty miles from here, so it’s a little out of our walking range. We can take my F250 crew cab pickup. Your bags can go in the back, and we will all fit up front. You guys need to be armed up. We may have our little town relatively secure, as the townspeople have banded together to do security patrols and—”

“You mean like the gentlemen that met us at the pier?” Jason interrupted with a crooked smile.

“Yes, exactly, but once we get out of our little world, the people venturing out of Wilmington may get in the way. They may see that we have gas and get a little grabby. Fuel is food right now. You can run a vehicle to go find food, and then you can run a generator with it to cook the food, or hell, just make a fire with it.”

Evan looked at Jim with a concerned expression. “Taking us out there isn’t going to burn too deep into your fuel supplies, is it?”

“No, not at all,” Jim replied. “I have a few fifty-five-gallon drums of stabilized high-octane pump gas and a hand pump in the barn with the plane. I had to be my own fuel supplier operating the airplane out of the farm. The Maule should be full of fuel already. We keep it topped off to keep moisture from condensing in the tanks. Ice in your fuel is a problem you’ll need to keep an eye on, running pump gas in your bird. So much of the pump gas these days has ethanol in it, which attracts moisture.”

Getting side-tracked, Jim mumbled, “Damn government subsidy-driven-mandates. Anyway, I’m gonna bring the extra fuel back with me, and we’re going to load them up and take them with us. The *Mother Washington* runs on diesel, of course, but the kicker motor on the *Little Angel* runs on gasoline, so it will come in handy for something."

Gesturing to his friend, Jim said, "Carl here, is gonna ride out there with us to help me with the barrels and to ride shotgun on the way back."

Looking at the sturdy fellow, standing nearly six-foot-five, was carrying an AK-74-style rifle that had been painted woodland camouflage with what appeared to be a rather durable coating such as Cerakote or Duracoat. The tube-style side-folding stock was wrapped in olive drab paracord. In addition, an EOTech 512 holographic sight was mounted via a quick detach upper rail that hinged from the front sight mount. The man Jim introduced as Carl also wore a Glock 35, which was painted to match his rifle, in a drop-leg holster. Based on his choice of equipment and his demeanor, Evan and Jason instantly felt Jim was in good hands for his return trip.

Exchanging handshakes and pleasantries, the group loaded their things into the bed of the truck and prepared for their journey to the farm.

Once everything had been loaded and secured, Carl said, "I'll ride in the back with the gear. That way, no one can reach in and swipe anything. Not to mention the fact that it would be a little tight in the cab of Jim's truck with six of us, especially considering it's a stick shift and all."

"That sound's good," replied Jim as he gestured for the ladies in the group to make themselves at home in the truck. Jason rode in the shotgun position up front with Jim, while Evan took the back seat behind Jim on the driver side. Judith and Peggy occupied the middle and passenger side rear seats respectively.

This arrangement gave them rifle coverage on both sides, as well as Carl being able to cover the rear from the pickup's bed or pop up and cover the front if need be.

As they got underway, each of the men kept their rifles handy and in plain view to warn anyone who may have nefarious intentions to seek their prey elsewhere. They were taking only rural, back roads to get to the farm. This would reduce the chance of having a run-in with any sort of non-local government types.

After a few miles, with all the occupants remaining silent as thoughts of the future and its unknowns raced through their minds, they came across several groups of wandering people. Some of the people in these groups barely acknowledged that Jim and his group were driving by. They had a blank, hopeless look about them. Others actively asked for help, waving their hands and carrying signs containing requests for food, water, or help of any kind.

Riding shotgun in the front passenger seat, Jason had a front row view of the hopelessness and the looks of desperation. "Damn, it's only been a week, and people have already run out of everything and are starving," he mumbled.

Sharing the sentiment, Evan replied, "Yeah, it's sad, really. And to think, over the past few years, the government has been putting people who were doing what it took to be prepared to be able to feed their own families on watch lists. That sort of behavior all but trained people to just have blind faith in the system, and to not prepare for themselves."

Nodding in agreement, Jim's eyes followed a group of people standing on the side of the road. In a split second, barely having time to react, he saw as someone in the group shoved a young boy of around eight or nine years of age out in front of Jim's F250. Slamming on the brakes while screaming a few choice expletives, Jim narrowly missed the boy.

Moving into positions around the truck, the group stood around the vehicle as if they were trying to keep Jim from driving away.

"Give us some food or fuel! We're starving. We've got kids. You have to share! It's not fair!" one of the men in the group shouted.

Raising his AR-15 and pointing it at the man, Jason could see Carl in the side-view mirror as he popped up on one knee to cover the rest of the crowd. Knowing he had backup ready to go, Jason uttered a simple command to the man through gritted teeth, "Move, or die."

With a disgusted look on the angry man's face, he shouted with spit flying from his mouth, "So you're gonna shoot women and children just to get them out of the way over some simple stuff? Just give it up!"

"There's nothing simple about survival, sir. Now, move your people, or I'll smoke you!" Jason again ordered, becoming noticeably more agitated by each passing second.

"Go ahead!" the man said in a taunting manner. "I don't want to live in a world where I can't feed my kids!" Suddenly, and without further provocation, the man reached into his waistband and pulled out a nautical-style flare gun and began raising it to Jason's open window, as if he were preparing to fire.

Without hesitation, Jason fired two rounds into the man's chest at nearly point-blank range. To Judith, this being her first glimpse of an armed conflict, it was like it all happened in slow motion. She watched as the rounds struck the man's chest, sending a spray of blood and particles out of the man's back.

Falling backward from the impact of the rounds, the man's reflexes released a screaming hot flare at the truck window, grazing off the top of the truck, ricocheting into the air.

Flooring the accelerator pedal, Jim sped away like a madman, causing the people blocking their path to dive out of the way to avoid being overrun by the rapidly accelerating F250. With gravel flying off the truck's rear tires, Carl covered the crowd with his rifle as they disappeared into the distance behind them.

"Damn it! Damn it! Damn it!" Jason shouted in anger, his voice full of emotion. "Why the hell did he make me do that?"

In a stern, collected voice, Jim said, "A lot of these people weren't on their game before all of this started to happen, so they just can't handle it. They have become the bad side of what modern humanity has to offer. Society has trained the provider out of a lot of men. In my opinion, any man who can't provide for his family—not just in an economic way, but in a physical way, like hunt, fish, or whatever it damn well takes—isn't a man; he is merely an adult male. We've got way too many adult males and not nearly enough men these days if you ask me."

In a sad and stress-filled tone, Jason said, "Yeah, well, I have a feeling our current state of things may just naturally thin the herd a little. Maybe when this is all over, people will realize the value of real skills, not just digital ones."

Looking over to Judith to try and reassure her that everything was going to be okay, Evan placed his arm around her as she cowered down in the middle of the seat, shaking and crying in terror. She was already in an emotionally weakened state by what had happened to her husband, and now she had just witnessed her first violent death, up close and personal.

Joining Evan in lending Judith her emotional support, Peggy held her hand tightly. Evan could tell that Peggy had changed quite a bit from the naive, young woman that she was just a week before. She was now the rock that Judith needed. He thought to himself how some people rise to the occasion when truly tested, and some people become a burden to those around them. Peggy was doing quite well, and Evan knew that if they were able to reunite her with her son, Zack, that would be exactly what the young boy would need.

Chapter Thirteen: Faith and Friendship

The rest of the drive to the farm where the airplane was kept was tense, yet uneventful. They only came across a few more groups of people along the road, in addition to one vehicle that was traveling the back roads as they were. It was a gray Nissan Pathfinder with four men on board who did not look like locals to the area. Generally, only people local to the area frequented the backroads they had been using. Most of the people who used these roads were local family-owned farm workers, which regardless of ethnicity, had a general look about them by the way they acted and dressed, as well as the tell-tale signs of working long days outdoors.

As the men in the Pathfinder passed by Jim's F250, uneasy stares from each of the vehicles were the only interactions. As they drove on by, Carl noticed that there was no license plate on the back of the vehicle, and the lock on the tailgate hatch had been damaged. He knew the odds were that they were from one of the major cities to their north and northeast and were up to no good. He only hoped they weren't headed back toward Delaware City in their absence.

Arriving at the gate to the farm, Jim honked the horn three times. As the truck came to a stop, Carl jumped out of the back, walked over to the gate, unlocked the large padlock, and held the gate open as Jim drove through.

"What was the horn for?" Evan asked.

With a chuckle, Jim replied, "Oh, that was just to make sure Charlie isn't surprised to see us driving across the field toward the barn. I don't want him to get trigger-happy or anything. He's not one to just walk up and chat with strangers. He'd rather deal with them from a distance."

Pulling to a stop just past the gate, Jim waited for Carl to hop back into the back of the truck before proceeding. Jim looked to his right, speaking to Jason in the passenger seat. "I'll drop you guys off at the barn and you can check the bird out and get her all dusted off. After I show you around, I'll drive back up to the house to explain what's going on to Charlie; then I'll be back down in a bit."

Pulling up to the barn, Jim shut the truck off, allowing everyone to exit the vehicle. He then led them over to the main doors, where he removed the old, rusty lock and chain. He and Carl then swung the barn doors open, allowing daylight to shine inside for what appeared to be the first time in quite a while.

With dust particles dancing around in the rays of sunlight shining through the gaps in the old hardwood planks, Jim fanned the dust in front of his face, and said, "There she is. She's dirty but solid."

Evan and Jason saw a Maule M5-235C parked with its wings diagonally across the barn to allow room for an old Ford tractor and a few old implements that looked as if they hadn't been used for quite some time.

Walking into the barn, Jim continued, "Like I said, she needs to be cleaned up a bit, but trust me, when we parked her, she ran and flew great. I just got a little busy and the next thing I knew, she was out of her required annual inspection. She's sat for the better part of the last seven or eight months. I imagine we'll need to put a charge on the battery, if not replace it, but other than that, I think you'll be happy with her."

Evan and Jason began walking around the old bird to go over the details. Looking to Evan, Jason asked, "Do you have any taildragger time? I've always been in tricycle birds."

"Yeah, I've instructed in and flown quite a few taildraggers from Citabrias to Stinsons, to the old tailwheel Cessnas. I've even got a few hours in a Pitts S2B. Now that's a squirrelly little rascal," Evan replied.

Patting Evan on the back, Jason said, "Good, you can do the takeoff and landing, then."

"A Pitts?" Jim asked, overhearing their conversation.

"Yeah," Evan replied. "I didn't get much time in one. I just took some upset recovery training in one as an excuse to do something cool and to satisfy biennial flight review requirements. Those things are easy to upset. I guess that's why they called them 'little stinkers'."

Laughing in agreement, Jim said, "Yeah, I'm too tall to sit in one of those little things, myself. But one of the guys back in town has an S1. Not sure if it's a C or S model, but it's the single-seater for sure. He flies it a lot. That thing always reminded me of a World War I biplane. I always joked that he just needed to add a machine gun."

"It basically is," Evan replied. "Curtis Pitts designed it in 1943, I believe, so it wasn't that far removed from the World War I era."

Leaving them to their work, Jim stood back as Evan and Jason looked over every inch of the old bird. Noticing that Jason was checking the engine's oil dipstick, Jim said, "There is a case of Aeroshell oil on that shelf in the back. You're welcome to whatever you want. Take it with you if you have room for it. I won't have a need for it anymore."

"Thanks," Jason said with a nod.

Raising the cowl and looking into the engine compartment, Jason joked, "And to think, I used to joke that these old magneto ignition systems were ancient junk. Now, I look at them as being EMP proof."

With a chuckle, Evan agreed and continued to check out the rest of the airplane. "What's the fuel capacity?" he asked.

"Forty gallons at a twelve and a half gallon per hour burn," Jim replied. "That should give you about three hours and twenty minutes at seventy-five percent power down low. When we bought it, we wanted the sixty-three-gallon, long-range tanks, but we got a sweet deal on this one. We just couldn't pass it up."

"Oh well," Evan replied. "Forty will do. It should only be about two and a half hours to Zanesville, so that gets us there with a little to spare."

Checking the flight controls from the cockpit, Jason watched as each of the control surfaces moved according to his inputs. With everything feeling tight and correct, he turned to Evan and said, "Looks good to me; how about you?"

"Oh, I love it," Evan replied. "You made a great trade, Judith," Evan said, looking at her with a smile.

"Well, at least I was able to contribute something," she said, returning the smile.

Looking at the group, Jim asked, "So, what's the plan? Are you leaving tonight under the cover of darkness?"

Looking at Jason, and then back to Jim, Evan said, "Under other circumstances, that would be a good idea. However, with what we are currently facing, with power outages being so widespread, we have to time it so that we arrive after sunrise since there won't be any functional airport lights, not to mention ground-based navigational aids. The problem with that is, that would put us at risk of morning fog where we're going. Not to mention the fact that hugging the terrain at night would be risky, and if we had a problem and had to make an unplanned, off-airport landing, we would be up the creek without a paddle. With the Maule being a bush-plane at heart, we're probably gonna be landing off-airport somewhere anyway to avoid detection. I'd imagine airports aren't the place to be hanging out at the moment."

Looking off to the western horizon, Evan continued. “Also, considering how late it is in the day already, by the time we get the battery charged, I think we’d be cutting it too close to getting there in the dark. I think our best bet would be to get it ready, get a good night’s sleep here in the barn, if that is okay with Charlie, of course, and head out in the morning. If we buzz the treetops all the way there, by the time anyone sees us, we will be out of their line of sight in a flash. And if we want to buzz the treetops for hours on end to stay out of any potential radar coverage areas, we will need the daylight, for sure.”

Taking in everything Evan had said, Jim replied, “That makes sense. If you want to get that old generator over there fired up so that you can power the charger, I’ll drive on up and tell Charlie what we’re doing down here and what your plans are. I don’t think he will have a problem with that, though.”

Jim watched as Carl began helping Evan and Jason drag the old generator out and get it running. It took quite a few pulls on the recoil starter, but it finally shook, shuddered, and roared to life. Seeing that they were in good shape, Jim started his truck and began his short drive across the farm to Charlie’s home.

~~~~

Pulling up to Charlie’s home, Jim stepped out of his F250 as his old friend met him on the front porch. “What’s all the racket down there?” Charlie asked.

“I’m getting that old Maule out of your way. I’m trading it for another boat,” Jim replied.

“Another boat?” Charlie asked. “Where’s yours?”

Taking a deep breath and sitting down on the porch steps, Jim began to explain in detail to Charlie what had become of his brother, and how he had met Evan, Jason, Peggy, and Judith. After detailing all their struggles, Charlie patted Jim on the
~~~~

back, and said, "I'm sorry, Jim. You and Damon were two peas in a pod, and I know you're hurting a lot more inside than you're letting us see. If you need anything, anything at all, you know we're here for you and Lori."

"Thanks, Charlie," Jim replied, tossing a pebble onto the ground. "I've got too much going on at the moment to get tangled up in the weeds of my own mind. If I got stuck in that mess, I'd never get out. I just need to press on. I need to help the folks of Delaware City as best I can, and then I need to get the hell out of here." Turning his head to Charlie, he said, "You do, too. You know that."

"And you already know the answer to that, my friend," Charlie said as he stood up, stretching his aching back. "Now, let's go meet your friends."

Climbing into the passenger side of Jim's Ford as he yelled toward the house, Charlie shouted, "I'll be back in a minute. We've got company. The good kind, this time."

Opening the old screen door on the front porch, Charlie's wife, Clara, answered, "I'll get started on dinner!" with excitement in her voice, pleased to have guests to entertain.

~~~~

Flipping through the airplane's pilot operating handbook and other documentation that was tucked into a seat back pocket, Evan stopped on a page of interest, and said, "Here we go." Chuckling, he continued, "I haven't used these old-school performance charts in years. Anyway," he said, tracing his finger across the chart from point to point, "it says here, at max gross weight, we can still get off the ground in six-hundred feet. Jim said the strip is around a thousand, so we should be fine."

Just then, he looked up to see Jim pulling up to the barn, this time, with a grizzled looking old man with a fuzzy gray
~~~~

beard in the passenger seat. Evan then heard Carl say, "Oh, that's Charlie."

Getting out of Jim's truck and walking over to the group, in a gruff voice, Charlie said, "Hell no, you ain't sleep'n in my barn! After what Jim told me you did, going through all the trouble to bring his brother back to him and his family with the world falling apart around you, there is no way I would let you sleep out here. You are all going to spend the night up at the house with the missus and me. She's gonna whip up a feast to send you all off right. After what you did for the Rutherford's, you are all friends for life, as far as I'm concerned."

Standing there with a big smile on his face, Jim said, "Now come on, everyone hop in the truck. We can come back down after dinner to shut the generator off. There should be a good charge on the battery by then."

With that, they all climbed in. Charlie took the front passenger seat, the ladies took the back seat, and Carl, Evan, and Jason jumped into the pickup's bed.

After the quick drive to the farmhouse, Jason took one look and said, "Now that is my idea of a dream home."

"Yeah, it's straight out of an old movie," Carl said. "Wait'll you see the inside."

The home was an old-style, two-story farmhouse with a porch that wrapped all the way around. It had a chimney on each side of the house, as it had four fireplaces, total, for wood heat during winter. Two fireplaces were located on each floor, one on each end of the house. As they went into the home, they felt as if they had stepped back in time. Oil lamps were in each room, giving them ample light, and there was no television or other modern devices around that anyone could see at a glance.

Charlie had an old Civil War Springfield musket hanging over the main parlor's fireplace mantel. Immediately catching

Jason's eye, he walked up to it, and said, "That looks like a real one."

"It is," replied Charlie, beaming with pride. "It's a model 1861 Springfield. That rifle has been in the family since the war. It has been handed down generation after generation. The missus and I never got around to having kids, though, so I'm the last of the line. I told her to just bury it with me," he said with a smirk on his face. "I just couldn't bear the thought of it ending up in some pawn shop or something after an estate sale when we're both gone. Besides, I might need it if the rapture doesn't go so smoothly."

Sharing a laugh, he then led them into the kitchen. Charlie's wife Clara, who he always simply referred to as 'the missus', looked as if she was right out of history as well. She wore a beautiful homemade dress, cooking over a real, antique, wood-fired stove.

"Wow," Judith said. "This kitchen is fabulous."

"Oh, thank you," she replied. "I'm Clara; pleased to meet you."

Running her fingers across the intricate details of Clara's stove, Judith said, "Your home is just amazing, and this stove is unbelievable."

Smiling, Clara said, "The stove was actually put in this house when it was built back in the mid-1800s. It's an antique, just like me," she said with a laugh. "I think you would probably have to tear down a wall just to get it out. And since we heat the house with wood anyway, we might as well throw a few logs on the stove every once in a while. It helps keep the kitchen warm, plus, it's always ready to use that way."

Looking to Charlie, Evan said, "You seem well prepared for this situation, Charlie."

"Well," Charlie said, looking for his words, "it's easy to be old-school when you never went new-school in the first place.

We barely notice what's going on out there. We do have to keep an extra eye out for thieves and looters, though. For some reason, some folks from the cities feel as if they can just come and take what we have once their precious supermarkets are emptied, which didn't take long, by the way. It's like they think farmers are here to serve them or something. But this is my damn farm and my damn food!" he said, clearly beginning to become agitated. "I'll die protecting this place from those filthy thieves and looters if I have to!"

"Now, just calm down, you old coot," Clara said with her hands on her hips, giving him the eye.

Turning her attention back to the task at hand, having gotten Charlie settled down, Clara asked Judith and Peggy to help her with dinner. The dinner she was planning consisted of fresh steaks from a steer they had just butchered, fresh-baked homemade bread, potatoes, carrots, and homemade apple pie for dessert. This was truly a feast for the entire group, as they had been living on tuna, oatmeal, and the like, ever since everything had gone down.

Meanwhile, as the men sat in the living room by the fire, Jim jokingly asked Charlie to come along with them on their boats. He said, "Charlie, you and Clara need to come along with us. You're way too close to Wilmington and Philadelphia here to not have some sort of problems from people as they desperately leave the city in droves, looking for food. They will be like zombie hordes."

With a huff and a puff, Charlie replied, "Hell no, I ain't leavin'!" with passion in his voice. "I've not got a whole lot longer on God's green Earth as it is, and I'll be damned if I'll spend that time running. This farm is where I was born. It's where my daddy was born, and where his daddy was born. I can't think of a better place to die than right here on my family's land, defending it to my last breath!"

All the men simply nodded in agreement and raised their coffee cups in a silent toast to honor what Charlie had said.

~~~~

Once everyone was finished eating, and yawns began to spread around the room, Clara said, "Well, ladies, if you'll follow me, I'll show you to your rooms for the night, where you can wash up, and get some much-needed rest. Charlie will take care of the boys."

"That's our cue, fellas," Charlie said as he pushed away from the table. Let's get everything wrapped up down at the barn."

"I'll take them down there, Charlie," replied Jim. "It won't take us but a few minutes. You and Carl get some rest."

Agreeing with a nod, Charlie retired for the evening, while Carl fished an old hand-carved pipe from his pocket, relaxing on the front porch in an old wooden rocking chair. "I'll hold down the fort," he said jokingly as Jim, Evan, and Jason walked to Jim's truck.

Arriving at the barn, Jim stepped out of the truck and then looked at both Evan and Jason as the noisy generator suddenly shut down on its own. With a silent nod to one another, the three men crept over to the barn. Looking inside, they saw three figures inside gathered around the generator, as if they were contemplating the best way for them to carry it away.

Evidently, the noisy generator had masked the sound of Jim's truck approaching, and the looters had yet to be alerted to their presence. With his heart skipping a beat at the realization that both he and Jason had foolishly left their rifles in the back of the Maule with their gear, Evan reached down to silently unholster his sidearm, which was securely in place on his right side.
~~~~

As one of the men began to reach into the back of the Maule, fearing what would happen if the man discovered their weapons, Evan fired a shot at his feet, screaming, "Down! Down! Down! Down on the floor or die!"

One of the other men immediately began running for the door. Jim quickly grabbed a shovel that was hanging on the wall and ran at the man, swinging it at him violently. The shovel connected with the man's head, making a loud, metallic thump. The man fell forward and plopped onto the floor of the barn like a rag doll.

Relentlessly continuing his attack, Jim began hitting the man in the back with the shovel over and over while screaming expletives in a fit of rage. He then ran over to the third man, who had dropped to his knees with his arms in the air, fearing that Evan or Jason would shoot him if he ran.

Ramming the shovel into the man's gut, Jim kicked him in the face, knocking him backward and onto the floor.

Jim now approached the man by the Maule, who was lying on his stomach, with his arms and legs spread. Grabbing him by the back of the head, Jim began smashing his face into the dirt over and over. Through gritted teeth with spit flying wildly from his mouth, Jim said, "I swear to God Almighty, if you or any of your looting scumbag friends ever come back here again, I will chop off your arms and legs, grind them up in a meat grinder, and force-feed them to you. I will kill you in the most horribly slow and disgusting manner that my war-torn, twisted mind can come up with. Do you understand me? Do you understand me?" he shouted.

Unable to answer due to the brutal beating he had received, the man just shook, reeling in pain. Evan and Jason looked at each other, shocked from seeing Jim snap as he had. They had never seen him act in such a way but understood what Charlie and Clara meant to him, so they were not about to judge his defensiveness.

Standing over the man and turning to walk to the corner of the barn, Jim retrieved a five-gallon jug of used motor oil and began pouring it all over the three men while they lay there on the ground, one of which remained unconscious.

Once the jug was empty, he poured a can of paint thinner on them. Then, taking a step back, he lit a cigarette. The cigarette's red glow shined ominously in the darkness of the barn and the evening's fading light.

Looking to Jason, Evan motioned that they needed to intervene before Jim took things a step too far.

Jim spoke to the men while twirling the cigarette between his fingers. "Now, you two pick up your buddy and drag his worthless ass off this property as fast as you can. If you're not moving fast enough, I will light your sorry asses on fire and laugh while I watch you burn to death."

As the men struggled to get up and retrieve their cohort, Jim added, "And make sure you tell all of your scumbag friends they will not get the nice treatment you just received. All warnings have been made. I won't waste my breath making more threats. Now, get moving!"

Struggling to pick up their unconscious accomplice, each grabbing an arm, the men began dragging him away. Following closely behind, Jim puffed on the lit cigarette, keeping the orange glow ready should he need to live up to his promise to burn the men alive. The ominous red glow of the cigarette kept the fear of that promise in the minds of the looters as they desperately continued dragging the other man along.

Confident that they wouldn't be stopping or turning around, Jim stopped and watched them for a moment. Raising his pistol, with only the moonlight to help his aim, Jim fired a shot into the ground behind the men, keeping them motivated and moving.

"Don't forget to tell the others the fate that awaits them," Jim shouted as the men disappeared into the darkness down the road.

Walking back to the barn with a look of disgust on his face, Jim made eye contact with Evan and Jason, and said, "Charlie wouldn't have been as polite and neighborly as I was."

"Damn, Jim," Jason said. "I sure would hate to be on your bad side."

"I take my loved ones seriously," he replied as he put the cigarette out on the dirty barn wall, flicking the butt to the dirt floor below.

"What war were you in?" Evan asked.

"Huh?" Jim said, not understanding the question.

"You mentioned your *war-torn mind* during your tirade. I was just wondering what war you served in."

"Oh," Jim said with a chuckle. "I was never in a war. Those bastards don't know that, though. I wanted them to think I was on the verge of snapping and reliving some God-awful day from my past."

"You had us convinced," Jason said shaking his head.

"The recruiters turned me down when I was nineteen," Jim said. "I was in a car wreck as a kid and took a pretty good lick to the head as well as a few too many broken bones. They medically disqualified me at the MEPS station. Such is life, I guess."

Hearing the roaring sound of a diesel tractor engine barreling toward the barn, the group looked up the hill to see one of Charlie's tractors with Carl hanging on to the step and Charlie behind the wheel. Slamming on the brakes and sliding to a stop, Charlie shut the tractor down as Carl jumped off.

Looking around with an old, double-barrel twelve-gauge shotgun in hand, Charlie asked, "What the hell was the shooting for?"

"There were a couple of thieves in the barn," Jim replied. "I guess they heard the generator running from a distance and decided to come and take it. They were looking around for other spoils when we caught them off guard."

With a crooked smile, Jason said, "Jim gave them a pretty good beat down and put the fear of God in them. I doubt they will be back."

"They might not," Jim said. "But others will eventually stumble across this place, without the benefit of the warning."

"Ah hell," Charlie said, resting his shotgun against his shoulder, holding on to the stock with one hand. "I'll just make a game out of them. It'll help me pass the time. We old guys have to keep busy, or we get bored and sleepy."

"Well, let's get everything secured here and get you guys to bed. You have an eventful day ahead of you tomorrow," Jim said as they began to retrieve Evan and Jason's gear from the Maule.

Having learned their lesson not to leave their gear unattended, Evan and Jason loaded all of their stuff back into Jim's truck to take back to the house with them for the night. Weaving a large chain through the gaps in the boards, they locked the barn as best they could. Once satisfied with their work, they climbed back into Jim's truck and headed back to the farmhouse for the night.

Upon arriving at the home, they barely got through the front door before Clara asked, "What was all the commotion was about?"

Speaking in a calm and reassuring voice, Charlie said, "Oh, Jim just saw a coyote. He hates those things. Sometimes it seems like they kill livestock for the fun of it. We don't need them around here, that's for sure."

Judith and Peggy were relieved by Charlie's reassuring answer, but Clara looked at Charlie with the stink eye, as she knew he wasn't being honest. He returned the look, and she understood.

"Well, let's all get some sleep," she said, and with that, they all retired for the night.

~~~~

Awakened to the smell of a freshly cooked breakfast emanating from Clara's kitchen, the group each made their way to the dinner table where Clara had prepared breakfast. She had cooked a country-style feast consisting of fried eggs fresh from their backyard chicken coop, homemade biscuits, and steak medallions from the same steer they had enjoyed for dinner the previous evening.

Gathered around the table, Clara asked them to stand and join hands for a special prayer before their meal. As everyone joined hands and bowed their heads, Charlie said a profound prayer that brought tears to many of their eyes.

With sincerity in his voice, he said, "Dear Lord, our Father in Heaven, thank you for the abundance of this meal that we are about to eat. Thank you for granting us the fortune of growing up in a time and place where we could learn the skills and acquire the work ethic that it takes to provide for one's self and one's family in such abundance. We appreciate that blessing, Lord, as we know so many are scared and hungry and are without the means or knowledge to provide for themselves. Lord, please have mercy on those who have become dependent on society for their sustenance in this modern age, who have recently found themselves without a hand to feed them. Please help them and guide them in what you need them to do, to carry on in these uncertain and challenging times. Grant them the strength and wisdom to carry on. Also, Lord, please help our new-found friends who have faced many difficult challenges,
~~~~

and who have found themselves together in this journey. Lord, we know the twists of fate that brought them together had to be guided by your hand, and the events that brought them to Damon, and for Damon to help guide them to us. We know that their journey is part of a greater plan of yours, so please be with them and keep them safe. We thank you again, Lord, for our blessings and our friendships and family. In your name, we pray, Amen."

Looking around the table, Jim thought it was obvious that everyone felt connected and somehow drawn together. When this chain of horrific events began, Evan, Jason, and Peggy were merely co-workers spending another day on the job together. Along the way, their lives had become intertwined with the Rutherford family, Judith, and now Charlie and Clara.

Standing there in awe, he reflected on their good fortune to have somehow managed to be surrounded and helped by so many wonderful people throughout their struggles. He couldn't help but feel that humanity wasn't lost, not yet.

"Okay, everyone. Let's eat," Clara said with a smile. And with that, they all sat down and enjoyed their excellent breakfast and their beloved company.

Pushing himself back from the table, his stomach now full, Evan said, "Clara, thank you so much for this feast. And to everyone, thank you for the hospitality. You've done more than we can ever repay, but we had better get going. We've got a long way to go to get to our first stop of Zanesville, and then on to Cincinnati and Tennessee."

They said their goodbyes to Charlie and Clara, thanking them again for their generosity and hospitality. Climbing back into Jim's truck, Jim, Carl, Evan, Jason, Peggy, and Judith made the short drive to the barn.

Once at the barn, Jim fired up the old Ford tractor and pulled it out of the way, allowing room to get the airplane out of the barn. Everyone lent a hand pushing the airplane clear of the barn and into the grass covered field.

Giving both Jim and Carl hugs goodbye, Peggy and Judith expressed their thanks. Judith took Jim by the hand, and said, "I'll say a prayer each day that the *Little Angel* keeps you and your family safe."

Shaking both Jim and Carl's hands, Evan looked Jim in the eye, and said, "Maybe we will see you guys again someday." Fumbling around in his pocket, Evan retrieved a small, folded piece of paper. He handed it to him and continued, "Here's a map of where we will be. If the islands don't work out, feel free to come looking for us. You'll always have a place to go in Tennessee."

With that, Evan, Jason, Peggy, and Judith climbed into the Maule for the next phase of their journey. Excitement and anxiety was obvious on their faces as they prepared to, yet again, venture off into the unknown.

Watching the airplane taxi onto the short, grass strip next to the barn, Carl turned to Jim, and asked, "Do you think they'll make it?"

"I don't see why not," Jim replied. "They've got their heads on straight. I just hope they make it home before the world around us unravels any more than it already has. Travel is about to become very difficult."

Hearing the engine roar to life as the aircraft entered the grass runway, Jim and Carl watched as the old Maule began its takeoff roll, accelerating and lifting the tail off the ground. Once it had built sufficient speed, it soon took flight, making a westerly turn as the aircraft disappeared over the tree line in the distance.

Happy to see that their new friends had gotten off to a good start, Jim turned to Carl, and said, "We'd better be getting back home. They're not the only ones that have an unraveling world to deal with."

Chapter Fourteen: Return to Delaware City

With Evan, Jason, Peggy, and Judith airborne and on the next phase of their journey, Carl turned to Jim and said, “You’re right. We need to get going. Not only do we have people filling in for us on our watches, but we’ve also got to get our butts in gear to get ready for our own potential bug-out. There’s lots to do and lots to prep.”

“Yeah. Yeah, I know,” Jim replied as he looked back in the direction of Charlie and Clara’s home.

“What?” Carl asked. “Do you think you can actually talk him into leaving? That’s not gonna happen. And Clara, she won’t leave without him.”

“I know, but—”

“But nothing. You wouldn’t let someone talk you into doing something that went against your grain, and neither will Charlie. It just ain’t gonna happen,” Carl insisted.

Kicking a rock with his boot, Jim said, “Well, let’s go say goodbye if nothing else.”

“That, we can do,” Carl replied, adjusting his olive drab green 5.11 ball cap.

Upon reaching Charlie and Clara’s home, Jim and Carl proceeded up the front steps to the porch where they were greeted by both Charlie and Clara. “Well, did they get off safely?” Charlie asked.

“Yeah,” Jim replied. “Yeah, they’re fine. Now, Charlie, I really think you should reconsider—”

Putting his hand up in protest, Charlie spoke in a calm, but authoritative tone. “Jim. We’ve been friends for a long time. I respect your advice; I really do. There aren’t many men in this world that I trust. You’re on that short list. That being said, there’s no way in hell I’m leaving the piece of land my family has been on for generation after generation. My father fell on hard times during the great depression and was forced to sell off a large chunk of our land to save the farm from the bank. He never forgave himself for that. He felt as if he had betrayed our entire bloodline. I'm not gonna make the same mistake and let this farm end up in the hands of some hoodlums."

Turning to face the house and pointing at it with his left hand, Charlie continued, "This house is older than both Clara and I put together. I ain't leavin' it to be burned and looted if things get as bad as you say they could. So please, do us both a favor and let's let this goodbye be with a smile and a handshake, not an argument."

Before Jim could answer, knowing he didn't have a chance of convincing them, Clara added, "And Jim, Charlie and I have been married longer than you've been alive; and you ain't no spring chicken. I'm not leaving him. Not for nothing. If he's staying, I'm staying."

With a smile, Jim nodded, and said, "Yes, ma'am, of course. Well, Carl and I had better be getting back to our neck of the woods. We've got a lot to do before what hit the fan reaches us in full force. We've been blessed to have been overlooked for the most part so far, but that won't last forever."

Reaching out to give Charlie a firm handshake, Jim pulled him in and gave him a hug, patting him on the back. Turning to Clara, he gave her a hug as she kissed him on the cheek. "You take good care of Lori," she said softly.

With a smile, Jim replied, "I will. She's my world."

Shaking Carl's hand, Charlie said, "Take good care of Jim, here. I've known him since he was a boy. He's got his head on straight. You'll be served well by your friendship with him with what's ahead. I may not have known you as long as I've known him, but any man Jim would trust with his life has got to be a pretty damn good guy. You're always welcome here if you ever find yourself back this way."

"Thank you, sir. I appreciate that," Carl said, returning the handshake with a nod and a smile.

Wiping a tear from his eye before Charlie could see it, Jim turned and walked to his truck. Once Carl was inside, he waved one last time before climbing in. Starting the Ford's diesel engine, Jim sat there for a moment, put the truck in gear, and drove away with the sight of Charlie and Clara fading from view in his rearview mirror.

Riding in the passenger seat of the truck, Carl double-checked that his magazine was fully seated and then pulled back slightly on the charging handle to verify that there was a round in the chamber. Seeing him do the same with his Glock 35, Jim jokingly said, "Are you paranoid, or something?"

"Nope. Not at all," Carl replied with a cross look on his face. "I just expect either your buddies from the barn or the group we ran into yesterday on the way here will not be too happy to see us driving back through."

"The one's from the barn, maybe. But the other folks, if they had a gun, they'd have used it instead of pulling a flare on us."

"Hell, I'd rather get shot with a .38 than a flare," Carl said. "That would seriously suck."

"Yeah, that was close," Jim replied, recalling the near-miss of the previous day, with the flare barely missing the open passenger's side window of the pickup truck.

Snapping out of his momentary daydream, Jim looked up in time to see a middle-aged woman step out in front of the vehicle, forcing Jim to slam on the brakes, swerving to miss her.

Unable to avoid going into the ditch on the left-hand side of the road, the truck slammed into a tree stump hidden in the brush, causing the rear of the truck to slide sideways, completely blocking the road with Jim's long, F250 Crew Cab.

“Damn it!” Jim shouted as he quickly kicked his door open, rushing out and behind the nearest tree for cover while they assessed the situation.

“You killed my husband!” the woman shouted with rage in her voice.

“No. I did not. You and your husband refused to get out of the way and tried to force us to give you what we had. That’s robbery!” Jim argued from behind the tree, covering the woman with his Kimber .45.

Hearing a rustling in the woods behind them, Carl spun around, scanning the area through the sights of his AK-74, ready to pull the trigger the instant a threat presented itself.

“Tell them to come out!” Carl demanded.

Ignoring Carl’s command, the woman walked closer. “Where is he?”

“Who?” Jim asked.

“The one with short hair. The one that shot my husband!” she shouted, growing more agitated by the moment.

“He’s long gone,” Jim replied. “But it doesn’t matter. He was defending us. Any of us would have done the same.”

“Defending you?” the woman argued, taking another step forward.

“Stay right there!” Jim shouted.

“He was unarmed. We had children with us. You killed him!”

“He wasn’t unarmed,” Jim protested.

Hearing the rustling in the woods again, Carl continued to scan the area, shouting, “I’m telling you for the last time! Tell them to come out!”

Just as he finished his sentence, a glowing red flare went screaming by his head so close that he could feel the heat as well as being disoriented by the bright flash of light.

Missing its intended target of Carl's head, the flare struck one of the barrels of fuel in the back of the truck, which he and Jim had retrieved from the barn. Instantly igniting the contents, due to the surrounding vapors emitted from the old barrels, the truck erupted in a violent inferno of flames and hot air, narrowly missing Carl as he dove into the ditch.

Now only steps from the truck and consumed by fire, the woman's high-pitched screams lasted mere seconds before succumbing to the heat and flames. Dropping to the ground, her burning body began to sizzle, emitting the stench of burning flesh. Both Jim and Carl knew there was nothing they could do for her, having been completely consumed by the inferno. Raising his rifle and taking careful aim, Carl released the woman from her agony, firing a single shot into the base of her skull.

Turning quickly and screaming into the woods, Carl shouted, "I swear to God you'd better run, I'll kill every last one of you and leave those kids as orphans in this screwed up world! Run you bastards, run!" he shouted as he fired several shots blindly into the direction from where the flare had come.

Stepping from around the tree, Jim looked down at the burning woman, smelling her cooking flesh. The stench combined with the stress of the situation nearly caused him to vomit. Signaling to Carl while covering his mouth with his shirt, Jim gestured for them to both get moving on foot.

After rounding the next bend, Jim removed his shirt from over his mouth, and shouted, "Damn it to hell! What's wrong with people?"

"Let's just keep moving," Carl said. "We've got about five miles to go, and on foot; that'll take a while. Oh, and Jim, never leave your house without a long-gun again. This just goes to show you that you don't know when a shit storm is coming. But rest assured, it's gonna be coming a lot from now on."

~~~~

After an hour of jogging, Jim and Carl passed by New Castle County's Southern Elementary School. Stopping to catch their breath, Jim bent at the waist, with his hands on his knees. Between his heavy breaths, he said,
"Damn...I'm...out...of...shape."

With a laugh, Carl said, "Hell, Jim. You're doing great for a fifty-five-year-old man who never exercises. When's the last time you went to a gym? That's why I always give you grief about including a workout regimen into your preps. How many people bugging out right now with their sixty-pound packs are only one mile into their journey and are ditching things they considered critical, because they aren't in shape to hump it?"

With his breathing becoming more controlled, Jim said, "First of all, I'm forty-five! Second, you can swim to the islands if you're in such good shape."

"Hey, man, don't be bitter when confronted by the truth," replied Carl with a crooked smile. Looking up at the school, Carl chuckled again, shaking his head.

Giving him a dirty look, Jim asked, "What's so funny now?"

Pointing at the elementary school, Carl said, "A month ago, or hell, a week ago, they'd have called out a SWAT team and the national news media if two men with guns were standing in front of the school like this."

Looking at the school with the sad realization that just a week before, this very facility was bustling with young children with minds filled with dreams of bright futures, Jim shook it off and changed the subject. "Okay, let's keep going. It's only another mile or so to the outskirts of town."

Turning on to Clinton Street, Jim and Carl heard an authoritative voice shout, "Stop right there!"
~~~~

Freezing in their tracks, they heard, “Lay your weapons on the ground and take five steps back.”

“Just do it,” Jim said. “If they wanted to kill us, we’d be dead.”

Reluctantly, Jim began to lay his pistol on the ground as Carl did the same with his AK-74, when they heard, “Ah hell, that’s Jim and Carl. Sorry, guys.”

Standing up and holstering his pistol, Jim looked over to see two of Chief Winsted’s officers stepping out of the brush that followed alongside the road. “Howdy, guys,” he said with relief both on his face and in his voice.

“Why are you guys on foot. Where’s your truck?” Officer Tim Foust asked.

“We had a little run in with a flare gun,” Jim said. “I guess people are resorting to whatever they can get their hands on for a weapon. Especially the people coming from the New York and New Jersey areas where strict gun control laws prevented them from having things on hand when it all started to go down.”

“You let someone with a flare gun steal your truck?” Foust asked.

“Uh, no,” Jim replied. “We were hauling gasoline back from a friend’s farm. Gas and flare guns don’t mix very well.”

Looking at each other and trying to play the scene out in their minds, Officer Carney said, “Sorry, Jim. Anyway, at least you’re okay. Where are you two heading now?”

“Home, ultimately,” Jim replied. “We wanted to stop by Town Hall on the way and talk to Chief Winsted, first.”

“He’s at the grill right now,” Foust said. “He was eating lunch when we left.”

“Which one?” Carl asked.

“Lewinsky’s on Clinton, down toward the water on Clinton Street,” answered Officer Foust. “They’re giving everything that hasn't spoiled away before they close the doors and head out of town."

"They're giving away free beer, too!" Officer Carney added with an upbeat tone in his voice. "It's warm, but the price is right."

Looking at Carl, Jim said, "I love that place. That's one of the things I'm gonna miss if this all doesn't get sorted out anytime soon."

"I always thought the name was brilliant," added Carl with a chuckle.

Trying to hold back a laugh, Jim said, "As much as I'd like to get drunk off my ass right now, we've got a lot to do. Besides, that's about the time some jihadists would start shooting up the town. And there we'd be, fumbling around, accidently shooting each other in all the confusion."

"I promise I won't shoot you if we can at least grab one," Carl said, only half joking.

Replying with a smile, Jim said, "Thanks for the info, guys. We'd better get a move on. It's been a very long day, and it's not even half over yet."

"You guys be careful," Officer Foust said as he and Officer Carney gave them both a nod as they began to walk away.

Continuing east on Clinton Street toward Lewinsky's, Jim and Carl remained silent as they observed the now empty businesses and homes along the way. The once bustling street filled with mom and pop businesses and homes now felt like a ghost town.

A sad example of what much of country must be going through, Jim thought.

Breaking the silence, seeing the hurt in Jim's eyes at the sight of what the small town he was born and raised in was going through, Carl said, "Hey, we've got it better than some."

"For now," Jim replied. "But yeah, you're right. At least we've got time to get our stuff in order. The people in the major cities that were hit didn't have that luxury. For that, I'm thankful. I'm just hoping these empty homes and businesses are merely a reflection of that. A reminder that the people who'd normally be waving at us through their windows must have had time to get somewhere safer before the mass exodus from the cities overflows into our streets."

Approaching Lewinsky's on Clinton, Jim and Carl could hear laughing and shouting from inside the restaurant. Looking over at Jim with a sneaky smile, Carl said, "It sounds like the free beer is still flowing."

"You do what you want," Jim said. "You know I love a good beer as much as the next guy, but I'm keeping my head on straight. We've got a lot to do to get everything ready. If I have one, I'm liable to have twenty. Besides, I've got to get home to Lori. She's probably been packing like a mad woman since we left."

"Maybe we can place a *to-go* order," Carl replied.

"Now that would be a different story," answered Jim with a laugh.

Arriving at the front door, Jim reached for the elaborately decorated door knob as the door swung open rapidly, striking him as he blocked it with his forearm.

"Oh! Hey, Jim. Sorry about that," Randy Carter said as he stumbled onto the sidewalk.

"It's okay, Randy," Jim replied. "No harm done."

"Well, it wouldn't matter anyway," Randy said, his tone suddenly darkening. "It's all going to hell, and we're going with it. The Chief was just telling us everything he knows. It's bad, man. Real bad. And his contacts with the state are no longer talking. We're screwed. We're all screwed. No food is coming. Our water supply is no longer flowing. No fuel. No—"

Interrupting Randy's tirade, Jim said, "Hey now, Randy. There's no reason to give up. We're not sure what's—"

"No reason? No reason?" Randy shouted, his anger building from his alcohol induced rant. "You and your guys stand all day down on the waterfront thinking you can stop something if it comes. That's just as futile as the chief thinking he can keep us safe here in town. When they come, and I say when, not if, they're gonna kill us all. They're gonna rape our women and do the same unspeakable atrocities to our children that they've been doing in the Middle East to the infidels that refuse to convert. You've seen it. You know what I'm—"

Raising his hands in the air, Jim pleaded with Randy, "Hey, man. Calm down. If we're gonna be able to take care of—"

"Damn it! Stop interrupting me, Jim! I'm sick of your Boy Scout bullshit. You're not gonna save the day. You're not gonna keep anyone in this town safe, you stupid son-of-a—"

Blocking Randy's swinging fist, Jim rotated Randy's arm behind his back, locking his elbow, and pushing his wrist forward to the edge of the breaking point as Randy screamed, "Let me go! Awwww, God, you're breaking my arm."

"I said calm the hell down, Randy," Jim shouted. "If you swing at me again, I'll—"

"Hey!" Chief Winsted shouted as the door to Lewinsky's flew open. "Damn it, Randy. I told you to go home and cool off." Placing his hand on Randy's shoulder, he then said, "Jim's gonna let you go now. If you fight me, I'll put you down hard. Do you understand?"

Nodding his head in the affirmative, Randy relaxed as Jim released the arm bar hold. Standing up straight, looking Jim in the eye as he worked his wrist around in an attempt to relieve the pain, Randy warned him. "This ain't over."

Shoving Randy backward and onto the pavement with a thud, Chief Winsted shouted, "Damn it, Randy. What did I say?"

Kicking him in the leg, he then said, "I don't have time for your shit. If you keep pushing me, starting crap with people, not only will I ban you from Lewinsky's, I'll lock your ass up."

"You can't ban me," Randy said with a slur in his voice as he began to sit up. "You don't have that authority."

Stiffening his face, Chief Winsted spoke through gritted teeth. "Who the hell is gonna stop me from doing anything I want to do to you, Randy? You're the town asshole. Everyone around here would be glad if I shut you up. Whatever form that takes. No one would care, and there's no one you could call for help." Kicking Randy in the leg, causing him to flinch, Chief Winsted kneeled down and asked, "Do you understand me," as he put his hand on his gun.

Nodding again, Randy began to scurry backward before he paused and turned sideways, vomiting all over the sidewalk.

Standing up, towering over Randy in his drunken state, Chief Winsted said, "Good. Now get the hell out of here and don't show your face on these streets until you've sobered up and cleaned up your attitude. People have enough crap to put up with around here without you adding to it."

Wiping his mouth with his sleeve, Randy lumbered to his feet and ran down the street toward his home.

"Sorry about that, Jim," Chief Winsted said, softening his tone. "I should have escorted him all the way home instead of just telling him to get the hell out of Lewinsky's. I should have known he'd be trouble. He never could keep it together."

With a chuckle, Jim said, "Yeah, remember the high school football game where he ran out onto the field, yelling and cursing at the referee. I'm pretty sure that wasn't soda in his cup. His son was horrified."

Nodding with a grin, Chief Winsted said, "Yeah, but the problem now is his behavior, as well as others like him, might not stay at the nuisance level. If they believe nothing's gonna fix this country anytime soon, they may not feel as if they need to struggle to keep it together for much longer. Let's face it. There are probably thousands of Randys out there who have already snapped, unable to bear it all, or have begun to act out what's in their twisted minds without fear of consequence."

"Yeah," Jim replied with reluctance in his voice. "Those folks I escorted out to Charlie's place have the right idea. They're on their way to some homestead in middle-of-nowhere Tennessee. Getting away from everyone else is probably a pretty good answer."

"Unless you're a higher up with the government," Chief Winsted replied. "They're still being taken care of. I'm sure of it."

"Is there any food left in there?" Carl asked, gesturing toward Lewinsky's.

"No, that's all gone," replied Chief Winsted. "All the good beer is gone, too. They're down to some lime flavored light beer and a cider, I believe."

With a laugh, Jim replied, "That's all for the best, anyway. I'd just get drunk and end up getting a *talking to* by you just like Randy did."

"Hell, Jim. One beer wouldn't—"

Just then, Chief Winsted was interrupted by a massive explosion to the north of town that rocked the entire city. An enormous fireball erupted into the sky, followed by billowing, black smoke. Before any of the men could say a word, the sound of fully automatic machinegun fire could be heard in the distance from the same direction as the devastating blast.

"The refinery!" Chief Winsted shouted. "They've just hit the refinery."

"It's getting closer!" Carl shouted, noticing the advancing sounds of automatic fire.

Opening the door to Lewinsky's, Chief Winsted shouted, "Everybody in the basement, now! Stay off the streets until I say otherwise!"

Closing the door quickly behind him and returning to Jim and Carl's position on the sidewalk, Chief Winsted said, "I need you guys."

With a nod, Jim said, "Of course, Chief," as he looked up, seeing a Chevy Silverado pickup truck rounding the corner. Three men stood in the back of the truck, hanging on to a ladder track and holding what appeared from a distance to be AK-style rifles with seventy-five round drums of ammunition rocked into place instead of the usual thirty-round magazines.

As the truck completed its turn and began to drive down the street, Chief Winsted, Jim, and Carl could now see that the men wore masks over their faces, hiding their identity. As one of the men shouted, "Allah Akbar!" they opened fire into the windows of the stores along Clinton Street. Carl raised his AK-74 to his shoulder, and Jim and Chief Winsted readied their handguns, as several people, including a young woman and her infant child, were gunned down as they began to scatter and run for cover.

Being the only one of the three with and long-gun and the ability to engage at such a range, Carl began firing into the windshield of the truck, as he was unable to get a good line of fire on the men in the back from its oncoming angle.

Swerving dramatically to the left, the truck impacted a light pole, sending the driver of the truck through the windshield and onto the pavement twenty feet in front of the vehicle. The impact ejected the three gunmen from the back of the truck as well, temporarily halting any return fire from the attackers.

Maintaining his barrage of fire, Carl immediately picked off one of the attackers as the masked man attempted to retrieve his weapon, still dazed from the crash. With several of Carl's sixty-grain 5.45-millimeter rounds striking the man in the chest, he immediately fell backward onto the pavement as one of the other men resumed fire on their position.

Ducking behind a Nissan Altima that had been parked alongside the street in front of Lewinsky's, Chief Winsted shouted to Carl and Jim, "Get behind the wheels!" as the car shook from the impact of what seemed like twenty or thirty rounds from the enemy's AK.

Laying on the pavement between the car and the sidewalk, with broken glass raining down on him as the car being used for shelter felt like it was being ripped to shreds, Carl aimed beneath the front bumper of the car while taking a deep breath. With intense focus, he sent several shots toward the attacker who was relentlessly firing on their position. Striking him in the ankles, sweeping his legs out from under him, the assailant fell violently to the ground. With two more well-placed shots, the man's struggles ceased.

"Where's the third?" shouted Jim, his ears ringing from the close proximity of Carl's muzzle blasts.

Answering as he stood and pointed, Chief Winsted shouted, "I think he ran between those houses toward Washington Street!"

With Clinton Street being near the waterfront, several of the watchstanders from the marina arrived on scene. Turning to see them approaching at a full sprint, Jim saw Paul Funk carrying his Smith & Wesson M&P 15 carbine, as well as Jackie Burnette with her Remington twelve-gauge pump shotgun.

"What the hell is going on?" Paul shouted.

Pointing at the truck, Chief Winsted replied, "Four men in that truck. Three are down. One is unaccounted for. He ran between those houses."

Turning to see Monica, the bartender from the restaurant come out onto the street, he pointed to the victims lying in the street, shouting, "Monica, get some help and check on the injured."

With a nod, she turned, running back inside to get help as he then said, "Jackie, go back to the marina and tell the others to spread out and begin to work this way into town, making a net. We've got to find that bastard. Jim, Carl, and I are gonna go after him, so don't shoot us if you come across us. Paul, that rifle will come in handy. You go with us while she gets the others."

As Jackie ran back toward the marina, complying with Chief Winsted's orders, he, Jim, Carl, and Paul ran southwest on Clinton Street in pursuit of the remaining attacker. "Jim, you and Carl go up Front Street. Paul and I will take William Street. There's a back lane between the two rows of houses. Get on that lane and push west, we'll come around from the east."

Complying with Chief Winsted's orders, Jim and Carl turned onto Front Street, running toward the back lane between the two rows of houses. Reaching the back lane, they turned onto it as Jim scanned the houses on the south side of the lane with his Kimber drawn and at the high ready, while Carl scanned the backyards of the homes on the north side while looking through the EOTech holographic sight mounted on his AK-74.

Seeing Chief Winsted and Paul round the corner on the far side of the lane, Jim and Carl worked their way toward them, visually scanning the surrounding areas as they went. Hearing a woman's screams coming from a house on their left, Jim and Carl ran toward the back door of the home as the screams became painfully distorted. Chills ran up Jim's spine as he could only imagine the horrors that were befalling the woman.

As the four men converged on the home, an object flew from the upstairs bedroom window, followed by the shouts of a man with a thick, Middle-Eastern accent, yelling the same ominous phrase as the shooters in the pickup truck, "Allah Akbar!"

As the object hit the ground with a thud, rolling toward Chief Winsted, he recognized the long, gray hair of an elderly woman as it came to a stop at his feet. To his horror, it was the head of Hellen Newsome. An elderly lady who had recently been widowed by the death of her husband of forty-seven years. Her head had been savagely cut from her body. Her eyes still showing the agony that she'd gone through during the evil and heinous act.

Running at a full sprint toward the back door of the home, Chief Winsted kicked it off its hinges and ran full steam inside, failing to wait for Paul, Jim, or Carl to serve as backup.

Looking at both Carl and Paul, Jim said, "Paul, you wait here and cover the home. Position yourself on the side of the house so that you can see both the front and back yards. Carl and I will go in with the chief. We can't let this bastard get away and do this again."

With a nod in the affirmative, Paul jogged toward the home, positioning himself as Jim directed. As Jim and Carl entered the home, Carl entered first, carrying his rifle at the low ready as he sliced the pie around each corner, clearing the home as they went. The pair worked their way through the kitchen, and then to the living room toward the stairs.

Scanning both the front and rear of the home as best he could from the side, Paul watched as a man ran out the front door, carrying what looked like an AK pattern rifle. Raising his M&P15, Paul sent three rapid-fire rounds in the direction of the fleeing attacker, dropping him instantly to the ground.

Hearing gunshots outside, Jim and Carl turned and ran toward the front door of the home, exiting onto the front porch, where they saw Paul standing in the front yard over the dead assailant's body.

Running over to Paul, Jim and Carl looked at the dead man who lay face down on the lawn. The man had two direct hits to the back, and one to the back of the head, shattering his skull, sending bits of bone, brain matter, and soft tissue onto the ground in front of him in a fan-like pattern.

"Where's the chief?" Paul asked.

"Damn it!" Jim shouted in frustration as he and Carl turned and ran back into the house.

"Chief!" Jim called out as they entered the home. Quickly clearing the lower floor, Jim and Carl ran up the stairs to find Chief Winsted lying in the hallway that spanned the width of the house between the upstairs bedrooms. They were horrified to see Chief Winsted lying there, his eyes wide open and his throat slashed from ear to ear.

"Damn it to hell!" Jim exclaimed as he kicked a hole into the sheetrock wall of the hallway.

Turning to Carl, seeing a look of anguish and defeat on his face, Jim said, "It's time. We've got to get the hell out of here."

Chapter Fifteen: Shattered Calm

Early the next morning, with the smell of burning petroleum filling the air from the destruction of the refinery and the ensuing fires, Jim and Lori were bringing supplies up from their basement in preparation to leave Delaware City and follow through with their plans.

Pausing on the stairs leading up to the main level of their home, Lori broke down in tears. "I can't believe it's come to this. I mean, we always planned on having to bug out if things got too bad, but I never really thought the day would come. I guess deep down inside I felt as if we were just trying to make ourselves feel better by having food storage, weapons, ammunition, and a plan. This is all too much. It's just too much all at once."

"I know," Jim said, taking Lori by the hand, pulling her close. "Deep down inside, I probably felt like you. Being prepared for whatever may come could have just been an excuse to justify buying guns and gear. I'm sure there are a lot of other gear whores like me out there who latched onto prepping as an excuse to buy cool stuff, subconsciously thinking we'd never use it but wanted it anyway. Hell, we men can justify just about anything to ourselves."

Noticing Lori giving him a dirty look, he continued, clearing his throat, "Well, regardless, I knew we'd be ready if this day came. When Carl and I made our trip with Evan, Jason, Peggy, and Judith to Charlie and Clara's farm, it all started to sink in for me. Then yesterday, when the attacks came right here to Delaware City—right in the middle of our own town in broad daylight—it hit me like a baseball bat. It's here. It's upon us. Whether this is the big one or not remains to be seen, but we aren't safe here in our little coastal town anymore."

"But why us? Why here?" she asked.

"My guess would be the refinery," Jim replied.

"But why the attacks in the middle of town, so far from the refinery?"

Holding her tight, Jim said, "Based on the events we've watched unfold, the consistent theme has been to hit us as a nation in ways that prevent or distract anyone from coming to the aid of those suffering from the brunt of the attacks. All across the country, from what we have heard, major infrastructure components are hit, and then the people in the surrounding areas are somehow hit as well.

"Take the municipal water supply poisonings for example. If people are suffering from the losses of their loved ones who drank the water before it was discovered, or if they are just struggling to find what little bottled water that hasn't already been hoarded by others, they don't have much time or energy to come to the aid or protection of their major points of interest. The way the terrorists are hitting us leaves everyone feeling vulnerable."

"Vulnerable is exactly how I feel, so it's working," Lori said.

"Precisely. Take yesterday for example. With us having to defend the town from a truck full of attackers, the last thing on our minds was the refinery. None of us ran toward the blaze to help. We fell for their diversion—not that we had a choice in the matter. They had what little response there would have been from us all tied up, giving them free reign to finish their carnage, unimpeded by first responders. At least, that's my uneducated theory."

Hearing a knock at the front door, recognizing it as Carl's signature rhythm, Jim released his and Lori's embrace and quickly answered the door.

Quickly closing the door behind him, Carl said, "It's a madhouse out there."

"What do you mean?" asked Lori.

“People are freaking out. Now that Chief Winsted is dead, the rest of the members of his department are nowhere to be found. I ran into Bruce, and he said he heard some chatter over the HAM that the federal government has been confiscating food and water resources for redistribution at FEMA facilities.”

“That matches what Evan and Jason said happened in the city as they were leaving,” Jim replied.

“Yeah, well, it’s spreading,” added Carl. Looking at the case of freeze-dried food sitting on the floor near the top of the stairs, he said, “It would be a shame for them to take all of what you’ve been squirreling away.”

“Which is precisely why we are leaving,” Jim replied.

“Is the plan still to leave after nightfall?” Carl asked.

“Yeah,” answered Jim as he got back to work. Heaving a crate of number ten cans of freeze-dried staples, he looked at Carl, and said, “Unless you have any new information or better ideas. I’ve already made my rounds first thing this morning to let the others in our group know we’re bugging out. A few were hesitant, which I just don’t understand. We’ve been planning for this as a group for a long time now. Things are getting bad—really bad. What the heck do they want us to stick around for? Lori and I were just talking about how the reality of it all is hard for us to grasp as well, but that’s not stopping us from following through with the plan.”

“You’ve got me, man,” Carl replied while shrugging his shoulders. “Maybe some of them just liked being in a doomsday club. Well, I just wanted to check to make sure the game plan hadn’t changed over the course of the night. I’ll see you at six o’clock, then. I’ve got some gear prep I need to do, as well as some goodbyes to say.”

“We’ll see you this evening,” Jim replied as Carl exited the home, rushing up the street.

~~~~

Arriving at the marina at nearly five o'clock that afternoon, Jim and Lori each pulled along a folding cart, carrying food and provisions for their journey. As they approached their boat, Paul and Marcie Funk walked up to them, and said, "Here, we can give you two a hand."

"We're fine," Jim replied with a smile. "But you can help us get it on the *Mother Washington* if you'd like to."

"Sure thing," Paul said. "By the way, did you see the Black Hawks running up the coastline earlier?"

Turning to Paul with a concerned look on his face, Jim replied, "No, I didn't. How many were there?"

"It was a big group. I counted eight. They were flying low and fast, too."

"North or south?" Jim asked.

"North. Why?"

"Because we're going south," Jim replied. "Eight, huh?"

Before Paul could say more, the group heard the rhythmic beating of helicopter main rotors from a distance. Looking out toward the river, they saw twelve more UH-60 Black Hawk's flying just feet above the water in a tight formation.

"Hell, that's a big group," Paul said, his eyes fixated on the helicopters.

"Yeah, and they're flying right up the river toward Philly," replied Jim. "Either something is going on up that way, or the government is staging and relocating its assets."

"For what?" Paul asked.

"Who the hell knows?" Jim answered with disdain in his voice. "They may be setting up something defensive, or..." he said, pausing.

"Or what?" again asked Paul.
~~~~

"Or they're...ah, hell, who knows? You can't trust the government. These days, it seems like they use disasters and attacks as an excuse to build government and restrict our freedoms, rather than looking after our best interests. It's hard to say. All I know is if the government passed a law called the Puppies and Kittens Protection Act, somewhere hidden in the three-thousand-page bill would be a requirement to kill all puppies and kittens. You know, just like when they put 'affordable' in the name and our costs go up."

Replying with a nod, Paul said, "Oh, and by the way, Thane said he and his family aren't coming."

With an unsurprised look, Jim said, "Yeah, I didn't get a warm and fuzzy about him when I paid them a visit. What did he say?"

"He wasn't very talkative. He just said they had decided to hang tight for now."

Mumbling under his breath for a moment, Jim collected himself, and said, "That still leaves, Lori and I, Carl, you and Marcie, Martin, C.J., Rick, and the Hildebrandts."

"Well, actually," Paul replied. "The Hildebrandts aren't coming either."

"What the...?" Jim said shaking his head.

"Oh, and you forgot to mention Carmen Wheeler. She and her boyfriend are coming along."

"Boyfriend?" Jim said, stopping in his tracks. "She's bringing a boyfriend?"

"Hey, man," Paul said, holding his hands up in front of him. "Don't shoot the messenger. I'm just telling you what she said. Besides, I'm the new guy to the group. Who am I to argue?"

Gritting his teeth, he asked, "Well, who the hell is this guy and why does she think it's okay to bring along a total stranger the rest of us haven't met? She knows that's not okay. I mean—"

Jim's rant was suddenly stopped by the sound of high-speed boats coming up the river from the direction of the Delaware Bay. "Those things are really moving," Paul said.

"What kind of boats are they?" Lori asked.

Watching as the haze gray painted boats with US NAVY markings on the side raced up the river, Jim said, "Those look like IBU boats. Sea Ark Dauntless, I believe."

"IBU boats?" Lori asked, seeking clarification.

"Inshore Boat Units," Jim replied. "They're the Navy's littoral force."

"Littoral?" Marcie asked.

"The shallows," Paul said.

"Yeah, the big boats stay out at sea," added Jim. "They draft too deep to get too close to shore, not to mention the fact that they would be big, slow easy targets in that close. The Navy uses smaller, faster, more maneuverable craft for the littoral waters. IBU units specialize in that theater of warfare."

"There must really be something going on up north," Marcie added as she shaded her eyes with her hand in an attempt to see them as they left their sight.

"Yeah, and *up north* is just around the corner from here, so we've got to get moving," Jim said as he continued toward his beloved Viking double-cabin cruiser.

~~~~

As the sun began to fade behind them, Jim and Lori sat on the aft deck of the *Mother Washington* as they looked into their beloved town of Delaware City. Neither of them spoke, but they knew that their world was about to be completely altered. Where they would wake up the next day, they did not know.

Watching the black smoke rise from the still-burning refinery in the distance, the only certainty that they had was that
~~~~

they would be leaving their town, and along with it, a lifetime of memories, to an uncertain fate.

At the sight of Carl and Paul jogging down the marina toward the *Mother Washington,* Jim stood.

"Jim!" Carl shouted.

"What is it?" he asked.

"There are two military patrol boats guarding the entrance to the bay," explained Carl. "It looks like a blockade of some sort. Will Clark tried to head out earlier in his Sea Ray only to be turned back by them."

"Are they the same Navy IBU guys we saw earlier?" Jim asked.

"Not our Navy," Paul replied.

"Huh?"

Looking up at Jim from the pier below, Carl said, "Will said they were foreigners. He didn't know from where. The boats were marked UN."

"UN? Damn it to hell!" Jim shouted, punching the stainless-steel railing of the vessel. "Well, that didn't take long."

"Our entire plan hinges on taking to the sea, and now some foreign soldier or sailor is gonna stop us before we even get going?"

Watching as Jim paced anxiously back and forth, Carl asked, "So, what now? We can't just shoot our way out. Even if we did want to do such a thing, I guarantee you those guys have contact with backup and air support that would be on us in minutes."

"I've got an idea," said Paul, with reluctance in his voice.

"What idea?" Marcie asked.

"We need a diversion. We need to pull them off station to allow the *Mother Washington* and *Little Angel* to slip by unnoticed.

"What do you have in mind?" asked Jim with a look of curiosity.

"I've got the Pitts at home in our garage," he replied.

"What?" Marcie shouted, interrupting him.

"Let me finish. Please," he said as he gestured for her patience while he explained. "Anyway, I've got the Pitts at home in the garage. I was putting an inverted oil system on it and doing a few other things, so I pulled the wings off and trucked it home. I've got it assembled in the garage to tweak with the rigging. I was going to have to pull the wings off and truck it back to the airport, but considering the circumstances, I can use a road for a runway and get her in the air. If I provoke those guys, they just might follow me."

"No way, Paul!" Marcie protested.

Curious, but doubtful of the plan's chance of success, Jim asked, "First of all, what about power lines? Second, if we slip out while you're creating a diversion, how the hell will you catch back up with us? It's not like you can do a carrier landing on a forty-seven-foot boat."

"Regarding the runway concern, I can use Jefferson Street. I'd have to taxi a few blocks, but that thing is so small it can fit between the parked cars on either side easily. There are a few places where there are crossing power lines and nearby trees, but I think I can get her out of there. Second, I always fly with a parachute. I'm a certified skydiver, so I know I can handle it. I can ditch the plane, and you guys can pick me up. Just don't take too long. That water is cold. I don't want to end up with hypothermia."

"What if you can't shake them?" Carl asked.

"You think I can't shake a boat with a Pitts?" Paul asked with sarcasm.

"Their pursuit may not be limited to a boat," Carl added.

"Well, there are a thousand potential scenarios, but one thing is for sure, the noose is tightening around our necks, and we need to get the hell out of here. Does anyone else have a better suggestion?"

Speaking up, Jim said, "He has a point. There has been increasing crime and terrorist activity in the area, plus the cities to our north seem to be turning into hotspots for government activity. The UN boats at the mouth of the bay say it all. Also, we know we can't travel by road in a group this large. We would need several vehicles and simply wouldn't have the fuel to make it happen. Besides, we haven't adequately planned for that. In hindsight, we should have planned for such a scenario, but we didn't. Unless you just want to shoot from the hip and head off blindly via car or foot, we have to get by those bastards guarding the river."

After a moment of awkward silence, Paul spoke up. "Well, it's gonna be dark soon. I'd better get going. Keep a keen eye out for me. I don't have navigation lights or landing lights on that thing. It's for daytime VFR use only. Once it gets dark, you'll only have the moonlight to find me, and like I said, that water will be cold."

As Paul turned to walk back into town, Marcie followed along, arguing with him as they walked. After having only gone just out of earshot, Marcie nodded and shed a tear as she hugged and kissed him.

As she returned and boarded the *Mother Washington*, Jim asked, "Is everything okay?" Immediately feeling guilty for his question, Jim started to apologize, but couldn't find the words.

"Yeah," she replied with a sniffle. "He knows what he's doing. I know he'll be okay. He said he'll fly with his dry suit on, too. It's just such crazy idea, I have a hard time wrapping my head around it."

Putting his hand on her shoulder, Jim said, "If I'd trust anyone to pull something like that off, it would be him."

At forty-four-years-old, Paul had spent most of his adult life tinkering with airplanes. Though an engineer by trade, his passion was for aviation. He was mostly interested in the old rag and tube taildragger types. Starting out with a Piper Colt, he'd worked his way through several classic airplanes before settling on the Pitts Special aerobatic biplane as his true love. Over the years, he had amassed hundreds of hours in his little red single-seater and had become an avid aerobatics competitor.

Turning back toward the group, as most everyone had now arrived, Jim said, "As you've all probably noticed, we've had a few no-shows. I believe we still have plenty people on hand for the trip, however. I've asked Martin to skipper the *Little Angel.* He's a very experienced sailor. He's got more time on the water than the rest of us combined. We plan on towing it, just like the others did when they brought her here. But just in case, we'd like a qualified crew on board. I'd like to ask for two volunteers to go onboard the *Little Angel* with Martin to help him to work the rigging if she has to get underway on her own."

Rick Parsons, a recent addition to the group, asked, "It looks like we will all fit onboard the *Mother Washington*, so why would we want to be slowed down by a sailboat?"

"Good question, Rick. I'm sorry you missed my explanations on that before. It's been a little hectic around here lately, you know," he said with a half-joking smile.

"Anyway, yes, we would all fit aboard the *Mother Washington*; however, we've got far more supplies and provisions than we can comfortably take on one boat. That and we don't want all our eggs in one basket. What if the *Mother Washington* becomes inoperative? She's a good boat, but she was made nearly forty years ago. She's simple and sturdy, but not bulletproof. Think of the *Little Angel* as a navigable lifeboat, pre-stocked with food, water, guns, and ammo. While under tow, we plan to maintain radio silence, except in the case of emergency. Martin will go over the light signals we've been working on. You guys will use those signals for basic communications with the *Mother Washington*."

Nodding that he understood, Rick replied, "Thanks. That makes sense." Turning to C.J., a large bearded man who had spent most of his life as a residential plumber, he then said, "Hey, man. You up for it?"

"Sure thing," replied C.J., wiggling his eyebrows as he talked.

"Thanks, guys," replied Jim with a smile.

Laughing at C.J.'s mannerisms, Rick shook his head and said, "C.J., you'll keep us from getting bored, that's for sure."

Not understanding the jab, C.J. shrugged his shoulders, and said, "Huh?"

Seeing Carmen Wheeler, the last member of their group to arrive, along with her unknown male counterpart walking toward them at a distance, Jim squinted trying to get a good look at the two.

"Looks like everyone's here," he said, attempting to refrain from passing judgment against her too early for bringing someone along who was not previously brought to the attention of the group—a clear violation of protocol. He had at least run the inclusion of Paul and Marcie by everyone beforehand.

At twenty-eight years old, Carmen was the youngest of their preparedness-minded group. She grew up on a small family farm, where her father taught her the ways of hunting and fishing throughout the years as she had grown. Moving to the Philadelphia area for college, Carmen felt vulnerable and out of place. The self-sufficient lifestyle of her past gave her a yearning to be around others who didn't see the city as the safe-haven of society, but rather a liability if things were to begin to fall apart.

Stepping up onto the small wooden steps alongside Jim's boat, she nervously said, "Hi, Jim. This is Jordan."

As he reluctantly reached out his hand, Jim looked the young man over. With a flat-billed hat, a designer t-shirt and jeans that, at least to Jim, were a bit too snug fitting for a man to wear, Jim's first impression wasn't a good one. Biting his tongue, he shook the young man's hand. "Hello, Jordan."

"Hey," Jordan replied. "Thanks for taking me along."

Looking at Carmen, Jim said, "I never said we were taking you along. I just said hello. That's all."

With the smile on her face quickly turning to a frown, Carmen protested, "But Jim, you can't just leave us behind."

"I don't plan on leaving YOU behind, Carmen, but nobody has talked to me about him," Jim said, gesturing toward the young man.

Hearing a shout from behind him, Jim turned to see Carl standing on the boat with a hand-held radio in his hand. "Hey, man, we've got to get going. Paul just radioed and said he's back at his place. We can't waste this opportunity."

Looking back at Carmen and Jordan, Jim took a deep breath, and said, "Okay, let's get going." Quickly turning toward the steps leading to the flybridge, Jim stopped. "Don't make me regret this, Carmen."

Chapter Sixteen: Death Race

Arriving at his home winded from the jog, Paul fumbled with his keys to unlock his garage door, sliding it up and out of the way. With only a twenty-foot wingspan, the little red biplane was small by aircraft standards, but was a bit wide for the garage of an average suburban home. Being a rabid Pitts enthusiast and homebuilder, Paul had fitted his garage with the widest garage door he could find. This allowed the Pitts to fit through, but only if he started on an angle and adjusted the aircraft as it passed through the opening. Though he couldn't normally fly from his home within the confines of Delaware City, he did disassemble and truck it there to work on it from time to time over the years and liked the option of being able to push it outside while assembled.

Quickly donning his parachute, Paul pulled the vinyl seat back from the airplane's only seat and tossed it aside. While wearing his parachute, he needed every inch of space he could get while flying the tiny airplane from the cramped cockpit, especially when wearing his thick, bulky drysuit. He even had to go as far as wearing shoes with the thinnest possible soles to give him an extra quarter inch of rudder pedal reach.

Pulling the aircraft forward by the propeller, he reached the edge of the doorway, where he quickly ran to the tail of the plane and cocked it at an angle, pushing it forward another inch, allowing the rounded wingtips to slip through the garage door opening.

Once the aircraft was clear, he stepped up onto the bottom wing and climbed inside. "I can't believe I'm doing this," he mumbled to himself aloud as he donned his combination helmet/headset.

Yelling, "Clear prop!" from his partially opened canopy, he chuckled to himself, thinking, *really...with everything that's happening I'm worried about the little things?*

Once the Lycoming IO-360 powered aircraft shook itself to life, he released the toe brakes and nudged the throttle slightly forward to begin his taxi onto Adams Street. *Wow, this is tighter than I thought,* he mused as he entered the street.

With the forward visibility of a Pitts while on the ground and with the tailwheel down and slow speeds being somewhat limited, if not non-existent, Paul taxied using S-turns to give him an occasional glimpse of what lay just in front of him. Turning left onto Williams Street, he slammed on the brakes as a minivan packed with people and supplies went speeding by, narrowly avoiding him.

"Damn!" he shouted as his heart pounded. "That's just what I need right now!"

Continuing onto Williams Street, he soon reached Jefferson Street, and with a jog to the right, he stomped the left toe brake and swung the tail of the aircraft around to line up on Jefferson Street in a westerly direction. Looking at the trees that lined the edge of the road and the power lines that crossed overhead two intersections down, he said aloud, "What the hell was I thinking?" as he pushed the throttle forward with his left hand while pushing the nose down with the stick in his right.

As the tail of the little plane quickly lifted off the ground, he held the nose down, keeping the plane on the ground until passing underneath the powerlines. As soon as he saw the lines go overhead and knew he was clear, he snapped the stick back and climbed as steeply as possible in order to avoid the next set of powerlines. Unable to see directly in front of him due to the steep angle and poor forward visibility of a Pitts, he held his breath as he prayed he would clear them. Seeing the rooftops of the neighboring homes through the ankle windows of the plane located by his feet, he looked around and breathed a sigh of relief.

"Now for the hard part," he said.

Quickly leveling off and flying at rooftop level, Paul looked down at his beloved small town below. He saw several buildings burning beneath him. The once crowded streets were occupied only by those who were frantically trying leave town to escape the danger and despair that had gripped them ever tighter as each day passed.

Seeing looters throwing what appeared to be a trashcan through the window of a local athletic shoe store, he shook his head in disgust. *I sure as hell wish I had guns on this thing. I'd strafe those bastards like a WWI fighter.*

Approaching the marina, he rocked his wings in a salute to his group as he passed overhead, then turned toward the southeast, heading for the mouth of the Delaware Bay. He stayed close to the southern bank of the river, flying a mere fifty feet above the ground to avoid being spotted too soon.

With the Atlantic Ocean now in view, he saw the silhouette of the patrol boats guarding the harbor. Looking down at a picture of Marcie that he kept clipped to his aerobatic competition sequence chart holder, he pushed the throttle forward and began speeding toward the boats mere feet above the water.

Seeing flashes of light ahead, Paul immediately banked left and pulled hard, the weight of his body being magnified as he pulled the high-G turn. Rolling immediately back to the right, Paul set his sights on the boats, heading straight at them, pulling up and into an inside loop just before impacting the lead vessel.

Rolling wings level at the top of the loop, now facing northwest, Paul buried the nose of the Pitts below the horizon, diving back toward the river, following it in the direction of Delaware City and ultimately Philadelphia to the north. Banking hard right, he descended toward the terrain and flew toward Cape May, which lies just on the north side of the mouth of Delaware Bay.

Looking in the direction of the boats, he once again saw flashes of light, which he assumed to be gunfire from the now pursuing vessels. Turning toward the north, he pulled back the power and slowed to one hundred knots to allow the boats to keep him in sight and in pursuit.

With a slight S-turn to the right to get a view south toward the boats, Paul turned back to the north to see two helicopters heading directly for him. Quickly rolling inverted, he loaded the wings, pulling into an inverted dive. Narrowly averting a head-on collision with the helicopters, he rolled upright and pulled out of the dive just before impacting the beach.

With his heart pounding and his pulse racing, Paul began looking over his shoulder to see the helicopters, now recognizable as a pair of two-seat, tandem attack helicopters. *What the hell? Those aren't...they're not Apaches or Cobras. What the hell are they?* he thought as he banked hard left in an attempt to blend into the terrain.

Dodging a cellular communications tower positioned on the ridge of the cape, he accelerated while turning back toward the south. Paul knew that whatever those helicopters were, their advanced targeting and weapons systems would take him down quick. His only chance was to push the extreme aerobatic capabilities of the Pitts to the edge of its limits.

Seeing a stream of glowing tracers streaking over his bubble canopy, Paul dove toward the water, reentering Delaware Bay. As his airspeed built rapidly, he pulled back hard on the stick, initiating another inside loop as the helicopters flew beneath him, unable to maneuver as aggressively as the Pitts.

Continuing the loop, he shoved his throttle forward, forcing the prop to claw its way around the top of the loop in an attempt to gain as much altitude as he could. He knew that having initiated the maneuver just feet above the water, his chances of impacting the bay once he reached the bottom of the loop were high.

Once again racing toward the water as he completed the loop, Paul saw the helicopters coming back toward him, having turned around in an attempt to re-engage. Rolling the Pitts over ninety-degrees, applying top rudder to hold the knife-edge pass, he flew directly between the oncoming helicopters, once again avoiding being on the business end of their weapons for too long.

Rolling his wings level, Paul looked at his engine cylinder head temperature gauge to see that he had been pushing his engine into the red, far exceeding its normal limitations. Backing off slightly, he dove for the coastline heading south, seeing a Viking cruiser moving in the same direction with a sailboat in tow.

"Yes!" he exclaimed, pumping his fist with excitement.

After his moment of bliss quickly passed, the realization set in that he had no chance of ditching the Pitts and parachuting down to his wife and friends without leading the attack helicopters right to them. He knew he couldn't shake his attackers and hold them off forever. His Pitts, although far superior to an attack helicopter in the realm of pure maneuverability, simply didn't have the ability to return the fight to them, forcing him on the defensive. And at a maximum structural speed of just over two hundred miles per hour, he couldn't outrun them, either.

As the sun's final rays of light disappeared over the western horizon, a feeling of sickness rushed through his body. He turned north away from his wife and friends and flew directly toward the oncoming helicopters.

He hadn't planned for this. He had planned to distract a few slow-moving patrol boats, but instead, he found himself in a life or death struggle with two amazingly deadly attack helicopters, who had undoubtedly had already radioed in for backup in the event that he was able to maintain his evasive maneuvers and keep avoiding their deadly fire.

As he slid his canopy open, preparing himself for an unplanned bailout, the sky in front of him lit up with flashes of lights as tracers streamed from the nose-mounted cannons of both of his pursuers. With what felt like the strike of a baseball bat, Paul felt blood running down his face as the roar of his engine went silent, his propeller shattered from several direct hits as his assailant's stream of incoming fire penetrated the swinging arc of his Hartzell prop.

Gliding silently into the darkness below, Paul turned out to sea, grabbed the hand grip in the center of his upper wing with his right hand, and released his five-point harness with his left as he pulled himself free from his beloved Pitts. Falling toward the cold, dark ocean below, he frantically pulled on the rip cord of his parachute to no avail. It simply would not open.

Chapter Seventeen: Underway

With the sun now gone, Jim piloted the *Mother Washington* south into the darkness of the night, remaining near the shoreline in an attempt to allow Paul to find them. Reluctantly flipping the navigation lights on, Jim heard Carl say, “Hey, man. The lights.”

“Yeah, I know,” Jim said in a defeated tone. “It’s so he can find us. It’s gonna be hard enough for him to bail out in the dark. He needs to be able to get close to us first so that we can get to him.”

Looking forward toward the bow, Carl could see Paul’s wife, Marcie, sitting alone just behind the bow pulpit with a blanket wrapped around her shoulders. “Is she okay?” he asked.

“I doubt it,” replied Jim. “Would you be?”

“No. Not at all.”

After a moment of silence, Carl placed his hand on Jim’s shoulder, and said, “You know we can’t stay this close to shore with the lights on forever. We need to run dark, and we need to be away from shore.”

“I know,” Jim said, reaching out to flip the navigation lights off. He stopped just short, leaving them on. “A few more minutes,” he said.

“Of course,” Carl replied, patting him on the shoulder.

After a few more moments of silence with nothing but the sound of the *Mother Washington’s* Detroit Diesels churning away down below, Jim reluctantly reached over and flipped off the lights.

Hearing Marcie begin to sob, Carl began to stand as Jim reached out to him. “Just let her be. Give her time.”

“I’ve got this,” Carl replied. “Go take a break.”

Nodding in agreement, Jim reluctantly left the flybridge and stepped down to the rear deck, entering the main salon of the vessel.

Once inside, he found Lori sitting with Carmen and Jordan on the sofa. Walking over to his wife's side, he waited for someone to make room for him so that he could sit beside her, only to receive no reaction from either Carmen or Jordan.

Turning around and sitting in the recliner behind the salon's lower helm, Jim began to speak as Lori interrupted, asking, "He's not coming back, is he?"

"I…I just don't see how he could at this point," replied Jim. "Maybe he ran into more trouble than we expected," he said as he held his head low. "I…I just don't know."

"Are you talking about the airplane guy?" Jordan asked.

Looking up at him, Jim said through gritted teeth, "That *airplane guy* as you so eloquently put it, got us out of there. That means without him, we couldn't have gotten your ass out here."

"He didn't mean anything by that," Carmen interrupted.

"Let him speak for himself," Jim snarled. "Who the hell is this guy, anyway? Why the hell did you bring a total stranger along? You knew the rules. We kept all of this hush-hush for a reason. We took a chance bringing you into our group, and this is how you repay us?"

"Jim!" Lori said sharply, interrupting Jim's tirade.

"No, let him finish," Carmen said. "We need to get this out in the open."

"I don't have time for this right now. We've got a lot going on," he said as he stood to leave.

"What can we do?" Carmen asked.

"For now, just sit here and guard the couch. I can't have someone I can't trust on the weather decks right now."

“Jim!” Lori again shouted as he walked up the short flight of steps to the aft main deck above.

~~~~

Turning to see Jim rejoining him on the flybridge, Carl said, “She hasn’t moved an inch.”

Looking forward to the bow, Jim could see that Marcie was still slumped over, sitting behind the bow pulpit with her head in her hands.

“What’s our heading?” Jim asked.

“Zero six five,” Carl replied. “GPS shows us about five miles offshore and continuing to pull away. How far out do you want to go?”

“No more than this.” Turning to look behind them, Jim was pleased to see the *Little Angel* towing along nicely, illuminated only by the moonlight. Giving Martin and his crew a wave, Jim smiled and turned back to Carl.

“Now that we’ve made it out of the bay and away from the authorities, it’s time to arm up. I’m gonna go down into the V-berth and get what we need.”

“Aye, aye, Captain!” Carl answered smartly with a hand salute.

Shaking his head with a grin, Jim climbed down from the flybridge and disappeared into the salon below.
~~~~

Chapter Eighteen: Coming to Terms

As the sun came up over the flat, featureless eastern horizon of the Atlantic Ocean, Jim watched from the salon's side windows as the vessel moved up and down with the gentle rolling of the ocean. Boiling a pot of hot water on the stove in order to make a cup of instant coffee, Jim looked over to see Carmen and Jordan sleeping quietly on the sofa.

As he poured the crystals into the hot water, stirring it with a small metal spoon, he savored the aroma as it wafted up to his face, riding on the warm, rising air. Pouring his concoction into a large stainless steel thermos, Jim took a sleeve of disposal paper coffee cups and walked up out of the kitchen, across the salon floor, and back down into the aft stateroom where Lori was still sound asleep.

Walking to her bedside, he sat down gently on the bed next to her, leaning down to kiss her on the forehead.

As her eyes opened, she yawned and smiled. Putting her hand on his leg, she said, “Good morning, my love.”

“Good morning, beautiful,” he said, returning the smile.

Pouring her a hot cup of coffee, he handed it to her and said, “I've been thinking long and hard about Carmen and Jordan.”

“And?” Lori replied with a crooked stare.

“And...I've decided that since I already made the mistake of letting her bring him onboard, I may as well make the best of it. I'll talk to them this morning. I need to see where his head is in the game. I need to look at how we can best utilize him. If he's gonna eat, he's gonna work.”

Replying with a smile, she said, “Good. I'm glad you've come around. Were you up all night?”

“Not all night,” he replied, the fatigue showing on his face. “But most of it. Carl and I have been solving all the world’s problems.”

“If only you two ran the world,” she said with a smile. “So, what’s the solution?”

“What solution?” he asked, confused due to his lack of sleep.

“The solution to all of the world’s problems. Duh. That’s what we’re talking about. You and Carl’s discussion?”

“Oh, right,” he said, snapping back into the moment. “Nuke it.”

“What?” she said, cocking her head to the side.

“The only way to solve all the world’s problems is to nuke it,” he replied. “But that, of course, would bring a whole new set of problems. So, I guess there really isn’t a solution. We’ve just got to keep plodding on along, making our way in this twisted mess of a world.”

Patting her on the leg, he stood up, and said, “I’m gonna get some coffee to Carl and check on the guys in the other boat. When our two young’uns in there wake up, send them topside, if you don’t mind.”

“Of course, Admiral Rutherford,” she said with a salute.

“Oh, stop it. You and Carl are just alike.”

~~~~

Dutifully watching the horizon for signs of threats, Carl heard footsteps coming up the steps behind him. Turning to investigate the source of the sound, he saw Jim with a thermos in one hand and a sleeve of coffee cups in the other. “Thank God,” he said, happy to see the warm brew on this cold, crisp morning.
~~~~

Placing the thermos and cups on the bench seat beside Carl, Jim said, “Pull both transmissions back into neutral, then bump reverse momentarily. Let’s let the *Little Angel* drift up to us.”

“Sure thing,” Carl replied. “Do you want me to just shut her down?”

“No, not this far from shore,” Jim said, looking off into the western horizon toward land. “Let’s just let her idle in neutral. If she didn’t start back up, we’d be screwed.”

“Roger that,” Carl said, bringing both of the *Mother Washington’s* shift levers to the center position, then aft, then to the center again.

Climbing down the aft ladder to the swim platform, Jim pulled the towline between the two boats in hand over hand, keeping it from getting tangled in the *Mother Washington’s* props and rudders underneath, as the slack in the line steadily increased. Once the *Little Angel* reached the *Mother Washington,* Jim reached out with his foot to slow its approach, feeling a slight bump as it came to a stop abruptly when the two boats made contact.

“Ahoy there!” he said with a smile on his face. “How goes it, Skipper?” he asked Martin.

“It’s going,” Martin replied. “But, do you have any air freshener?”

“Air freshener?”

“Yeah,” Martin confirmed, looking back at the other two men. “C.J. got a little green last night. He’s not quite got his sea legs yet.”

Watching C.J. hang his head in shame, Jim said, “Hey, that’s nothing to be ashamed about. Why don’t you guys come aboard for breakfast? I’ll cook up something for C.J. to spread all over your cabin later.”

“Ha ha, very funny,” C.J. replied with a look of discomfort on his face.

"I'm just messin' with ya, man," Jim said with a chuckle. "But seriously, this boat doesn't move around as much as that little thing. Come and take a break."

Hearing Carmen's voice from the rear deck above, Jim looked up to see Jordan and her leaning on the railing. "Lori told me you wanted to see us?" she said.

"Yeah, I'll be right up," he said. Turning back to Martin, Rick, and C.J., he said, "You guys go make yourself at home in the galley and get yourself something to eat. If there's something you can't find, just ask Lori. We've got most things or at least some freeze-dried representation thereof. The butter powder tastes like butter; you just can't spread it on toast as well," he said with a smirk.

Climbing up the ladder from the swim platform, Jim looked at Carmen and Jordan, and said, "Let's take a walk."

Reaching the bow of the *Mother Washington*, Jim leaned back on the deck railing and began to speak as Carmen asked, "Where's Marcie? Is she okay?"

"She's in the forward V-berth right under your feet," Jim said. "We'll just let her be and give her time to come to terms with things. Lori will be checking in on her from time to time."

"Jim," Carmen said, attempting to cut him off before he could speak, "I'm sorry, but I just couldn't leave Jordan behind. He—"

Holding his hand up to stop her mid-sentence, Jim said, "Don't. Look, you don't have to explain at this point. I allowed him onboard, so there's no reason for me to keep beating you up about it." Seeing a look of relief on her face, he continued, "He's here now, and we all need to make the best of this."

Looking at Jordan, he asked, "So, in a nutshell, what's your resume?"

"My resume?" Jordan asked, confused by Jim's question.

"Yeah, your resume. Act as if you're trying to get a job in this group. We've been getting together for a long time, working on our preparations for what we felt was inevitable. We've trained together. We've studied together. We've pooled our funds to stock these vessels with food and supplies. So, given the fact that you weren't a part of that, what makes you an asset to us? What's your background?"

"Well, I'm majoring in Urban Studies at Temple University. Well, actually, I just changed my major to Urban Studies from Art History. I—"

"Were," Jim said, interrupting him.

"Huh?" Jordan uttered, again confused by Jim's blunt speech.

"You *were* a student at Temple," Jim replied. "That world is gone. At least for the foreseeable future. Step one to becoming a part of this group is to get your head on straight. Our nation, and the world for that matter, has been on a collision course with collapse for some time now, accelerating dramatically in recent years. The writing was on the wall for anyone who was willing to see it. Massive and nearly incomprehensible public debt, divide and conquer politics, and engineered civil unrest have all been a part of a globalist agenda to 'reset' our way of life."

Pausing for a moment, watching as Jordan rolled his eyes, Jim said, "What? What's the problem?"

"Well, nothing, but..."

"But what?" Jim asked.

"Well, no offense," Jordan said, "but that seems like an overly simplistic way to see the problems the world faces that have been caused by decades of corporate greed."

"Are you kidding me?" Jim said, looking at Jordan and then to Carmen as if she was responsible for his statements.

With an embarrassed look on her face, Carmen hesitated as Jim looked Jordan directly in the eye.

"Is that what your professors told you? The same professors that probably told you to seek a safe space when someone said something offensive to you? The same professors that encouraged you to disrespect our nation's founding and flag?"

"Well...I—"

"Shut up," Jim said, cutting off Jordan's incoherent stammering. "Now you listen to me and listen good. I don't know how you were raised. I don't know what environment you've spent your life in that made you such easy clay to be molded by the 'university elite' who have never even been in the real world, but let me ask you something. Where are those professors now? Did they have the wisdom and foresight to stockpile food and supplies for such an occasion? Do they have the tools and skills needed to defend themselves while the world collapses around them?"

"Well—"

"No! Of course, not. They probably made snide remarks in class, degrading anyone who didn't believe in the wonder and majesty of big government and the security it supposedly provides. They probably openly opposed our right to bear arms."

Jim's eyes swept over the boats and the sea before he calmed down enough to continue.

"Right now, I'd imagine those who you allowed to fill your head with false truths are either dead or standing in a government food line somewhere, desperate for a handout that may not come. We, on the other hand, the people that took you in and evacuated you from the world that has begun crumbling down around you, have food. We have well-equipped transportation, and we have weapons. We have those evil guns that your professors probably told you that only government should have to oppress you with. You know—the evil black ones.

You'd better do a control-alt-delete and reset your pre-programmed mind and open it up to the reality around you. You'd better open your mind to the fact that it's not reliance upon government, but reliance upon the individuals who are around you right now, of their own free will, who will keep you fed and safe in the foreseeable future. Don't peddle that crap around here. I promise you, not one person in this group will give you the time of day if you do."

Turning to walk off, he said, "Oh, and one more thing. I need a replacement for C.J. He needs a break. He hasn't gotten his sea legs just yet, and Martin needs a full crew on the sailboat. I need you to fill in for the rest of the day once we get underway again."

Seeing the look of protest on Jordan's face, Jim asked, "Is that a problem?"

"No," Jordan sheepishly replied. "No, I'll do whatever you need me to do."

"Good," Jim said, calming his voice. "Look, I'm not trying to be a hardass, but we all need to be on the same page. I don't care what you think of me, but I need to know we can trust you, regardless of your feelings. I need to know that you've got the best interest of everyone on these boats in mind. If you think you were merely hitching a ride, taking handouts from us, you were sorely mistaken."

Looking back to Carmen, Jim said, "Shadow Carl on the bridge for a while. He'll teach you everything you need to know to man...er...staff the helm. We need to get everyone trained to be able to give everyone the time off they need to recharge."

Turning to walk away, Jim heard Carmen's voice. "Uh, Jim?"

"Yes," he replied.

“Um...I’m sorry. I’m sorry for causing all this trouble. But trust me, Jordan really is a nice guy. I wouldn’t have brought him otherwise.”

“Being a ‘nice guy’ when times are good is easy,” Jim said. “Being a ‘good guy’ when times are hard, isn’t. Keep that in mind.”

Chapter Nineteen: Dark Skies

Later that evening, as the skies began to darken, Martin used light signals to communicate with Jim about the approaching storm. He instructed Rick and Jordan to help him lash everything down securely onboard the *Little Angel.*

"Okay, guys," he said. "Everything big or small needs to be secured. Once this boat starts rocking and riding the waves, things that you thought weren't gonna move will be moving right at you. Big stuff will knock you out cold. Little stuff will be carried by water into pump intakes or jam hatches as you're trying to close them. We don't want any gear adrift once we start taking on water. Understood?"

In a frustrated and concerned voice, Jordan asked, "Taking on water? What do you mean, taking on water?"

"Plan for the worst, hope for the best," Martin said. "You can't go into a storm in a small boat like this and not expect to take on water. There's no nine-one-one to call out here. We have to be prepared for whatever may come, and the waves, I promise you, they will come."

Doing as Martin asked, Rick and Jordan quickly helped get the little boat as ready as they could for the coming storm.

As the winds began to pick up and the waves began to break, smashing water against the boat's fiberglass hull, dousing them with a cold, saltwater spray, Jordan frantically asked, "Why don't they pull us in? We need to get on the big boat. They can't leave us out here!"

"Relax," Martin said. "We'll be fine. Trust me. I've faced worse, much worse. Besides, if the boats are too close together, they could collide when things get rough, sinking us both. No, we've got to keep our distance, and if things get too rough, we'll need to cast off the line. If the storm gets too bad, the towline could rip a cleat right out of the fiberglass."

Wiping the blowing saltwater off his face as he struggled to speak, Jordan exclaimed, "What do you mean *cast the towline off*? You mean just drift out here on our own, getting blown to who knows where? What the hell?"

"Relax, kid. If it comes to that, they'll find us."

"Like they found Paul?" Jordan quipped.

"Hey, watch your mouth!" snapped Rick, not at all happy with Jordan's insinuation.

"We can argue later, boys," replied Martin, trying to defuse the situation. "Right now, let's get down below, get out of this wind, and stay dry."

After an hour had passed, the sea state had intensified to the point where Martin was afraid they must do what he'd feared, and set themselves adrift. Feeling sharp tugs from the towline as the two boats crashed over different waves, he feared the jolts would become more than the fiberglass hull could handle.

Taking the radio's microphone in hand, Martin said, "I'm gonna let Jim know we're gonna cast off. We can't take much more of this." Another sharp jolt from the towline bounced him against the bulkhead.

"*Mother Washington*, are you up?" he asked, releasing the push-to-talk button to listen for a reply. "*Mother Washington*, are you up?" he asked again. After several moments and several more attempts to no avail, Martin hung up the mic, and said, "Either the radio isn't working, or the winds are drowning us out. Regardless, I've got to cut us loose."

"What about the line?" Rick asked. "Don't they need to pull in the slack?"

"Yeah, under normal conditions, but right now, we have to be concerned with the integrity of our hull—"

Interrupted by another sharp tug of the towline, accompanied by the sound of cracking fiberglass, Martin said, "I've got to do it. Hopefully, they'll notice and reel it in."

Opening the main hatch leading out of the berth and on deck, Martin stepped outside, only to be pummeled by the high winds and water from crashing waves. A flood of water entered the boat, soaking Rick and Jordan, who were still inside. Frantically closing the main hatch behind him to ensure the watertight integrity of the boat, Martin struggled to maintain his footing. Gripping firmly onto the railing, he worked his way forward toward the tow cleat. With the hood of his jacket blowing off his head, the wind and salt spray pelted his face, forcing him to close his eyes. Reaching for one of the mooring lines coiled neatly between two of the side cleats, Martin untied and freed it, securing one end to his belt and the other to the hand railing.

Reaching the bow of the boat, Martin struggled to hold on with his left hand while untying the towline with his right. Unable to loosen the knot under its heavy load, he removed his knife from its sheath and began sawing furiously.

Once his blade had penetrated the line over halfway, it snapped as they rode a wave upward, pulling the line tight against the opposite motion of the lead vessel. As the boat rode the wave to its pinnacle, Martin held on tightly as it seemed to freefall, crashing down into the base of the next wave. The impact of the boat's hull against the powerful wave sent a wall of water over him, causing him to lose his grip on both his knife and the railing.

From inside the *Little Angel*, Rick watched as his friend, Martin, was washed overboard by the force of the wave. Shouting over the sounds of the raging winds and seas, Rick said, "Man overboard! Man overboard!" as he rushed to the hatch and out onto the main deck.

Frantically trying to see his friend in the water, Rick grabbed the life ring with his right hand, while holding on with his left. “Martin! Martin!” he shouted, his voice drowned out in the violence of the storm.

Seeing a flash of the reflective strip on Martin’s raingear, he tossed the life ring to him but overshot. The wind carried it further than planned, missing Martin by several feet. “Damn it!” he shouted. Seeing the taught rope tied to the hand rail going into the water toward Martin, Rick grabbed the rope and began pulling with all his might. Outmatched by the heavy seas, Rick struggled to gain ground.

“Help me!” he shouted, looking over his shoulder to see that Jordan wasn’t there.

Turning his attention back to his friend, he pulled and pulled on the rope, slowly making headway until Martin managed to reach up, grabbing the handrail with one hand, while Rick reached out for the other, pulling him aboard.

Falling on top of Rick, as the waves washed the two men across the deck, Martin attempted to speak, but couldn’t, shivering violently from the cold.

Scurrying to his feet, Rick dragged Martin to the hatch, struggled to open it, and then pulled him inside.

Slamming the hatch shut behind them, keeping the winds and rain from crashing in on them, Rick turned to see Jordan huddled with a blanket in the corner. “Where the hell were you?” he shouted. “We’re a crew. You left me out there alone. He could have died. I needed you, you coward!”

Tugging on Rick’s arm, Martin signaled for him to stop. “It’s okay,” he said. “He’ll learn in time.”

Starting the propane heater to warm his friend, Rick sat across from both Martin and Jordan as a feeling of awkwardness filled the cabin.

Three hours later...

As the worst of the storm had now passed, Martin broke the silence. He asked Jordan, "Have you ever been on a boat before?"

"Just ferries and small fishing boats when I was a kid," Jordan replied. "I've never been much for the water. I grew up in an apartment raised by my grandmother. She never took me to the beach or anything. She always complained about her figure, and didn't want to be seen in a swimsuit."

Will a smile of understanding, Martin said, "Tomorrow, we'll go over the basics. I know you were thrust into this situation and didn't plan on it. But there will be times that you'll need to act, fear or not."

"Yeah, I know," replied Jordan, hanging his head low. Looking up to Martin, he then asked, "So, how long have you been a sailor?"

"I made my first solo oceanic voyage at thirteen," Martin replied as if such a feat wasn't at all noteworthy. Noticing that Jordan was looking him over, he added, "I'm sixty-eight, if you're trying to do the math in your head."

Bewildered, Jordan asked, "But how did you make a solo oceanic voyage at thirteen? Were you a fisherman back in Mexico?"

"I'm not Mexican," Martin replied. "I was born in Cuba in 1950. It was a wonderful place back then. When I was only nine-years-old, the revolution began."

Nodding with a smile on his face, Jordan seemed as if he was familiar with the history of Cuba.

"Anyway," Martin continued, "I basically grew up in the middle of the worst of it. My father and most of my family were killed by Guevara and his ilk."

Confused, Jordan asked, "Che?"

Pausing for a moment, Martin replied, “Yes, Ernesto Che Guevara, the murderous Marxist socialist that helped Castro turn Cuba into a communist prison. He murdered my father for opposing the rule of the communist party.”

“But...he...he was a hero of the revolution, wasn’t he?” Jordan stammered. “He was fighting back against the capitalist exploitation of Latin America by the U. S.”

“Hero? Maybe to some brainwashed middle-class American college student who’s been fed that line of bull by their professors. Professors who’ve never seen the real world outside their cozy and safe university. No, in real life, Che Guevara was a terrorist mass murderer. He didn’t earn the name, ‘The Butcher of La Cabaña’ for nothing.” Martin waited for Jordan to respond, but he didn’t.

Clearing his throat, he continued, “This is just one story, but it shows who the socialist *hero* who adorns your generation’s t-shirts really was. According to eyewitnesses, Che packed over eight hundred prisoners in a space where no more than three hundred could humanely be held. The prisoners were former Batista military, police, journalists, businessmen, and merchants. The revolutionary tribunal was made up of Che’s militiamen. Che Guevara himself presided over the appellate court. They executed many innocent people in the name of advancing their socialist agenda. He never overturned a sentence. He let them all die or rot in prison.

“Later, he went on to set up the forced labor camp, Guanahacabibes, in 1960. That camp would set the stage for the later systematic confinement of those he saw as unfit. I think it was 1965 in the province of Camagüey, where he imprisoned dissidents, homosexuals, AIDS victims, Catholics, Afro-Cubans, and other such scum, as he saw it. He would herd those poor souls into buses and trucks, where they would be transported at gunpoint to concentration camps, organized just as he had set up Guanahacabibes.

"Some would never return. Others would be raped, beaten, or mutilated; and those who escaped death would be traumatized for life. Your *hero* executed children as young as fourteen. No, your *hero* wasn't a mere revolutionary. He was cut from the same cloth as Mao, Hitler, and Stalin. It's a shame how history, or modern revisionist history, has been re-written, altering the perspectives of an entire generation."

Pausing to give Jordan another chance at rebuttal, but getting no response other than a blank look, he continued. "After he murdered my father, I left my once beloved homeland of Cuba on a homemade raft, pieced together from what most would consider garbage. I set out with my aunt, but she didn't survive the journey.

"When I arrived in America, I was granted political asylum and allowed to remain. I've always been thankful to the sea for delivering me out of the hands of evil, and to America, where my freedom was guaranteed by the constitution. I've remained an avid sailor ever since. I feel a connection to those I lost when I'm out on the water, particularly when alone, just like that fateful voyage so many years ago."

"I...I don't know..." Jordan mumbled, tripping over his words.

"You don't need to respond," Martin replied, releasing Jordan from his sure to be failed attempt at a college lecture driven rebuttal. "I didn't tell you that story to alter your opinions of the world, although it sounds like you may need it. I started telling you the story of my youth to explain to you why I feel such a connection to the sea. If I tell you it will be okay, I want you to believe me. I've been through worse, and the sea—she's always delivered me safely through it all."

Looking to his shipmates, Martin said, “It’s dark outside now. There’s nothing we can do until sunrise. Once we meet back up with the *Mother Washington*, we can rotate you guys out for a break.”

“I’m good,” Rick quickly replied. “I don’t need a break.”

“Me, too,” Jordan added. “I’ll stay. I can tell I’ve got a lot more to learn.”

Chapter Twenty: An Uncertain Dawn

Opening the hatch and stepping out onto the main deck of the *Little Angel*, Martin looked around at what was now a dead calm sea. Seeing that the rigging of the small boat was in disarray, he thought to himself, *oh well, no wind anyway. We've got time to get things in order.*

Scanning the horizon with his binoculars, Martin heard Rick's voice behind him. "Do you see anything? The *Mother Washington*?"

"Nothing yet," Martin replied. "It'll be okay, though. I expected to be a good distance from them this morning. They would have kept motoring into the storm, in order to keep their bow pointed in the right direction to avoid rolling to the side with the waves. That, and since we weren't in communication with them when we cut ourselves loose, there's no telling how far they went before they realized we weren't there."

"Surely they noticed right away," Rick said, trying to reassure himself.

"They would have been thinking the same thing we were, regarding the stress on the towline. Martin replied. "So, I'm sure you're right. For now, we'll just spend the day getting ourselves something to eat and straightening out this mess. They'll find us. They've got radar."

Joining them on the main deck after overhearing the conversation, Jordan asked, "Can't we just fire up the engine?"

"If it comes down to it," Martin replied. "But that little thing is more for docking than anything else. Besides, we may just get ourselves farther from them and not help the situation at all. I think the best bet is for us to just let them come to us. It's harder to find a moving target."

Accepting Martin's decision, Jordan and Rick got busy with the tasks at hand, helping Martin get the boat rigged for sail in the event it should come to that.

Six hours later...

Scanning the horizon with his binoculars, Martin turned to Rick, and said, "At some point, if we don't see them, we're gonna have to rig the sails and get underway. I was hoping they would have found us by now."

"What do you think could be holding them up?" Rick asked.

"Who knows? There are too many variables to guess. We can't just sit here forever, though."

As he began to lower his binoculars, he caught a glimpse of something on the horizon to the west. "What the...?"

"What is it?" Jordan asked in an excited voice. "Is it them?"

"Just a sec," Martin said, watching the object as it appeared to be getting closer. "It's a boat for sure."

"Is it them?" Jordan impatiently asked again.

"Hang on a minute," Martin replied.

Adjusting the focus, he said, "Rick, get the rifles from below."

"Who is it?" asked Rick.

"I'm not sure, but it's not them," Martin said as he lowered his binoculars and looked at both Rick and Jordan.

As the vessel approached, the men could see that it was a center-console fishing boat a little more than thirty feet in length. The boat had two large outboard engines mounted on the stern, causing Rick to say, "We're not gonna outrun that thing."

"Nope, we sure as hell aren't," replied Martin. "Hell, we couldn't outrun a canoe."

Quickly retrieving the rifles from the compartments below the V-berth's mattress, Rick kept one for himself and handed one to both Martin and Jordan as well. Seeing Jordan stare at the weapon with a confused look, Rick said, "Have you ever shot one of those?"

"I've never shot anything," Jordan replied.

Holding the rifle in front of Jordan, pointing to it as he spoke, Rick said, "Your magazine is already inserted. It holds thirty rounds, so don't worry about running out. If you take your time and aim well, that will last you through anything survivable on this little boat. Are you familiar with how to aim?"

"From video game guns," Jordan replied.

Scrunching his forehead, Rick then said, "Here," as he took the rifle. Cycling the charging handle, Rick let the bolt go home and ensured that a round was indeed in the chamber with a slight pull to expose brass. Bumping the forward assist to set the bolt securely back into battery, he said, "Look here," pointing at the safety selector. "Safe and semi are your only options; this ain't a machine gun. It's on safe, click it like this with your thumb to make it ready, then aim, squeeze the trigger, and hope like hell that we are as badass as we wish we were."

Nervously, Jordan reached for the rifle. "Okay. Got it."

With the vessel now closing to within fifty yards, they could see three men standing in the forward area of the boat, just ahead of the center console. Behind them, the driver and two other men stood under the shelter of the fiberglass top.

Adjusting his ball cap, Rick turned to Martin, and said, "I'm not happy with how the math is adding up here."

Replying with a nod, Martin said, "I just hope our subtraction skills are up to speed."

"Ahoy there!" one of the men shouted, waving his arm.

Waving back with his left hand, Martin held his AR-15 with his right, and said, “We’re fine, thanks. We don’t need any assistance.”

Ignoring his statement, the boat slowed to idle and continued toward the *Little Angel.*

“What are you boys doing way out here all by yourselves in that little thing?” one of the men on the front of the boat asked.

With a serious look on his face, Martin said, “This boat is big enough to go anywhere in the world, with the right sailor at the helm, of course.”

“Well, now, I didn’t mean to insult your little boat there,” the man said, laughing along with the others.

“What can we do for you?” Martin asked. “We were just getting ready to rig the sails and get underway. So, if you don’t mind, daylight is burning.”

“Now, hold on, fellas. There’s no need to be in such a rush,” the man said. “Things are getting hard to come by back on shore, as I assume you’ve noticed. We’re running low on a few things, and were just hoping you guys would be willing to do a little trading.”

“We’ve not really got anything to spare,” Martin sternly replied.

Seeing the nervousness on Jordan’s face, the man looked at him, and said, “Since your hombre there isn’t in the mood to do business, maybe you are. What do you boys have that we may be interested in?”

As Jordan began to speak, Martin interrupted. “This ain’t his boat. He’s just a friend. If there were to be any deals made, it would be through me. And I assure you, we won’t be making any deals.”

Ignoring Martin’s protest, the man looked again to Jordan, and said, “Whatcha got, boy?”

Looking at Martin, Jordan's heart now pounding in his chest, he said, "We've not got anything of value. Just food for ourselves."

"Well, hell, boy. Nothing is as valuable as food these days. I'd like to offer you a trade."

Interrupting, Martin said, "We've not got anything to trade."

With an aggressive voice, the man shouted, "I'm not talking to you, asshole. I'm talking to your young friend there. Now, I've been trying to be nice, but that's not working. I guess we're gonna have to come aboard and see for ourselves what you have."

Quickly raising his AR-15 and leveling it at the man's head, Martin gritted his teeth, "That's not going to happen. Now, get the hell away from us. Just leave us be."

With an evil grin, the man said, "What the hell is wrong with you? We've got six men, you've got three." Looking at Jordan, he said with a sly grin, "Okay, maybe you only have two and a half. You're not really in a position to be giving orders today. You had better lower that rifle. If any of you show yourselves to be a threat to us, we will deal with you in kind."

Refusing to lower his rifle, Martin said, "Like you said, things are hard to come by these days. Food is life. We will treat it as such. Now, you back away and leave us be. There's no need to die over anything today."

Chuckling to himself, the man said, "You're right. There's no need to die over anything today, but it looks like you will anyway."

As the man finished his sentence, Martin's AR-15 shattered the silence of the calm, clear day with the supersonic crack of a high-velocity 5.56mm projectile as it smashed through the man's skull. As the bullet exited his head, splattering blood and bits of tissue sprayed the windshield of the center console behind him.

With gunfire erupting from both vessels, Jordan raised his rifle to his shoulder, quickly aimed, flipped off the safety, and for the first time in his life, felt the impulse of recoil through his shoulder as he watched one of the men fall before him. Screaming inside his own mind with both fear and rage, he pulled the trigger over and over and over again as his world seemed to move in silence and slow motion.

Chapter Twenty-One: Red Seas

Looking out over the now calm seas, Jim and Lori sat on the flybridge, both scanning the horizon with their binoculars and the *Mother Washington's* radar. "Where the hell are they?" Jim shouted in frustration.

"Hey, guys," Carl shouted from the swim platform on the stern of the vessel.

"What's up, Carl?" Jim replied.

Pulling himself up to the main rear deck, still dripping wet and dressed in his wetsuit, Carl said, "I finally got the towline untangled from the screws and rudders. Any luck finding them?"

In a defeated tone, Jim said, "No. Not yet."

Pointing into the salon amidships, Carl said, "We've pretty much got the mess cleaned up. What else do we need?"

"We need to—" Interrupted by a glimpse of something on the boat's old technology, green radar display, Jim held up his hand as if to halt the conversation.

"What is it?" Lori asked, looking over Jim's shoulder.

"Right there," he shouted, tapping on the screen. "There's something...no, wait. The return just split up."

"What?" Carl asked as he jogged up the steps to the flybridge.

"Okay, we've got a stationary target and a moving target. They were one return, but diverged into two."

Scratching his chin, Carl said, "That sure as heck isn't the *Little Angel* moving that fast."

"No. You're right," Jim replied, putting a plan together in his head. "Carl, you yell down to C.J. and Carmen to get up here. Lori, if you could go check on Marcie. I know she's still pretty torn up over Paul's unknown whereabouts, but we're gonna need everyone on this."

"What? What are we doing?" asked Lori with anxiety in her voice.

"We're gonna check out what's going on there. The location of the stationary boat could be the *Little Angel,* if you add all the variables for drift and time. Martin would have known not to get underway but to hunker down and wait for us, so as not to complicate things."

"What's up, Jim?" Carmen asked as she and C.J. joined them on the flybridge.

"I've got a radar return we need to check out. Something's fishy. Go into the V-berth and pull up the mattress cushions. In the compartments underneath the cushions, you'll find several M1's. Bring those up, as well as that Barrett M82 of C.J.'s.

"C.J., I want you to get your Barrett setup here on the flybridge. You've got the range, and the elevation will give you a nice long area to work with.

"Carmen and Carl, I want you to use the M1's to lay down a suppressing fire if we get into a scuffle, allowing C.J. to work his magic with the fifty."

"Eight-round M1's instead of thirty round AR's?" Carmen asked.

Looking her way, Carl replied, "Those AR's are cool and all, but they lack punch. The M1 Garands may be dinosaurs, but they're hard-hitting dinosaurs. If you look at the ballistics of 30-06 vs. 5.56NATO, there's simply no comparison regarding hull penetration."

As Jim pushed the two transmission levers into forward, followed by the throttles, he brought the two big supercharged Detroit Diesels to life, pushing the bow of the large vessel up and out of the water, leveling off with the hull on plane. After getting his heavy Barrett rifle into position and ready to fire, C.J.

scanned the horizon with binoculars as Jim guided the vessel toward the radar return.

"There!" C.J. said, pointing to the horizon.

Adjusting his course slightly, Jim said, "I see it. It's a sailboat."

"It's them," C.J. said, looking through the binoculars. Lowering them to his chest, he said, "It's the *Little Angel* all right, but I don't see anyone."

Pressing on, Jim brought the *Mother Washington* to within thirty yards of the *Little Angel* and chopped the power, pulling the transmissions into neutral, and then bumping reverse to slow the forward momentum of the heavy boat.

Scanning the deck through the sights of their rifles while standing on the bow, Carl and Carmen were horrified to see blood and fiberglass fragments everywhere. The hull of the *Little Angel* was riddled with bullet holes.

Drawing his Kimber .45 from its holster, Jim ran down the stairs of the flybridge and onto the main deck, jumping over the railing and onto the *Little Angel.* Frantically searching for survivors, Jim shouted, "Martin! Rick! Jordan!" as he jerked open the hatch leading into the cabin of the small vessel.

Lighted only by rays of light shining through the holes left behind by the projectiles that had penetrated the hull during what appeared to be a ferocious firefight, Jim saw no bodies or any sign of survivors.

Rushing back to the main deck, Jim looked to Carl and Carmen, who were now tying the *Little Angel* to the *Mother Washington,* and said, "They're not down below. Where the hell are they?"

As he wrapped the mooring line around a cleat on the *Little Angel,* Carl looked into the water, seeing a line running underneath the boat. "What the?" he mumbled as he visually followed the line underneath and aft. Standing up and walking slowly to the stern of the boat, Carl noticed a trail of bird activity behind the boat.

“What the hell is that?” Carl heard C.J. shout from high up on the flybridge of the *Mother Washington*.

Seeing that C.J. was pointing toward the bird activity, in the direction of the line, he reached into the water and began pulling on the line. His heart sank as he felt the resistance of weight. Something was floating at the end of the line.

Pulling the line toward the boat hand over hand, Carl said in a metered voice, “Um...can you two come here?”

“What is it? What did you find?” Carmen asked as she and Jim joined him.

The three were horrified to see three, bullet-riddled bodies tied to the line, trailing the boat as if they were chum.

Violently throwing up over the side of the boat, Carmen heaved her breakfast into the ocean as Carl and Jim stood there, silently. After a moment, Jim said in a cold, monotone voice, “Cut the lines. Get back on the *Mother Washington*.”

Without saying another word, the three rejoined C.J. on the flybridge. Jim violently shoved the transmission and throttle levers forward, turning in the direction of the fleeing craft.

Once the *Mother Washington* was up on plane, C.J. asked, “Was that what I thought it was?”

Without breaking his cold, silent stare ahead and toward the horizon, Jim said, “Yes. Yes, it was.”

“We’re going after them?” C.J. asked.

“Yeah,” Jim replied.

Pushing the *Mother Washington* to its threshold of performance, the engine’s water and oil temperatures began to rise into the danger zone.

“She’s gettin’ kinda hot,” C.J. said.

Jim’s cold, silent stare did not waver. Looking at his radar display, he said, “If we get them in range, take out the engines.”

"Will do," C.J. replied.

"There they are!" shouted Carl as the other boat began to come into view.

"Can you reach them from here?" Jim asked.

Looking through his Schmidt and Bender scope, C.J. replied, "Yeah, but what if they didn't do it? They may have stumbled across them like we did."

"Then we'll apologize," Jim said.

Staring at Jim for a second, thinking over what he had asked him to do, C.J. cycled a round into the chamber, adjusted his hold, and gently pressed the trigger, letting a massive six-hundred-and-forty-seven-grain, full metal jacket projectile fly. Striking the right rear corner of the craft, the brutal impact of the massive fifty-caliber round sent fiberglass shards into the air, but failed to disable the boat.

"Damn it!" C.J. shouted as he once again took aim. Adjusting his hold, he let another one fly. "Boom!" he shouted as the fleeing vessel's now shattered starboard, outboard engine's cover popped off from the direct hit. It flew into the air, splashing down into the boat's wake.

Watching as the vessel veered momentarily to the right due to the loss of thrust from the right engine, he added, "Got one."

"One to go," Jim said coldly.

Taking his third shot, the boat then began to slow, pushing a wave of water in front of it as its hull settled off of plane and into the water.

"Be ready to sink it," Jim said to C.J. as the *Mother Washington* bore down on the disabled craft.

With Carl and Carmen taking their positions on the forward deck with their M1's, covering the occupants of the boat, Jim stood up and shouted through the bullhorn kept on the bridge, "Place your weapons on the deck. Then, place your hands on top of your heads where we can see them. Move one damn inch more than that, and you all die!"

Frozen in their tracks, the men looked to one another as if they were looking for options. One of the men spoke up, saying, "Do it, guys."

As they placed their rifles on the deck, Jim slipped through the railing on the bow pulpit of the *Mother Washington* and down onto the stern of the now-disabled center-console fishing boat. "What are these from?" Jim asked, pointing to holes and blood splattered on the console. "It's still wet," he added, wiping his finger through the blood.

"We came across a sailboat that appeared to be in distress," one of the men said, holding up his hands. "We asked them if they needed help. The next thing we knew, they just opened fire on us for no reason."

"Is that a fact?" Jim said tersely as he quickly searched the boat. Pulling open one of the boat's storage compartments, Jim recognized his very own, long-term storage packed foods, complete with his handwriting with the date it was packed away—the food being carried by the *Little Angel.*

Slowly standing, Jim looked at each of the men. With a cold, hard stare, he said, "It looks like you guys have plenty of food to eat. You must have worked hard to store all of this," he said, walking back toward the stern of the boat.

Taking his knife, he reached down and cut the fuel lines going to both of the boat's engines, allowing fuel to spill onto the deck.

Reaching up and pulling himself back onto the bow of the *Mother Washington*, Jim walked in a very deliberate manner across the forward deck, around the salon, and back up onto the flybridge. Shouting down to Carl and Carmen, he said, "Cast us off."

With a nod to Jim, Carl loosened the mooring line around the forward port cleat as Carmen did the same with the line on the forward starboard cleat. Pulling the *Mother Washington's* transmissions into reverse, the old cruiser began to back away from the now disabled fishing boat, while C.J. held his sights on them with the fifty caliber Barrett. Once they had adequately distanced themselves, Jim picked up a forty-millimeter flare gun from the emergency kit kept in the under-seat storage of the flybridge. Aiming it in the air and toward the fishing boat, he pulled the trigger, releasing a flaming hot signal flare.

Watching the white-hot flare arc through the sky, traveling up and then gently down toward their adversaries, Jim never blinked. The flare landed in the center of the craft, followed by the flash of igniting gasoline fumes. As one of the boat's occupants began screaming in pain as his clothes were ignited by the flash, Carmen cringed, looking at Carl, confused by what she was seeing with her very own eyes. *Is all this really happening?*

With the boat now fully engulfed by the ensuing flames, Jim didn't flinch as the light flickered in his eyes. He watched calmly as each of the men jumped helplessly into the water, one by one. Listening callously to their screams for help, Jim shifted the *Mother Washington's* transmissions into forward, slowly turning the boat to a southerly heading, and began a nine-knot cruise toward their original destination.

The burning vessel disappeared, the flames extinguishing as it slipped beneath the surface, taking with it the lives of its crew.

Chapter Twenty-Two: A New Course

After a quiet and somber night, following the revelation that the Martin, Rick, and Jordan had been lost on the *Little Angel,* C.J. dutifully manned the 0200 to 0600 watch at the helm. As the sun began to shine its first rays of the new day over the eastern horizon, he yawned and struggled to focus his eyes. He heard Jim exit the salon and step up onto the rear deck and turned to see what he was doing.

Tiptoeing across the deck in an attempt to avoid waking Lori, who was sleeping in the aft stateroom below, Jim reached the ladder leading down to the swim platform as he heard C.J. say through half a yawn, "Good morning, Jim. Watcha doin'?"

Turing to C.J., Jim looked down at the paint can in his hand and then back up to C.J. "We're erasing who we are, or who we were."

"What?" C.J. asked, confused by Jim's statement.

Taking a moment to gather his words, Jim said, "Things aren't the same, anymore. More so than we first thought. If nothing else, the events of yesterday taught us that our once polite society has quickly become dog-eat-dog. Those men killed our friends simply because they were stronger and our friends had what they wanted. We, or I rather, changed the game when I took matters into my own hands."

Interrupting, C.J. said, "I fired the shots that stopped them, Jim. You didn't act alone."

"Either way, things are different now," Jim said, holding his head low. "I managed to go my entire life without killing another human being. Then last week, I had to take a life. And then another. It started out as purely self-defense or the defense of others. Yesterday, well, that was different. I took things to a different level. I killed for revenge.

"I thought about that all night. How did I turn away from what I had been my entire life, and so fast? How did I, in such a calculated and deliberate manner, set a disabled craft ablaze with its crew still on board? No, things aren't what they used to be. The game has changed, and with that, we must erase the trail that leads back to who we were—just in case this all blows over, and life somewhat returns to what it was before. We don't know what we're going to get ourselves into, and having a trail that leads back to us just isn't wise. I'm going to paint over the ship's name and place the extra decals I had down below over the existing decals to alter her registration numbers."

"What's the new name?" C.J. asked.

"New name?"

"Well, if we do come across authorities of some sort, having the name on the back of the boat simply painted over will look like we stole it. You need to replace it with something that looks legit at a distance."

"Hmm," Jim mumbled. "That makes sense. Do you have any ideas?"

"Uh, well, she's a Viking, right?"

"Yeah, a Viking Double-Cabin Cruiser made by Viking Yachts," Jim replied.

"Use that in the name," C.J. suggested. "The *Angry Viking,* or something like that?"

Looking at the back of the boat, Jim said, "Let's keep it simple. Let's call her *Viking One*."

"She's your boat, Skipper," C.J. said in agreement.

As Jim made the finishing touches on his new stern art, he climbed the ladder leading from the swim platform to the main deck above the aft stateroom. As he topped the ladder, he saw Lori talking to C.J. on the bridge.

"Good morning, dear," Jim said with a smile as he walked over to her, giving her a warm hug and a kiss on the cheek.

"It's good to see you acting like yourself again," she said.

"I'm sorry," he said. "Yesterday kind of took me by storm."

"These past few weeks have pushed us all to the edge and back several times," she said. "Knowing the burden you must bear, keeping the group together despite our losses, handling everything that comes our way...well, I can't imagine how you're holding up as well as you are."

Hearing footsteps coming out of the salon, Jim, Lori, and C.J. turned to see Carl, Marcie, and Carmen joining them on the flybridge. With a thermos of coffee in his hand, Carl said, "I brought the essential part of breakfast. Who brought the filler? You know, the oatmeal."

As the group shared a chuckle, Jim said, "I'm glad you're all here. Especially you, Marcie. I'm glad to see you're hanging in there," he said, placing his hand on her shoulder with a warm smile.

After an awkward pause, he added, "I've made a few changes to the boat and our potential plan, which I'd like to go over with everyone."

"Changes to the boat?" Carl asked in a curious tone.

Holding up the bucket of paint, Jim said, "She's no longer the *Mother Washington*. I renamed her *Viking One,* as well as changed the registration numbers on the bow, so that if things blow over, our actions won't be traced back to us. I think it's obvious to everyone here that the game has changed. We planned and strategized, or should I say, fantasized, about how we saw things going down in what was the inevitable collapse of our once polite society. Maybe it was just me, but I always pictured a post-collapse world to be devoid of government control, sort of like a zombie apocalypse movie where everyone is on their own."

"Same here," Carl said with a nod.

“From what we saw at the mouth of the bay, there is most certainly government control; it’s just not the government we’re used to. We have to assume there will be more conflict ahead of us. Considering all those things, we’ve got a lot of miles to go to get down to the islands, and the odds of us passing by all the major ports and military installations situated along the coast between here and there unmolested are slim. Add to that, the fact that we’ve already lost four of our finest in the first few miles of the journey, as well as at least forty percent of our provisions, and I’d say we’d be hardpressed to make the voyage as planned.

“I reacted horribly to yesterday’s situation,” Jim said, lowering his head. “Not only did I endanger the rest of you by seeking revenge, I recklessly let some of our provisions go down with that boat. I just couldn’t think straight. After what we saw—”

“Jim,” Marcie interrupted. “None of us were prepared for what we saw yesterday, or the day before that, or any of the days since this all started. You reacted how you reacted. Lord knows I wasn’t. We understand. There isn’t a standard here that anyone can expect each other to live up to, except to stand with one another and persevere.”

“Thanks, Marcie,” Jim said with a smile.

“So, what do you recommend we do?” Carmen asked.

Pulling out a chart of the coastline, he tapped his finger on their location and then traced the coastline south. “I think our best bet is to make land somewhere along the coast in one of the more sparsely populated areas, and then work our way inland. If we can get to the Smoky Mountains, we may be able to find a place to set up a long-term camp. There, we can hunt, fish, and forage for food. The area is teaming with wildlife.”

“Look, Jim,” Carl began to speak with uncertainty in his voice, “I know things haven’t worked out according to plan, but scrapping everything and changing plans...well, it seems a little knee-jerk to me."

"We're not prepared to trek inland on foot!" Lori exclaimed, confused by her husband's change of heart. "We stocked the boats for a trip by sea, not by land. We headed out to sea to escape the horrors awaiting us back there. We've got everything we need here. We have food, we have water, and most importantly, we have each other."

"Martin, Rick, and Jordan had each other, too," Jim added. "That didn't help when the wrong people showed up. At sea, if you come under attack by wanna-be pirates—as they did—or heaven forbid, some sort of well-armed and not so well-meaning government authority, you're screwed. You can't run and hide. Sure, you can fight back, but a few inches of fiberglass-covered wood doesn't make for a good bunker. The boat was perfect for getting us out of the northeast, but even that came with a high cost. Escaping on foot or even by vehicle in the northeast would have been hell on Earth. There's just too many people in too small of an area."

Patting the boat's railing with the palm of his hand, Jim looked the boat over, and said, "She did a good job getting us out of there. And she's well suited to the task of getting us ashore, somewhere that will help us avoid the chaos of the masses, but I just don't feel good about thinking we can avoid trouble all the way to the islands. It was a romantic notion, to escape to the islands and live out our days in paradise, but now that reality has hit us in the face like a baseball bat, my focus has turned to keeping those of us who remain safe and sound."

With a nod of agreement, Carl asked, "Where do you think we should go?"

Spreading the chart out on the table on the aft main deck, Jim said, "We have to get as far as the Chesapeake, if we're going to be able to make it anywhere on foot. If we make land before then, we'll be forced to work our way all the way north back to Delaware just to get around the bay. That's simply not an option."

Pointing at Norfolk, Virginia on the chart, Carl said, "The problem with that, is that on the south side of the Chesapeake Bay lies Norfolk. You don't get much more of a naval presence than that. We know the area, including the base, was hit by the attacks based on what Evan and Jason's group told us, but the bulk of the fleet probably remains untouched."

"That's not necessarily a bad thing," C.J. said. "They are still 'our' Navy. We aren't up to no good. What would they have against us?"

"So quickly you forget the patrol boats that were controlling the Delaware Bay?" Jim replied. "Whether they are 'our' Navy or not, they'll be following orders passed down from who knows where. Based on the situation, they are probably putting things on lockdown. They aren't just going to escort us safely through. If anything, they would escort us to a port where we'd be processed into a FEMA camp or the like as refugees or even worse, detainees. We have to base our decisions on what we know, and what we know is that it would be best to avoid other people, especially government authorities."

Clearing her throat, Carmen interjected. "So, you're saying we're painted into a corner? We have to go south to get around the Chesapeake, but the Chesapeake presents a very real and present danger being a naval stronghold. What the hell? You guys were so sure of yourselves at our meetings and get-togethers, but now everything is a lost cause?"

Looking up to the sky, Marcie pointed and said, "What are those?"

Looking up to see the contrails of a formation of four hi-altitude aircraft, each emitting four distinct contrails, Jim said, "They're flying in formation, and they've each got four engines, so those aren't airliners. They're too high up to identify, but I doubt United Airlines is running 747 passenger service in formation. Hell, I doubt United Airlines is running at all, unless it's by government contract or government order. The last we heard, the national airspace system is closed for private and commercial use. My guess is they are military transports of some kind."

Turning, Jim walked over to the railing, looking north in the direction of the aircraft high overhead. "We have a place to go, you know."

"Tennessee?" Lori asked.

"Yeah," he replied. "Evan made the offer. It's always an option."

"We'd have to cross the entire width of Virginia or the Carolinas to reach Tennessee. That's a long way," she added.

"That would certainly be a long-term goal," replied Jim. "I think we need to piece together a series of manageable short-term goals that, in the end, will get us where we need to be."

With an exasperated look on her face, Carmen spoke up. "What the hell? I didn't sign on with this group to run off to Tennessee if shit hit the fan, I joined it to go to the islands. How can you just change the plan now? That's not what we planned and discussed all this time!"

Understanding Carmen's argument fully, Jim calmly and politely said, "Trust me. I'm not making this recommendation based on my own personal needs and desires. I'm considering the losses we've already suffered, going from ten to six people in less than forty-eight hours. We've seen that traveling even this short distance hasn't worked out quite the way we planned. The purpose of our preparedness group was to have a group of people who could come together during a time of crisis to help each other survive. Of course, heading down to the islands was our plan because we had to have something to base our preparations on, but the islands were basically a placeholder for whatever achievable goal may come when things played out. Sure, that's where I want to be, but I just don't think it's prudent at this time. I want the rest of us to make it. I don't want us to all die, trying to follow a plan for the sake of sticking with a plan."

Jim paused to give Carmen a chance to respond, but she ignored him.

"Have you ever heard the phrase, 'no plan survives the first contact with the enemy?' or something along those lines?"

Crossing her arms in frustration, she replied, "Yes. Why?"

"That actually comes from Prussian Field Marshal Helmuth von Multke, who said—"

"Who?" she interrupted with contempt in her voice.

"He was a military leader back in the late 1800s. What he actually said was: '*The tactical result of an engagement forms the base for new strategic decisions because victory or defeat in a battle changes the situation to such a degree that no human acumen is able to see beyond the first battle*'."

"You remember that word for word?" she asked sarcastically.

"I read a lot about history. I believe you can learn a lot from those who have lived and learned, if you listen to them," he replied.

Watching as Carmen rolled her eyes at him, he continued. "But anyway, our scenario is not all that different. Our ultimate mission is survival, whereas theirs was victory over the enemy, but the same principle applies. You can have plans, but when it all starts to go down, you have to have a willingness to deviate from that plan in order to meet the situation that actually lays in front of you, not the situation you wish laid in front of you.

"When we made our plans, we didn't know what was going to happen. We had no clue. All we knew was that the world couldn't continue on its current course without something having to give. So, when we made our plan to bug out to the islands, the primary objective of that plan was to escape the population masses that were situated just a few miles north of us and the ensuing chaos their hunger and desperation would bring. It wasn't until we realized that the Delaware Bay was blockaded by patrol boats that our entire plan had been potentially tossed out the window. We're lucky to have even gotten out of there by sea."

Pausing while looking to Marcie, he corrected himself. "No, we're not lucky. We're blessed to have had Paul and his willingness to do whatever it took to help us get underway." Looking back to Carmen, he said, "Without his diversion, we would still be back there. Plans don't override reality."

"And the others would still be alive!" Carmen shouted.

"Maybe, maybe not!" Jim barked. "You don't know that. You have no idea what's going on back there right now. You can't 'coulda shoulda woulda' everything and think that your gains and losses have been in vain. You have to look at the hand you're holding and be damn thankful for the cards you have yet to play. At some point, you're gonna have to come to grips with that, Carmen.

"We've still got options. Sure, we could put all of our chips on the table and bet it all, trying to make a run all the way down to the islands, but in my opinion, that would be foolish with what we know now."

"As much as I hate to say it, he's right," Lori said. "We need to consider—"

Storming away before Lori could finish, Carmen left the group, working her way to the bow of the boat. Leaning on the railing, she stared off into the distance, her eyes getting lost on the horizon.

"Give her time," Marcie said, wiping tears from her eyes. "We all need a little time."

Chapter Twenty-Three: Unwelcomed

Two days later...

Stepping up onto the flybridge, Jim patted Marcie on the shoulder. When she turned to respond, he snapped to attention, and with a hand salute said, “Seaman Rutherford reporting for duty, ma’am. You are hereby relieved.”

With a chuckle and a smile, Marcie said, “Seaman Rutherford? Don’t you mean Admiral Rutherford? It’s your boat.”

“If you’re gonna look at it that way, it would be Captain Rutherford at best. I lost my star when I lost my fleet,” he said in a defeated tone.

Seeing the change in his facial expression, she placed her hand on his, and said, “You’ve done an excellent job, Jim. You’re not to blame for anything that’s happened to us.”

Looking her in the eye with a half-hearted smile, Jim replied, “When Carmen pointed out that the others would still be alive if we hadn’t gotten underway, it was a real kick in the gut because I know she could have been right.”

“Stop it!” Marcie said in a strong, motherly tone. “Maybe you need one of your own pep talks or speeches.”

“Speeches?” he asked. “I give speeches?”

With a smile, Marcie turned to see Carmen walking up to the flybridge. Simulating a yawn, Marcie waved her hand over her mouth and said, “Well, I need to get some sleep.”

“Make sure you grab breakfast before you hit the rack,” Jim insisted.

Turning to walk down the steps toward the aft main deck, she replied, “I will. I’m starving.”

Once they were alone, Jim looked to the horizon, feeling the breeze blow through his hair. “It’s a beautiful morning, isn’t it?”

Standing alongside him, holding her hand over her eyebrows to provide shade from the glare of the morning sun, Carmen spoke softly, “Yes. Yes, it is.”

Without breaking her stare, she said, “I’m sorry, Jim.”

“You’ve got nothing to be sorry for,” he quickly replied.

“I shouldn’t have argued with you like that,” she said, turning to look him in the eye as her long, blonde hair blew into her face. Pushing it back, she said, “I’m lucky you guys let me into the group with nothing to offer. I’m glad to be here. I really am. I don’t regret it for anything. I just wish—”

“I know,” he interrupted. “We all wish things could have worked out differently, but the most valuable resource we have right now is each other. We have to focus on that, and you’re just as valuable a resource as anyone on this boat. Don’t ever say you’ve got nothing to offer. If we hadn’t seen something special in you, we wouldn’t have brought you into the group. Just remember that. You’ve got a fire inside you that will get you through whatever may come.”

Replying with only a smile, she turned into the wind and closed her eyes as she felt the breeze blow through her tangled hair. After a moment, she asked, “How far have we gone?”

“Well,” he said, “We’re running on the right engine only, with the left shut off and the transmission in neutral to conserve fuel. We’re cruising at a leisurely seven knots.”

Quickly doing the math in her head, Carmen said, “That’s around a hundred and sixty miles per day, right?”

“I wish,” he replied. “You see, the Gulf Stream flows up from Florida and follows the coastline to around North Carolina and Virginia, where it splits off and heads away from the coast. We’re far enough out to sea to be feeling its effects. I wanted to stay far enough from the coast that we weren’t harassed by any authorities that might be protecting the Chesapeake and subsequently, Washington D.C. That has its drawbacks, though. Being as far out as we are and being on the edge of the Gulf Stream, it's slowing us down a bit."

Sliding his navigational chart over to her, he traced the chart with his finger, tapping it at their current location. "We're about right here."

"That's it?" she asked with a surprised tone in her voice.

"Well, we haven't been doing seven knots the entire time. We had to slow it down a bit yesterday when the swells picked up. That and being on the edge of the Gulf Stream, at times, we've been lucky to hold our position without actually going backward. The Gulf Stream can get up to about five knots. We're at maybe three knots of current here, based on the differences we can see in our GPS derived speed and our indicated speed."

"Hmmm," she replied, taking it all in. Turning around and looking behind them, she said, "I sure thought we'd be—"

Noticing the pause in her sentence, Jim asked, "Thought we'd be what?"

"Uh...further, but I think I see something."

Turning around, he squinted and asked, "What? What do you see?"

"On the horizon. That way," she said, pointing to the north.

Picking up his binoculars, Jim scanned their northern horizon, and said, "Damn, I sure wish I had your young eyes."

"Why?" she asked.

"Because you're right. There's a boat behind us." Lowering his binoculars, he looked at her, and said, "I'd have never seen it if it weren't for you. Go get the others. But let Marcie sleep."

"Okay," she replied as she ran down the steps onto the aft main deck, then turned to go down the steps leading into the main salon below.

Entering the salon, Carmen found C.J. spread out on the sofa, sound asleep, snoring like a chainsaw straining to saw through a thick, wet log.

Seeing Carl and Lori standing in the galley, she quickly joined them as Carl reached out to her with a hot cup of coffee. “Here, you could use this.”

“Maybe later,” she quickly replied. “Jim wants us all topside. There’s a boat in the distance.”

Quickly placing the cup of coffee on the table, Carl grabbed his rifle, and asked, “Is it following us?”

“I don’t know,” she said as she turned and ran back through the salon.

Kicking C.J.’s feet, Carl said, “Wake up, man. There’s a boat!”

“Huh? What?” C.J. asked, rubbing his eyes.

“There’s a boat in the distance. Jim wants us topside.”

Just then, they could hear the port-side Detroit Diesel begin to crank beneath their feet.

Hurrying up to the flybridge, Carl asked Jim, “What’s up?” as he scanned the distance, looking for a potential threat.

“We’ve got company, and the damned left engine won’t start,” he said, continuing to crank as the starter motor began to slow.

“Let the starter cool and the batteries charge back up,” Carl said. “She’s slowing down. Probably getting hot, too.”

“It’s probably the damned injection pump. It loses its prime every now and then and doesn’t want to fire back up until you crank it long enough to get fuel back up to the injectors. I don’t know if that old injection pump is shot or if the fuel is bleeding back to the tank from the check valve. Either way, this is awful timing.”

Still searching frantically for a threat, Carl said, “Where is it?”

"Back here," Carmen shouted, pointing behind them.

Taking Jim's binoculars, Carl said, "Oh, yeah, I see it. Has it gotten any closer?"

"I don't think so," Carmen replied.

Giving up on starting the port engine, Jim grumbled, "I should have never shut the damn thing down this far out to sea. That was stupid."

Turning the steering wheel a quarter turn to the right, Jim said, "I'm altering course to see if it follows."

"What if it does?" Carl asked.

"We'll cross that bridge when we get to it," Jim replied.

Reaching down to turn on the boat's radar, Jim and Carl watched the offending vessel's radar return, in order to determine its track. After a few moments, Carl said, "It looks like it turned."

"Yep, I was afraid of that," Jim replied in a frustrated tone.

Taking the wheel, Jim turned it all the way to the right to the rudder's stop.

"What are you doing?" Lori asked.

"I'm not getting shot in the back!" Jim exclaimed, remembering the story of the fate of Damon, his brother, as he evaded a pursuer on this very boat. "There's no way to outrun anyone on one engine. We may as well square off with them and take a defensive position rather than simply waiting for them to catch up with us."

Nodding in agreement, C.J. added, "Yeah, that'll put them in the position of either breaking off or making a move. But at least it will be on our terms, instead of being snuck up on from behind."

"Here's what I want everyone to do," Jim said in an authoritative voice as he adjusted his Ford Trucks ball cap. "C.J., you know I'm gonna want you on your fifty. I'll back you up with my Bushmaster.

"Carl and Carmen, get the M1 Garands and get plenty of those pre-loaded eight-round clips of .30-06 and position yourselves to lay down suppressing fire if they get within range and show themselves to be a threat.

"Lori, I want you to be on the lower controls in the salon. If it goes down ugly, I'll be too busy shooting to steer the boat. Keep us pointed toward the threat. Don't let them get behind us. Also, go ahead and wake up Marcie. Have her be our supply runner, taking orders for ammo or the medical kit if need be. Have her stay below until we call for something, but have it all laid out in the salon so that she's ready for whatever we may need."

Joining Jim on the flybridge with his fifty-caliber Barrett, C.J. sat his rifle on its bipod and pointed it toward their target and asked, "Are you a believer in firing warning shots over their bow?"

Turning up the volume on the radio, Jim said, "Let's keep our ears open as well as our eyes. Remember how Evan and Jason said they met Judith?"

Pausing as C.J. nodded in reply, Jim continued, "They thought her boat was a threat at first. Just like us, they were ready for the worst, as they'd an encounter that didn't end well. If they weren't listening to hear her distress calls, they might have opened fire on her as she approached."

"Hell," C.J. responded. "A distress call could be a ruse just as easily as it could be a legitimate call for help."

"Yes. Yes, it could. But, we need to hold off on putting holes in a hull until we determine it's our only remaining course of action. What if we had a medical emergency and were desperate to find another vessel in search of help? It could happen."

"Whatever you say, Skipper," C.J. replied with a nod, redirecting his attention to his rifle scope.

"Jim," Carl shouted from the main deck. "Where do you want us?"

"Both of you get several sacks of flour or grain from below," Jim said, looking down at them from the flybridge. "You can use them as both makeshift rifle rests and as a ballistic barrier. Sort of like an edible sand bag. Position yourselves on each side of the forward hatch that leads down into the V-berth. That'll give you an additional point of egress if you've got to get below while keeping your heads down. Also, if you need ammo or first aid, Marcie can hand what you need up through the hatch without you having to expose yourselves."

"Roger that," Carl replied as he and Carmen began to make their preparations.

Looking to C.J., Jim said, "Watch the helm for a moment. Keep us pointed directly at them. Don't get broadside and give them too big of a target. I'll be right back."

"Sure thing," C.J. said, adjusting his cheap sunglasses to filter the rays of the rising sun.

Hearing C.J. chuckle, Jim turned and asked, "What is it?"

"Oh, I was just thinking how if they were smart and actually trying to sneak up on us, they'd have approached from the east, not the north. We'd never see them in all that glare."

"Assuming we didn't have radar," Jim replied.

"Radar didn't alert us to them, Carmen's eyes did," C.J. added with a sly grin.

"That, sir, is correct. Technology can never replace good people," Jim said as he continued down the stairs and into the salon below.

Walking up to Lori, Jim embraced her and swayed side to side. He kissed her on the cheek, and said, "If things don't go well—"

"What?" she interrupted.

“If things don’t go well,” he continued, looking directly into her big, blue eyes, “head west as fast as she’ll go, but don’t push the only engine we’ve got running too hard. Watch her gauges carefully. If you go west long enough, you’ll either encounter authorities, which may or may not be a bad thing depending on your, uh, our situation, or land. Either way, if you’ve got to get help, you’ll find it one way or another if you head west.”

“Why are you saying that—like that?” she asked, refusing to accept the scenario he was painting in her mind.

“We can’t be foolish enough to think we’ll always prevail,” he replied. “We’ll always try. We’ll always give every situation everything we’ve got. But, if it comes down to it, there always needs to be a course of action in the back of your mind. Something to act on, no matter how grief-stricken you or any of us may be at the time.”

“That’s nonsense,” she replied. “But I understand what you’re saying.”

Kissing her on the forehead, he said, “Well, back to the task at hand. Remember, I’ll keep us heading in the direction of the threat for now, but stay down here at the salon controls, because if shooting starts, it will be on you to maintain our course. You should be able to see good enough from down here to keep us heading directly at them.”

“I’ll be ready,” she said as he turned and headed back up to the flybridge.

Reaching the bridge, Jim asked C.J., “How goes it?”

Looking through his scope, C.J. replied, “I can reach them from here,” as if to offer Jim his services.

“Not yet,” Jim said. “We don’t have justification for that as of yet.”

~~~~
~~~~

After waiting impatiently another fifteen minutes, Carl looked to Carmen to his right, and said, “I wish whatever’s gonna happen would just happen. I hate waiting.”

“Me too,” she replied. “Only, if someone else is gonna die, I’d rather that not happen sooner than it needs to.”

Looking through his binoculars, Carl said, “Is it just me, or are they not getting any closer?”

“I was just thinking the same thing,” she said. Turning to look up at Jim and C.J. on the flybridge behind her, Carmen shouted, “What the hell? Are we playing some sort of twisted waiting game, or what?”

Shouting in reply, Jim said, “It looks like a Hatteras. It’s not a coastie or a government type boat from what we can tell. It does look like they’re just sitting dead in the water, holding their bow on us as we are them.”

“So, what now?” she asked, craning her head back toward Jim and C.J.

“We keep playing the game,” he replied. “Not much else we can do.”

Looking to the radio, Jim picked up the mic, pressed the push-to-talk-button, and transmitted. “Hatteras approaching from the north, this is *Viking One*. I recommend you alter your course.”

Hearing no response, C.J. muttered, “Maybe they’re not monitoring this freq?”

“Maybe,” Jim said. “But who the hell would be playing such a game without wondering what the other vessel might have in mind?”

Waiting several minutes without hearing a response, Jim keyed the mic once again. “Hatteras approaching from the north. Identify yourself and state your intentions. This is *Viking One*. You are within our defensive range. We will take any action we deem necessary to ensure our security.”

Hearing the click of a mic, momentarily transmitting carrier only with no voice, Jim repeated, "That transmission was not received. This is *Viking One*. We are on a one-seventy-five bearing from a Hatteras to the north. If you are onboard said Hatteras, identify yourself and state your intentions."

Hearing the radio key up once again, a gravely middle-aged man's voice replied with simply, "I don't think I will, Viking."

"I can hit them from here," C.J. again suggested. "It's at the edge of the abilities of Miss Fifty and me, but I can hit 'em."

Watching through his binoculars, Jim said, "No. They're backing away."

"Are you sure," C.J. asked.

"Pretty sure. Either way, there's no need to start trading hull damage if we can avoid it. It's a long swim to shore for either of us."

Chapter Twenty-Four: Danger on the Horizon

Later that evening...

Watching the sunset over the western horizon, Jim stepped down onto the rear main deck and shouted into the salon, “Can everyone come up here for a few minutes?”

“Burr,” Lori said as she felt the chill of the night’s air on her exposed arms as she stepped out of the salon and onto the aft main deck.

“You need a jacket,” Jim said, wrapping his arms around her to keep her warm.

Looking up at the clear night’s sky, Carl added, “I bet it’s gonna be a cold one tonight.”

“Yes, and a long one,” Jim replied.

“What do you mean?” asked C.J. as he and Marcie joined the rest of the group.

“Let’s all squeeze onto the flybridge, so that we can keep an eye out while we talk,” Jim said as he and Lori climbed the small flight of stairs leading upward.

“What’s wrong?” Marcie asked.

“You think we’re gonna have more trouble out of that boat, don’t you?” asked Carmen with a raised eyebrow.

“Well, to be honest,” Jim replied, “I just don’t have a good feeling about the whole thing. The way they taunted us earlier, it’s almost as if they were probing, trying to see our reaction. And to answer on the radio like that guy did, whoever the hell he is, well, the only reason for that was intimidation.”

With a concerned expression, Marcie asked, “Who do you think it is?”

“Argh, Pirates,” C.J. interjected with a chuckle.

"You laugh, but that's exactly who I think it is," Jim replied. "Look, we know how things were back in Delaware City. We are aware how things were going in New York and elsewhere. This mess has gone on long enough for the less-than-desirables to have realized that whatever it is the government is doing, they're too busy to deal with petty crime. I'm sure they're working three shifts around the clock to guard critical government facilities and personnel, or whatever else is in their best interest, but the rest of us are on our own.

"Those less-than-desirables know they can get away with a lot right now, and I'd imagine many have set out to do just that. The food supply, the fuel situation with the refineries being taken offline—I'd imagine whoever that was saw that we were maneuvering and in control of our vessel, and therefore have fuel and more than likely other resources. With no prying eyes out here to stop them, they're probably pillaging by the sea, just as others are doing so on land. So, yes—pirates."

Turning to look at C.J., Jim asked, "Any luck troubleshooting the port engine?"

Adjusting his New Holland farm equipment ball cap, C.J. replied, "No. There's definitely no fuel working its way to the injection pump. There is fuel down the line, but the pump just isn't getting it. There's hardly any suction on the inlet side of the pump, so I'd say it finally let go. The lift pump doesn't seem to be moving fuel either, which is probably where it all went wrong. A lot of times the lift pump will go bad, and as a result of the injection pump not receiving the pressure it needs from the lift pump, it goes bad as well. That's what I'd imagine happened here. But then again, I'm not a professional diesel mechanic. I'm just a guy who's had a bunch of worn out diesel trucks over the years that I had to fix myself. I may be missing something."

"Well, thanks for trying," Jim said, patting C.J. on the shoulder. "Folks, with that in mind, we need to beef up our watch and start working our way toward the coast. We need to be closer in than this with only one engine. If something were to happen to disable us any further, we could be carried out by the Gulf Stream so far that we wouldn't have a chance. We can't float around out here forever in a crippled boat."

"Back to the point of calling you all out here, I'd like to double up on watches, so that we can have someone to man...uh, I mean, staff the helm," he said, correcting himself after remembering that three very capable women were on his team. Seeing them each respond with merely a chuckle and a rolling of eyes, he continued. "Anyway, I would like to have one person at the helm, monitoring engine temps, oil pressure, and fuel flow, as well as minding our heading and position at all times. We've got to baby our one good engine until we get the coast in sight. The other person can act as a lookout, continuously scanning the horizon and the radar. We can't afford to have someone sneak up on us in the dark."

"How far can we see with that radar?" Marcie asked.

"Well, it's an older unit. It has a relatively low power output compared to the newer recreational units available. I've also got it mounted fairly low in relation to the water. If an antenna is mounted high up, you get further range, but then you get a blind spot in close. Lori and I were most concerned with maneuvering in low visibility when we installed it, so we mounted it as low as we could. Considering that, we would probably get five miles out of it, best case scenario. If you're talking about rocks and steel, that is. A fiberglass boat hull doesn't reflect radar as sharply as a denser object like rocks and piers. A boat like we saw earlier may only show a good return at three or four miles. Also, considering that my old green display doesn't show detail, and all we've got is a fancy trip wire at best."

"So, what's the plan?" Carl asked.

“Like I said, I want to double up on the watches. Also, I’ll leave the only night vision-equipped rifle we have on board on the bridge, in the event something goes down in the dark. It’s an AR-15, so everyone should be familiar. As far as the scope goes, it’s an electronic unit. Just fire it up like you would a red dot, flip open the lens cover, and adjust the IR illuminator all the way out to the max.

“Carl, you and Carmen have been working well together. Let’s keep that going. Lori and I can stand our watches together as well. Heck, she’s probably the only person here who can stand being around me that long,” Jim said, grinning in Lori’s direction.

“I guess if someone’s gonna suffer, it may as well be me,” she replied with a flirty smile and a wink.

Looking to C.J. and Marcie, Jim said, “You two can stand the third watch together. Marcie, keep an eye on C.J. You’ll turn your back on him for a second, and he’ll end up fishing off the stern or something.”

With a laugh, Carl added, “Yeah, you can take the country boy out of the south, but well, maybe they should have just left him there.”

“Hey now!” C.J. replied, pretending to be offended. Laying on his thickest southern accent, he said, “Y'all are about to offend my delicate sensibilities.”

Looking at C.J., trying to figure him out, Carmen asked, “Where are you from, C.J.?”

“’Murica,” he replied with a smile.

With the group sharing a good laugh, Jim said, “Alright then, Carl and Carmen, you are up to bat. Everyone else, sleep with your socks and shoes on and ready to leap out of your rack at a second’s notice. Carl and Carmen, don’t hesitate to get me up and out of bed if anything at all comes up.”

"Roger that," replied Carl as he took the helm and made adjustments to their heading.

After the group dispersed and everyone went to their respective racks, Jim and Lori retired to the aft stateroom. Lying in bed and unable to sleep, Jim stared at the ceiling and aft bulkhead, taking note of each and every bullet hole that had torn through the fiberglass hull of the vessel during his brother's deadly encounter with Evan, Jason, and the others. *This ol' girl just wasn't meant for this,* he thought while visions of what had been and what could be swirled in his mind.

After several sleepless hours had passed, Jim heard a knock at the door. Leaping from the bed, he answered it, seeing Carmen standing there with a look of urgency on her face. "What? What is it?"

"We've got something on radar," she said.

Slipping on his shoes, Jim ran up the steps and out of the salon, turning to climb the stairs to the flybridge where Carl stood with his AK-74 in hand.

"What have we got?" Jim asked.

Tapping on the green radar screen, Carl said, "About four miles to the east. If we keep heading toward the coast, we'll cross paths with them."

"Do you think it's them?" Carmen asked. "The boat from before?"

"There's no way of telling," Jim replied. "Come left about twenty degrees and shallow out our intercept angle with the coast. We'll see if they continue their current course or if they make adjustments to meet ours. We'll develop a plan of action based on that."

"Roger that," said Carl as he made the course adjustment.

Jim watched the display while Carmen scanned the dark horizon with her naked eyes, and Carl dutifully held their course.

After about fifteen minutes, Jim said, "They've adjusted course. It looks like they intend to intercept. Come right to three-four-zero."

Doing as he was instructed, Carl asked, "What's the plan?"

"Carmen, can you wake the others?" Jim asked calmly.

With a nod, she replied, "Sure thing," as she quickly descended the steps from the flybridge to retrieve the others from below.

Once everyone had gathered on the flybridge, Jim said in a serious tone, "We've got a return. It was on a course to intercept us, we adjusted course, and it followed. We've come around to a northwesterly heading to cut in behind them while still heading toward the shore. They've reversed course to follow. Carl, pick it up to around nine knots. That's about as fast as we can go on one engine without feeling adverse effects from having off-center thrust. C.J., you know we need you and the Barrett up here. I'll take the helm up here while Carmen and Carl take up their previous positions up top and Lori and Marcie take up their previous positions down below as well. From now on, if something goes down, just assume those positions as your assigned GQ station."

"GQ?" Marcie queried.

"General Quarters," Jim replied. "Sorry, that's a naval term. It's what some B-rated Hollywood movie would call 'battle stations'."

"Gotcha!" she said as both she and Lori turned to go back down below.

Stopping just short of the steps, Lori turned and gave Jim a quick kiss, saying, "Love you."

"Love you, too," Jim replied.

Getting down to business, Jim watched as the radar return tracked to the northeast, on a direct intercept course with *Viking One.*

"They're gonna cut us off long before we reach the coast," Jim said to C.J., who was occupying the bridge next to him.

"Yep. What now, boss?"

Looking at C.J. with a crooked smile, Jim said, "You know, the longer we're away from Delaware, the more your southern accent comes back."

"Damn straight," C.J. replied. "Your northeastern snobbery isn't holding me back anymore. I'm embracing my inner redneck, now that the need to avoid the mockery is gone."

Replying with only a smile, Jim turned and looked out into the darkness of the night. He said, "I sure wish we had a full moon. The sky is too dark tonight to see any distance at all."

"This is gonna go down, isn't it?" C.J. asked.

"I reckon so," Jim replied.

Chuckling, C.J. said, "It sounds like you're embracing your inner redneck as well."

"Na, that's my inner Josey Wales," Jim replied.

"Ain't nothin' wrong with that."

"I'm glad to have you here, C.J."

"I'm happy to be here, Jim."

After a moment of silence, while watching the radar display, Jim said, "Screw this," and brought the wheel around to a heading of zero-eight-zero, steering away from the pursuing radar return.

"What?" C.J. asked.

"Not right now," Jim said. "There's no reason to fly right into the spider's web. Not just yet."

After a few moments heading in an easterly direction, Jim and C.J. watched as the radar return adjusted course once again, matching theirs.

"Damn it," Jim exclaimed.

"What now?" CJ asked.

"I don't like being on the run. This isn't working out as I'd hoped," Jim said as he focused on the radar display. "Damn it! Damn it! Damn it to hell!" he shouted in a frustrated tone.

Seeing what Jim was upset about on the radar display, C.J. muttered, "Ah, hell."

Tapping on the screen, Jim snarled, "Another damn boat! They weren't there before we turned!" Smashing his fist on the console, he continued his rant. "Those bastards have intentionally shown themselves to get us to focus our attention on the prospect of having only one pursuer, all while their cohorts laid in wait off the screen in the darkness. Damn it!"

"Like the raptors on Jurassic Park," C.J. added.

"What?" Jim said with confusion, giving C.J. a squinted look.

"You know, how one of the raptors would show itself to its prey to get attention focused on it while the others moved in for the kill. It's the ones you don't see that'll eat you."

With a chuckle, Carl spoke in the darkness from his position. "Well, if we're going by the Jurassic Park tactical manual, then I guess that makes sense." Shaking his head, he added, "You're such a goofball, C.J."

Shrugging his shoulders and raising his eyebrows, C.J. said, "Hey, it don't matter if I got it from a movie or one of those damn tacti-cool magazines you can't seem to put down. If it makes sense, it makes sense."

"You're both right," Jim said, interrupting the two. "Carl, you're right, C.J. is a goofball. And C.J., you're right, those raptors are about to try to eat us. Now, let's get back to the task at hand."

Looking around, Jim turned back to the group, shouting, "General quarters, everyone! This is not a drill! This is not a drill! All hands, man your battle stations!"

"Do you have to be so dramatic?" Lori asked as she kissed him on the cheek before heading down to the salon bridge below.

Turning toward her as she went, Jim said, "It worked, didn't it? I mean, you are going. Besides, how exciting would life be without a little drama?"

Chapter Twenty-Five: Making Contact

With his feet propped up on the console, leaning back in the captain's chair on the flybridge, Jim scratched his chin while staring off into the darkness.

"Um, well?" C.J. asked.

Leaning forward and placing his feet flat on the floor, Jim looked at C.J. and said, "I think we need to make a run for the coast. We need to head straight for the decoy vessel and try and shoot our way past them. If we're gonna get shot full of holes and sunk, I'd rather reduce the mileage of our swim to shore as much as we can. Turning back out to sea will accomplish nothing. We could get sunk farther out, or we can be crippled and set adrift with the Gulf Stream as it makes its turn out into the open Atlantic. No, we've got to make a run for the end zone."

"Sounds like a plan," C.J. said, raising his eyebrows up and down repeatedly.

Seeing Jim reply with a chuckle, C.J. said in a defensive tone, "What? What's so funny?"

"Nothing man. Nothing at all," Jim replied, shaking his head while smiling.

"When we get into a range that you feel comfortable making your shots with that fifty, let me know. I'll slow her up to let you get a few good shots off. If we can give them some grief, maybe we can slip by before the others catch up to us."

"Hell, yeah! I'll give 'em some grief," C.J. said as he adjusted his bipod. "I need a little more movement in it than normal," he said. "I'm not used to shooting from a moving platform. I need to be able to float her over the target. Can't have the bipod too stiff."

Pushing the starboard engine's throttle forward, Jim felt the boat surge forward and begin turning slightly to the left.

Adjusting the trim tabs and turning slightly to the right to counter the turning tendency of the off-center thrust induced by their single-engine situation, Jim said, “Twelve knots is about all we can get on one engine, and that’s pushing her to the max. We just can’t get up on plane like this.”

“You just give ’er all she’s got, and we’ll give ’em all we got, Skipper.”

~~~~

Feeling the deck rise beneath them as Jim brought the Viking’s starboard engine to life, Carl looked to Carmen beside him on the forward deck, and said, “Well, here we go.”

“I don’t like this one bit,” Carmen said, placing her forehead on the deck, only to have it bounce off with a thud as the boat hit a small wave. “Damn it!” she shouted in pain and frustration.

Chuckling under his breath, attempting to hide his laughter, Carl said, “I’m sorry. If that were anyone but you, that would be funny as hell.”

“It sure looks like you got a kick out of it either way,” she snarled.

“You gotta be able to laugh to get through the rough stuff,” Carl replied.

“Oh, yeah, and what rough stuff have you been through, mister?”

“I’ll tell you what, after we get through all of this, I’ll sit you down with a beer or a stiff drink and detail every minute of it. Right now, though, I’d rather laugh it off. I don’t want to go into a crap storm reliving a different crap storm in my mind. But trust me, sarcasm and humor will take you a long way when life serves you a crap sandwich. Sure, you may look like a jerk to everyone around you, but you’ll be a jerk that makes it.”

With a smile, Carmen said, “Crap sandwich.”
~~~~

“What?” Carl asked.

“That’s your new nickname, Crap Sandwich,” she said, focusing her attention toward the darkness laying ahead of them.

After an awkward moment, Carl laughed, saying, “See? You’re getting the hang of it already.”

“Or Crappy Carl. Crap man. Craptastic. Na, Crap Sandwich works. That’s what I’ll go with. They say to stick with your first instinct. Crap Sandwich it is.”

“Okay, okay, you’re a master at it already. I get it.”

“I’m a twenty-eight-year-old woman who’s grown up surrounded by bleeding heart millennial boys who can’t change a flat tire. I’ve got disappointment-based sarcasm and cold-heartedness down to a science.”

“Disappointment? What? I’m disappointing?” Carl asked in dismay.

Carl felt her grin at him in the dark. He laughed an uneasy laugh, saying, “Damn, girl. You’re a Jedi master.”

“I’ve had to run off a few boys in my day,” she said in a firm, confident tone.

“You had to run them off, or you ran them off?” Carl asked with a crooked smile.

“Touché, Crap Sandwich. Well played,” she said. Pausing for a moment, she added, “Just don’t go gettin’ yourself killed. I want to finish this conversation over that shot of tequila you offered.”

“Tequila?” Carl asked.

“Hey, you offered me a drink. I’m just placing my order.”

~~~~

Gathering her first aid supplies, as well as ammo for the resupply of those above decks, Marcie asked Lori, who was
~~~~

sitting dutifully at the helm of the salon bridge, "Do you think this is enough? Am I missing anything?"

Lori looked everything over and said, "The trauma packs should do for first aid. Anything beyond that will be done down here anyway. You've got Garand clips, AR mags...uh, how about fifty-cal ammo?"

"C.J.'s got all of that with him already," Marcie replied.

"I think you're good, then. We're all good, Marcie. We're gonna be fine. Just relax."

Answering with only a nervous smile, Marcie once again began nervously going over her replenishment supplies, double and triple-checking everything, as well as going over the best route through the boat to reach each station.

"Okay," she mumbled to herself, "Through the V-berth and up the forward hatch for Carl and Carmen, and up to and out on the rear deck, then up the steps for Jim and C.J. .30-06 up front, and 5.56 up top."

~~~~

"Any minute now," Jim said, anxiously looking at his radar display. "You should be getting them in sight any minute."

Just then, seeing a flash of light followed by the thunder of a large caliber rifle off in the distance, C.J. jumped as a chunk of the boat's fiberglass shattered next to him. "Damn it!" he shouted. "They've got range, too!"

Quickly getting back to his rifle, C.J. took aim in the direction of the source of the flash. He found a murky gray silhouette barely lit by the night's sky, and let one of his six-hundred-and-forty-seven-grain, fifty-caliber projectiles fly.

Immediately cycling the action, chambering another round, C.J. saw another flash of light as a section of fiberglass exploded
~~~~

between Jim and him, sending shards and fragments all over them.

Firing another shot, C.J. recovered from the recoil and quickly cycled a tracer round into the chamber and let it fly. Watching the tracer race across the night's sky, they watched as the flash of light erupted into flames on the deck of the offending vessel.

"We must have hit somethin' good!" C.J. said, cycling another round.

With the flickering flames providing a visual target for the old iron sights of the .30-06 Garands, Carl and Carmen joined C.J. by adding an alternating but steady volley of fire against their aggressor. As soon as the 'ping' of an empty clip ejecting from the top of a Garand was heard, the other would begin rhythmically emptying the eight rounds in their clip while the other shoved another clip in the top of their rifle, quickly pulling their hand free as the bolt slammed forward, chambering another round. They would then maintain a steady rate of fire until their ping was heard, once again alternating the cycle.

Feeling the shutter of a heavy round hitting the side of the flybridge, Jim shook it off, and shouted to C.J., "We threw them off a little, if nothing else. They were getting way too close for comfort. Speaking of too close for comfort," he said, tapping on his radar display. "I expect to start taking hits from the rear any minute now."

Looking back into the darkness that followed them, C.J. started to speak as a stream of full-auto fire came raining in on them from a distance, falling just short of them in their wake.

Turning sharply to the right, Jim shouted below for Lori to take the helm at the lower bridge and to begin evasive maneuvers while continuing their general course toward the coast.

Hearing another loud thump from C.J.'s fifty, Jim heard C.J. shout, "I think I got 'em good that time!"

Flipping on his Gen 2 night vision scope, Jim switched on his extra IR illuminator and faintly painted one of the pursuing vessels off in the distance behind them. "I knew this thing would come in handy eventually," he said as he began pulling the trigger, refocusing his aim after each recoil impulse.

"You ain't gonna scare 'em off tossing BB's at 'em," C.J. said, cycling another massive fifty BMG round into his rifle.

"No, but I just might keep their heads down enough that they don't get a good line on you."

"Carry on, then," C.J. said, releasing another punishing blow against the boat ahead of them.

Seeing the vessel ahead and to their left begin to alter its course, Jim said, "I think we're putting a hurt on them."

"I think it's a bit more than a hurt," C.J. said, just as they watched the boat burst into flames. "Hot flames or cold water, boys? Take your pick!" he shouted.

Ignoring C.J.'s biting humor, Jim shouted, "Carl! Carmen! Make for the aft main deck!"

Dropping into the forward hatch, Carl and Carmen quickly worked their way through the V-berth, into the galley, up the small flight of stairs into the salon, and up the final steps to the aft main deck.

As each of them rushed past Marcie, they took a battle pack of loaded Garand clips from her as she held them out as they passed.

"Thanks!" Carl shouted as the small double-doors leading to the aft main deck slammed shut behind him.

Looking up to Jim, Carl heard him shout, "Good job! Now, don't let those bastards get too comfortable back there."

With the vessel behind them now in sight, Carl and Carmen took prone positions on the aft main deck and began their rhythmic, steady volley of suppressing fire.

Firing one more shot into the now-fleeing vessel in front of them, C.J. picked up his big rifle, grimacing from the burning sensation in his hands from the heat the large weapon was now radiating, and propped it up directly on the seatback behind him. With the bipod dangling behind the seat, C.J. sent one of his massive rounds into the pursuing boat.

"Don't scratch my seat!" Jim shouted over the barrage of gunfire.

Answering with only a grin, C.J. cycled yet another round, only to be interrupted by the rapid deceleration of Viking One, followed by screeching sounds from the starboard engine's transmission.

Quickly pulling the operative engine's throttle to idle and the transmission into neutral, Jim looked frantically over the side and seeing nothing, jumped from the fly-bridge to the aft main deck and then down to the swim platform, causing Carl and Carmen to temporarily halt their fire.

"Damn it, Jim! I almost shot you!" Carl shouted.

"The damn prop is fouled!" Jim yelled back.

"What?" Carl responded, confused.

"Fishing net! That bastard in front of us must have been stringing fishing net out on the surface while the other boat pushed us right into it. We're screwed. I can't fix this while they're shooting at us."

Hearing a voice over the radio, C.J. turned his attention to hear, "*Viking One*, we don't want to sink you. You have things we want. But we will, if you force our hand. Place all of your weapons on the aft deck and move your entire crew to the forward main deck. No one is to be left below. All hands must be above decks and on the forward main deck awaiting boarding.

Any resistance will be dealt with in the harshest possible manner. Do you understand?"

Seeing Jim walk up alongside him, C.J. shook his head in disbelief as Jim picked up the radio. "This is *Viking One*. Identify yourself."

Feeling a sharp thud impact the side of *Viking One's* hull, Jim flinched as he heard the voice shout over the radio, "Did I not make myself clear? How many holes can you take? You're dead in the water. If you continue to resist, we will sink you. We will not risk the lives of any more of our men if you remain hostile. If you surrender, you will be given quarter."

Feeling another shockwave from yet another impact of a large projectile, the voice on the radio said, "That was the final warning. All further shots will be made below the waterline."

With his hand trembling, Jim gritted his teeth, pressed the push-to-talk button, and said, "We surrender."

As C.J. sat there in disbelief, Jim dropped the microphone, turned to Carl and Carmen. "Shout down to Lori and Marcie. All hands on deck."

Chapter Twenty-Six: Surrender at Sea

As the vessel approached, Jim, Lori, Carl, Carmen, Marcie, and C.J., all gathered on the forward main deck, unarmed and afraid. Whispering to Jim, Carl said, "We should have fought to the last breath, Jim. This is insane. They're gonna kill us."

"This ain't over yet," Jim replied softly.

Looking to Carmen, Carl said, "Don't worry, we're still having that drink."

"Damn straight," she replied. "I'm not letting you back out over something simple like this."

Turning to C.J., Carl then asked, "So, what's the Jurassic Park tactical manual say about this?"

"Shut up, Carl," C.J. muttered under his breath. "You know, there's a reason the guy who's told to shut up in all those military memes is always named Carl. There's something about Carls. But if you must know, I'm pretty sure it says the guy named Carl gets eaten by the raptors while everyone else gets away."

"Guys!" Jim snarled. "Keep it together. There will be an opportunity somewhere, and we have to remain on our toes to see it."

As the boat drew near, they could see several rifles trained on them. Two men stood ready to lash a rope around the cleats along the port side of *Viking One.*

Stepping onto the main deck of *Viking One,* a gruff, weathered man with a scruffy gray beard, wore a black, boonie-style hat and Navy-style digital BDU's. He carried a Saiga AK-based twelve gauge shotgun with a drum magazine. Pointing it at Jim and the crew, he said, "Well now, that was a lot easier than continuing your futile resistance, wasn't it?"

Studying the group, he seemed to take a mental note of each one of them. Waving the barrel of his shotgun back and forth, pausing on each of them, he asked, “Who’s the skipper of this once fine vessel?”

“I am,” asserted Jim as he took a step forward.

Quickly bringing the Saiga to bear, the man leveled the barrel at Jim, and said, “Take another step, tough guy. I dare you.” Following a tense, awkward moment, he then said, “I guess I misspoke, I should have asked, who *was* the skipper. Because you are not in charge anymore. This is not your boat anymore. You’re now just a member of the crew, my crew, so I suggest you act like it.”

Seeing terror in Lori’s eyes, the man looked at Jim with a twisted, sadistic smile, and said, “I see. You must belong to her. Well now, I guess you’ve got a good reason to do as I say then. I won’t just have my sights on you; I’ll have them on her as well. Understand?”

Answering with just a nod, Jim kept his firm, unrelenting stare on the man.

Walking toward Lori, the man raised the barrel of the shotgun, pointing it squarely at her chest, shouting, “I asked you if you understand? Sound off like you really understand, or I’ll be forced to show you folks the hard way that I’m not messing around here!”

“I understand! I understand!” shouted Jim.

Lowering the barrel of the shotgun, the man said, “Damn, I was hoping you would keep up the tough guy shit. I wanted an excuse to spray her guts all over the deck. Well, maybe you’ll give me that excuse yet. There’s still a lot to be done here.”

Turning to his crew on the other boat, the man said, “Manny, Wallace, you two clear the boat below.”

Quickly boarding *Viking One*, the men entered the salon and began searching the boat for others who might be hiding below. Emerging after a few moments, the one called Wallace said, "All clear below."

"What do we have?" the man in charge asked.

"There is food and ammo, as well as a few gadgets that may be useful."

"Fuel?"

"Yes, sir. Manny checked the tanks. There's half a tank starboard and three-quarters of a tank on the port side."

"Outstanding," the man said as he turned back to the group. "Manny, escort the women below. Have them pack all of their food and supplies topside. The men can watch as they hump it over to our boat right here in front of me. I don't want to let any of these bastards out of my sight."

Watching as Manny led the women below with the barrel of his AR-15 pointing the way, the man in charge looked around and said, "It looks like you used to have a nice boat here. Well, before it was ripped to shreds by our boys, that is."

"You can't lay claim to all of the holes in this old boat," Jim said. "She's encountered others."

"Is that so?" the man asked. "Where are my manners?" he said with a smile. "My name is Captain Cobb. You can just call me Captain, though. There's no need to get too intimate here. We won't be around long enough for that."

Looking squarely at Jim, he said, "The proper response to anything I say is, 'Yes, Captain', do you understand?"

Swallowing his pride, Jim said, "Yes, Captain."

"Good," Captain Cobb said with a smile.

Turning to the weapons arranged on the aft main deck, Captain Cobb said, "Well, look at what we have here. You guys have guns that range from old relics to some damn fine weaponry. That fifty will look good on my bridge."

Seeing C.J.'s eyes twitch, Cobb said, "Oh, she must be yours. You must have been the one who sent my friends on the Hatteras to a watery grave. Am I right?"

"I was just doing what I had to do to defend us," C.J. replied. "It ain't my fault you attacked us."

"Very true. Very true," Captain Cobb acknowledged. "I can't blame you for that. Still, I feel as if I owe you some sort of punishment for what you've done. You see, if I let you go, knowing that the result of your actions led directly to the deaths of my friends, then, what kind of a captain would I be? How could my crew still respect me? You've put me in a bind here."

"I'm sure they understand what self-defense is," C.J. replied.

"Never the less, I feel like something needs to be done. Nothing personal, of course."

Seeing Jim's desire to intervene, Captain Cobb looked at him, and said, "You're going to give me an excuse to kill her yet, aren't you?"

Turning his attention to Carl, Captain Cobb asked, "So, what's your story? Which one of those pretty ladies is yours? The blonde or the brunette?"

"I'm single," Carl answered calmly.

"I understand why you would say that, but let's be serious. Three men and three women on a boat out to sea and you expect me to believe you're all just friends? What kind of a fool do you take me for? Well, it doesn't matter, I guess. You'll give it away soon enough."

Turning as Manny forced Lori, Marcie, and Carmen out of the salon at gunpoint, each of them carrying an armload of supplies, Captain Cobb said, "Here we go. Back to business. We can have our fun in a moment. Ladies?" he said, getting their attention, "Hand what you have over to our boys on the other boat, then scurry back down for more. We've not got all night, you know."

Keeping a taunting eye on Jim, Carl, and C.J., Captain Cobb watched as the ladies made trip after trip down below, until Manny said, "That's it, Captain."

"Very good, Manny," he replied. "Now, ladies, if you would be so kind as to carry that final load over to our boat. Manny will show you where to put it down below."

Seeing Jim cringe, Cobb smiled. "Well, gents, it's been fun," as he turned to step back onto his own vessel. Stopping just short, he turned back to the men. "I almost forgot. We have an unfinished piece of business to take care of," he said, shooting a crooked smile at C.J.

"Wallace, Javier, give me a hand, would you?" Cobb said as the two men joined him aboard *Viking One*. "Javier, get me forty feet of mooring or anchor line. Wallace, get me something heavy. Not too heavy. I don't want to rip his leg off and spoil the fun."

Cringing, C.J. looked to Jim and Carl with fear in his eyes.

Returning to the main deck with one of the vessel's twelve-volt deep cycle batteries, Wallace asked, "Will this do, Captain?"

"Yes, that will do nicely. Now, flake out twenty feet of line and lash it to the chubby one's leg," he said, pointing to C.J., "to the line at that point, then tie the battery at one end, putting the other end on that bow cleat."

Seeing fight in C.J.'s eyes, Captain Cobb asked, "Would you like one of your ladies to join you in your fate? Or maybe all three?"

Relaxing his posture and acquiescing to his fate, C.J. allowed the men to tie one end of the rope securely to his leg just above the ankle. Watching as they tied the other end of the rope to the cleat, C.J. closed his eyes and said a silent prayer.

Lord, if you don't see fit to save me, please be merciful and take me quick. Please don't let me suffer, and please don't let them hurt the others.

With a nod to Javier and Wallace, Captain Cobb walked toward to his boat, stepping aboard as he watched them toss the battery into the sea. C.J.'s eyes grew wide as the slack in the other twenty feet of rope was quickly whisked off the deck by the sinking battery, yanking his leg, pulling him into the cold water of the Atlantic and into the darkness below.

As Wallace and Javier boarded their boat, another man tossed an open gasoline can onto Viking One's deck.

"Good luck, gentlemen," Captain Cobb said as he launched a flare onto the deck, igniting the fuel.

Sprinting to the cleat from which C.J. dangled, held under water by the weight of the battery, Jim and Carl feverishly pulled on the rope, barely making headway as the weight of C.J. and the battery made it almost too much for them to lift.

Inch by inch, they pulled him closer and closer to the surface. Turning to see the flames growing ever closer, Jim shouted, "Pull, damn it! Pull!" at the top of his lungs, as he and Carl heaved and heaved.

Feeling C.J.'s struggle with the line begin to fade, Carl said through gritted teeth, "Don't give up on us, C.J. Not now, man. We need you. Hang in there, buddy."

Hearing the sound of a vessel approaching, unrelenting in his struggle to save his friend, Jim raged. "Those bastards must be back to watch!" as the heat from the flames began to burn his back.

Feeling the flames turn into steam as a mist of water covered both he and Carl, Jim turned to see a United States Coast Guard forty-seven-foot Motor Life Boat extinguishing the flames as several of its sailors leaped aboard the now sinking *Viking One*.

Chapter Twenty-Seven: Taken

Hearing Carmen's screams in the next room, Lori and Marcie held each other tight while the men guarding them took turns peeking into the room, laughing and watching the hell being inflicted upon her. Turning to look at them, the man called Javier, said, "Don't worry, ladies. You won't miss out on the fun for long. Once the captain has his go, the rest of the crew will make sure you get put to good use."

"You bastards! Leave her alone, you dirty sons of bitches!" Lori shouted as she ran at the man, swinging her fist, catching him with a right cross.

With his head whipping back violently from the blow, she attempted to wrestle his rifle from his hands as he kicked her squarely in the chest. Watching as she flew across the room, the man turned to his left and watched as Marcie drew the black, eight-inch knife from his belt, thrusting it between his ribs. Feeling the searing pain as the knife penetrated his lung, deflating it like a popped balloon, he fell to his knees. His last vision being that of Lori pulling his rifle from him and firing into his friend who had been watching the assault on Carmen taking place next door.

As the deafening sound of the high-velocity, 5.56 NATO rounds discharged in the small, confined space, Cobb's crew were stunned, but soon came to the aid of their comrades.

"Drop it!" one of them yelled, pointing his rifle squarely at Lori.

Returning the favor with a cold, icy stare, Lori said, "Drop it, or you die, you son of a bitch!" as she aimed the smoking barrel of the AR-15 at the man.

He could see the rage in her eyes. She wasn't bluffing. She was a woman with nothing else to lose. She had witnessed many tragedies in recent days and would be damned to stand by and be forced to witness one more injustice or unnecessary act of violence.

With both Lori and the man resting their fingers nervously on the trigger and their guns pointed squarely at one another, the tension in the air was interrupted by a sudden burst of fully automatic machine gun fire and the sound of the superstructure of the boat being ripped to shreds. As the man turned to look toward the ladder leading to the upper deck, Lori took advantage of the diversion, dove to the right, and squeezed the trigger, sending a sixty-two-grain full metal jacket projectile screaming out of the barrel of her AR-15, propelled forward by the deafening supersonic crack of escaping gasses.

As the high-speed projectile collided with the man's sternum at such a close range, his heart was pulverized in an instant as the bullet entered his body, tumbling wildly, crushing his heart and lungs as it went, finally exiting out his back and becoming lodged in the wall behind him. The man was dead before the expended shell casing bounced off of the boat's old, wooden deck.

Kicking the cracked door fully open, Lori rushed into the room where Carmen was held, looking through the rifle's sights. As a man's head entered her sight picture, she pressed the trigger, sending a red mist onto the wall behind him as he fell to the floor.

Entering the room behind Lori, Marcie fired several shots into another man from the rifle she had quickly retrieved from Lori's would-be assailant in the other room.

Turning to look at the two blood-crazed women with sheer horror in his eyes, Captain Cobb stood, turning to face them, with his pants down to his knees. Lori and Marcie looked to the cot in front of him to see Carmen naked and tied to the cot face down, her legs spread apart.

In a fit of rage, Lori pointed her rifle at Captain Cobb's groin, and said, "Beg. Beg for your life, you dirty son of a bitch."

Shaking in fear, unable to speak, all Captain Cobb could say before Lori pulled the trigger was, "N—n—n—n—nooooo!"

Before he could complete his plea for mercy, a round shattered the hand he held over his exposed groin, smashing into his testicles, causing him to drop to his knees, screaming out in unimaginable pain.

Hurrying to untie Carmen, Lori helped her collect herself and don her clothes, while Marcie guarded the door. Looking back to both Lori and Carmen, Marcie said, "We've got to take this boat and go back to find the guys."

"We're gonna have to deal with whatever is going on up top first," Lori answered as Carmen struggled to her feet, wiping the tears from her eyes.

Picking up a porcelain coffee mug from the table, Carmen smashed it across Captain Cobb's face as he shuddered in pain, laying prone, bleeding out on the floor. Shattering from the brutal impact, all that remained in her hand was the mug's handle and a sharp, jagged fragment remnant of the mug. Slashing it across his face, Carmen split his face wide open as he fell over, unconscious from the pain-induced shock that his dying body descended into.

"Finish him," Carmen said in a cold, heartless tone.

"Just let the bastard bleed out," Lori replied. "Don't end it for him so quickly."

Picking up Cobb's shotgun, Carmen looked at Marcie and Lori, and said, "Let's go. Let's go get the guys."

Climbing the ladder leading to the main weather deck of the vessel, Lori poked her head out of the hatch and began to scan the area.

She drew back as a spotlight shined on her, with an amplified voice saying, "Drop your weapons and keep your hands above your heads. You are now in the custody of the United States Coast Guard."

A feeling of relief and uncertainty swept through her body as Lori dropped her rifle and climbed up and into the light. Placing her hands on top of her head, she nodded for Marcie and Carmen to show themselves and comply as well.

Hearing footsteps approach them in the shadows, the women heard a voice ask, "Are you ladies from the Viking cruiser that was attacked and boarded earlier tonight?"

"Yes. Yes, we are," Lori answered cautiously.

"Are there others?" he asked. "Are there threats remaining aboard?"

"Dead or dying," she said, looking around to see the bodies of the rest of Cobb's crew strewn about the deck, riddled with bullet holes from the Coast Guard's deck-mounted, M240 machine-gun.

As several uniformed men rushed past her and descended into the vessel with weapons at the ready, the man said, "I'm Petty Officer Cooper, ma'am. We've got four men who are anxious to see you. Please come with me."

Chapter Twenty-Eight: Miracle at Sea

"Welcome aboard, ladies," said a man in a set of blue Coast Guard BDUs with anchors on his collar. Reaching out to them, he said, "I'm Chief Prosser. We came across a few gentlemen you may know. Please, come with me," he said as he led them inside and onto the bridge.

Lori's heart fluttered wildly as she saw Jim standing there with a hot cup of coffee in his hands and a blanket around his shoulders. Next to him stood Carl and—"Paul!" Marcie shouted as she rushed past Lori and leaped into her husband's arms. "Oh my God, I thought you were dead!" she cried as she felt over his body. Noticing some partially healed lacerations on his face, she asked, "What happened? How did you get away? Are you hurt?"

"Your husband is quite the pilot, ma'am," said Chief Prosser. "We saw the whole thing. I never thought I'd see the day when some little biplane would give two Eurocopter Tigers a run for their money."

"It was insane," interrupted Petty Officer Cooper. "It was like watching a crazy airshow where one of those nut-job aerobatics performers flies loops and spins, but add to that two attack helicopters trying their best to shoot him down at the same time. We thought they smoked him when the plane hit the water. Then, one of our guys said they saw him bail out. We searched the water till we found him. He was near hypothermic, but otherwise in good shape despite a few cuts and bruises."

Releasing Marcie from his tight, loving embrace, Paul said, "I almost flew my last flight that night. My prop must have caught a few of their rounds as it shattered and covered me with metal fragments. That's what I believe cut my face up a bit."

Marcie touched his face lightly.

"Once I bailed out, the chute wouldn't open. I pulled and pulled, but nothing. Then, and the last possible second, it just opened on its own. I had given up, but I guess the chute hadn't. The impact pretty much knocked me out."

Marcie pulled him back into a tight hug, saturating his shirt with a stream of tears.

"The next thing I knew, I was looking up at these guys as their corpsman was giving me mouth to mouth. I told them all about you guys and why I was flying the diversion, and they offered to head south to find you."

"Speaking of our corpsman," Chief Prosser added, "he's with the other man now."

"C.J.," Carl said. "The other man is C.J. He's gonna be fine. These guys showed up just in time to save our butts. Those bastards sank C.J. with that battery before they lit the boat on fire. Our choice was to save ourselves from the flames and let C.J. die, or save C.J. and possibly all of us die."

"There really wasn't a choice for us," Jim said. "We pulled and pulled on the rope with everything we had," Jim said, showing the blisters on his hands. "C.J. isn't a small man, and that thin wet rope, well, it just wasn't working. The flames were getting closer and closer. We could feel the heat and then, there they were."

"The boat?" asked Lori.

Jim took Lori in his arms and looked into her baby blue eyes. "The *Mother Washington*...uh, I mean *Viking One* is lost, along with everything we owned. But you know what, I couldn't care less. We've already lost a lot as a group. I'd give anything to get Martin, Rick, and Jordan back. I'd trade everything I'm ever gonna have for that. No, the boat and everything that went down with it isn't worth anything to me without all of you on it."

Chapter Twenty-Nine: Resolve

Early the next morning after they had all eaten breakfast, Chief Prosser stood on the bow of the boat with Jim and said, “So, what’s your plan? Where can we take you guys before we head back? We’re gonna have to come up with one hell of a story as to what we’ve been up to and why we left our assigned operational area.”

“Operational area?” Jim queried. “What could they have you doing alongside those foreign patrol boats that were guarding the bay?”

“No vessels were to be operating off the coast in the New York area. We were assigned basically the same tasks as those patrol boats. To be honest, though, we don’t really like where things are going. We’re living under a mushroom of information right now. We really don’t have a clue what the big picture or the current agenda is, given the state of things, but we don’t like what we see. We’ve talked amongst ourselves, and if it gets much worse, we may just run this boat ashore, change into our civies, and hike home.”

“Good luck with that,” Jim said sarcastically. “You’re probably safer out here. It’s getting pretty nasty back there.”

“Yeah, well, our families aren’t safe out here with us,” Chief Prosser replied with an uncomfortable expression.

“I’d ditch this thing then, Chief. There is nothing more important than family,” Jim said, as he watched the sun peek over the horizon in the distance to the east. “Hell, I assumed your families would be taken care of.”

With a grumble, Chief Prosser said, “Only the political class are getting that treatment.”

“That would seal the deal for me for sure, then,” said Jim.

Changing the subject, Chief Prosser asked, “So, what're your plans? Where can we drop you off?”

“Any uninhabited tropical paradise will do, I guess,” answered Jim with a chuckle. “Short of that, anywhere along the coast away from a major population center will do.”

“Where are you headed?”

“Well, our plans were to bug out to the islands. We started out this little journey with a compliment of two boats and lots of food, supplies, and weapons. All that is gone now, including three of our finest,” answered Jim, pausing to gather his thoughts. “I guess that puts the islands out of the question.”

“What’s Plan B, then?”

“I think I see Tennessee in our future,” Jim said. “It’s a long shot, but hell, what isn’t these days?

The End

A Note from the Author

Here I sit here in our little temporary home finalizing this book, thinking of the crazy whirlwind our lives have been over the past year. From major career changes to moving full-time to our farm/homestead, this year has been something else, to say the least. I guess it's good timing to say "this year" as tomorrow is New Year's Eve and our calendar is about to start anew.

I've got several uncompleted books trying to burst out of my head that will make the shelves in 2017. If you enjoy *Viking One,* as well as my other works, I hope you check them out.

If I have not had the honor of making your acquaintance and if you like my work, please find me on Facebook at http://facebook.com/stvbird
and at my blog at http://www.stevencbird.com. You can also follow me on Twitter at http://twitter.com/stevencbird. In addition, my Amazon author page can be found at http://www.amazon.com/Steven-Bird/e/B00LRYYBDU/ where you can see all of my available work.

I look forward to hearing from each and every one of you, and may God bless you and your loved ones in all of your future endeavors.

Just as Jim resolved to set out on what seemed to be an impossible new mission at the end of this book, may you take the steps to set out on a new mission for yourself this year as well. The only difference between those who do and those who don't is that those who do, lace up their boots and get started.

About the Author

Steven Bird was born in 1973, deep in the Appalachian Mountains of Harlan County, Kentucky. Upon graduation from high school, he joined the U. S. Navy where he served eleven years on active duty, obtaining the rank of Chief Petty Officer before transferring to the Navy Reserves. Transferring to the reserves allowed him to pursue a professional flying career while continuing to serve his country. He ultimately retired with just over twenty years of service.

While on active duty, he earned a BS degree in eBusiness as well as all the professional flight certificates necessary to begin his new career. Once in the reserves, he worked as a flight instructor, charter pilot, airline first officer, airline captain, and is currently the captain of a super-midsized business jet based out of Knoxville, Tennessee.

Steven, along with his wife and two young daughters, currently live on a farm on the Cumberland Plateau in Tennessee where they raise cattle, sheep, chickens, ducks, and bees, as well as growing their own fruits and vegetables. In addition, they are currently pursuing their dream of building an off-grid, self-sustainable home, as well as developing the land to suit their desire for a true self-sufficient lifestyle.

Over the years, he has been heavily involved in competitive shooting, off-road motorcycle racing, snowboarding, hiking, camping, hunting, fishing, and, of course, writing.

Steven Bird is a self-sufficiency-minded individual with a passion for independence and individual liberty. He puts this passion into his writing where he conveys the things that he feels are important in life, intertwined with action-packed adventure and the struggles of humanity.

Made in the USA
Columbia, SC
05 October 2020